P9-DCD-518

WYOMING
LEGEND

Also available from Diana Palmer

Long, Tall Texans

Fearless
Heartless
Dangerous
Merciless
Courageous
Protector
Invincible
Untamed
Defender
Undaunted
Unbridled

Wyoming Men

Wyoming Tough
Wyoming Fierce
Wyoming Bold
Wyoming Strong
Wyoming Rugged
Wyoming Brave
Wyoming Winter

The Morcai Battalion

The Morcai Battalion
The Morcai Battalion: The Recruit
The Morcai Battalion: Invictus
The Morcai Battalion: The Rescue
The Morcai Battalion: The Pursuit

For a complete list of titles available by Diana Palmer, please visit www.dianapalmer.com.

DIANA PALMER

WYOMING LEGEND

HQN™

Recycling programs for this product may not exist in your area.

ISBN-13: 978-1-335-04108-1

Wyoming Legend

This edition published by arrangement with Harlequin Books S.A.

For questions and comments about the quality of this book, please contact us at CustomerService@Harlequin.com.

www.HQNBooks.com

Printed in U.S.A.

To my sweet editor, Patience, with love.

To my best friend, Ann, who rode on camels in Morocco and ate sushi in Osaka and sunbathed on the Mediterranean and toured Brussels and boated through the Amsterdam canals and sweltered in the Montana and Arizona heat to see historical places with me… Thanks for the memories, kid. It was a great ride. Thanks to our husbands, who refused to travel, we got to see the world. You were the best companion anybody ever asked for, and the best friend anybody could want. Love and hugs, Diana Palmer.

Dear Reader,

I've watched figure skating all my life, and loved it dearly. I had favorites. I named my heroine in this novel after two of them who were gold medalists: Katarina Witt and Irina Rodnina. It has been a privilege to watch such talented people on the ice, when my whole knowledge of skating was in roller rinks, where I went entirely too fast. I could skate forward and backward, do crossovers, almost anything you could do on roller skates. But I'm from Georgia and back in the '50s there weren't any ice rinks near me. Roller skating was all we had.

Nevertheless, I would have given a lot to have had the opportunity to put on ice skates and learn those beautiful moves that come from so much practice and pain. Skating is a big part of this novel, but it's also about two people with tragic events in their pasts. It brings together an injured skater who's afraid to get back on the ice, an embittered former skating coach who buys an ice rink in Catelow, Wyoming, near the big ranch where Karina gets work and a young girl who wants to skate but who has only her father's cold and unpleasant fiancée to teach her.

It has been an amazing story to tell. Along the way, I got a real education in ice skating and the difficulty that all contenders face when they start down the long road of training that leads eventually to nationals, world and Olympic competition. I had a ball writing this book. I hope you enjoy it.

Love,

Diana Palmer

CHAPTER ONE

SHE HEARD THE cheering of the crowd, as if it was close by. Lights flashing from dozens of cameras in the spectator stands. Music, beautiful music. The sound of her skates on the ice made smooth by the Zamboni. The perfect lifts and tosses by her partner as they soared toward the gold medal in the World Championships. The reviewing stand. The medal looped around her neck, the exultation as she faced the news media and shared her struggles and tragedies that had led her and her partner to the medal. Then, so soon after, the new tragedy that had put her in the hospital just days before they were to start training new programs for the National Championships and then, if their luck held, the Olympic Games. The hope of that Olympic gold medal in pairs figure skating, however, was already fading in the distance. Her hopes and dreams, crushed as the surgeon labored to reduce the damage in her ankle. Gone. All gone. Hopes and dreams of medals were lost like the dream that faded as she woke in her own bed, in her lonely apartment.

Karina Carter went to the kitchen to make coffee. It still felt awkward to walk without the cast and supporting boot she'd sported for five months. She had sports therapy for the break, which was healing. But her partner, Paul Maurice, was forced to practice with another skater, one not in her class. If the woman performed well, he would break up his partnership with Karina—with her permission, of course—and prepare for the Nationals. He and Karina had placed in the top tier at both the Grand Prix and the Four Continents events earlier in the year, which, added to the Worlds gold medal, would surely give them a spot on the Olympic team. It had been just after the last of the international competitions that the accident in training had happened.

Now, in October, almost six months after the accident, Paul was going to have to break in a new partner. That would mean that both he and Karina would sacrifice the Envelope—the stipend awarded by the United States Figure Skating Association to high-level contenders. Paul and Karina had been in Tier 1, the highest level of all. But if Paul officially changed partners, which he hadn't done yet, both he and Karina would lose their financial help.

With that in mind, Karina was looking at job possibilities. Her expenses would be much less since she was out of competition, perhaps forever. She had a career decision to make and it was going to be a hard one. Paul understood. He'd always supported her, whatever she did. She hoped that his new training partner worked out, so that he could compete again in figure skating. If he worked hard, he and his partner would work their way through sectionals and

Nationals to the big events next year. It would mean missing the Olympics, because a new team had to practice a lot to get to even the early competitions. Pairs skating was the hardest of all the disciplines in figure skating, because there had to be such perfect unison in the movements.

But that no longer concerned Karina. She'd given up. Her doctor had convinced her that it was madness to get back on the ice. That suited her, because she was afraid to try to skate again. The fall had been nightmarish.

There was a job interview later today, in Catelow, Wyoming, north of Jackson Hole and the small town where she'd been born. She'd lived with Paul's family just after the tragedy that had cost her parents their lives. Her parents had been gone for three years now. They'd died, ironically, in a plane crash on their way home from watching their daughter compete in the last Olympic Games. That tragedy had crushed her spirit. She and her partner had worked so hard. But they'd placed only eighth in the last Olympic Games. But this year, they'd won the Nationals, the Grand Prix, the Europeans, and then the gold in world competition. If it hadn't been for Karina's fall…

That gold medal in world competition had fired them up, made them hungry for the events that would lead them back again to the Olympics. But the accident, in training of all things, had robbed Karina of any hope that she might participate again. Paul felt guilty because he'd thrown her so high in one of their signature moves; but she'd landed badly. It had been her fault more than his.

Their new coach had comforted her. She needed several months to recuperate after the surgery to repair her ankle. She'd be back. She needed to keep up with the physical therapy, see her sports doctor regularly and then get back on the ice. She could do it, even if it took a whole year, which it might. The coach, an accomplished skater himself, insisted that one accident wouldn't rob Karina of her chance at Olympic gold. After all, wasn't she named for two famous figure skaters? Her name, Karina, was a combination of Katarina, for Olympic gold medalist Katarina Witt, and Irina, for Irina Rodnina, who'd won a record total of ten Olympic gold medals in her career. Both skaters were heroines of Karina's late mother.

Karina had smiled wanly at the coach's optimistic outlook and said that she'd do her best. But at night came the fear, eating up her self-confidence. What if there was a physical reason that her ankle broke? After all, the same leg had suffered a compound fracture in the plane crash that had killed her parents, a crash that only she had survived. What if it happened again, and crippled her for life? Those beautiful high jumps, the Salchows, the Lutzes, the triples, sailing high in the air and spinning—they looked so pretty to people in the audience, but they were the most dangerous part of figure skating. Many skaters had incurred life-changing injuries, some of them head injuries that meant they could never skate again. It was daunting. Although Karina was used to bruises and contusions—every skater fell now and again—the injury to the same leg was worrying.

She'd lost her confidence during the months of her recovery. She was afraid to even go on the ice again. The fear kept her from trying. She'd been doing physical rehab for five months, six months the following week, so that she'd be able to walk again, at least. She held out no hope that she might skate once more. She wouldn't heal in time for the Nationals, which were only three months away. She'd need to get back into training and regain the ground she'd lost. It was a daunting thing, even so. A nightmare of exercise and training.

Nationals would be held in January of the following year, just before the Olympics in Pyeongchang, but she was sure that she'd never be involved in them ever again. She and Paul had placed high in the international events, especially the Worlds. Those competitions added to the chances of being chosen for the Olympic Games. Now Paul was trying out a new partner. It was so depressing.

Her finances were iffy and she needed this job she was applying for, to tide her over until she could decide what to do with the rest of her life. Since she and Paul would lose the Envelope, which was based on scores a skater earned and didn't apply to new teams just starting, money was going to be a problem. She might go back to college. She'd done three years on her undergraduate degree in history. She had good grades and she wasn't afraid of hard work.

There were scholarships available and she knew how to apply for them. She might graduate and, with a bachelor's degree, teach as an adjunct at a college. Sure. She might fly to Mars…

It was a sad set of choices. She and Paul Maurice had been partners since they were ten years old. It wasn't a romantic partnership, because he was like a brother to her. They were best friends and still kept in touch. Karina was godmother to the twin boys he had with Gerda, another figure skater whom he'd met during the world competition five years ago. Karina loved the twins. She envied Paul and Gerda their happy marriage and their children. But she was sure that it wasn't for her, that kind of commitment. Not yet, anyway.

Poor Paul. He'd offered to stay out of competition, but Karina had insisted he take another partner. She wasn't sure that she'd ever skate again, or want to. In order to stay in competition, he'd have to have a new partner. Karina would sit out until her injury healed, or possibly, forever. A broken ankle was dangerous if it didn't heal completely. Her doctor wanted her out for six months to a year. In fact, he said flatly, she should give up skating professionally and find a less dangerous occupation. Her leg already had minor joint issues because of the breaks three years ago. The broken ankle would probably ensure some further pain in that joint. Since it was her main landing leg that was affected, continuing in competition could be deadly, he added.

His attitude had depressed her even more than the

injury. Now she wasn't certain that she could ever find the nerve to put on skates again. Incredibly, except for bruises and pulled muscles, she hadn't had a serious accident in all the years she'd been on the ice. And she'd skated since she was three years old. Her accident-free record was a source of amusement to other skaters, most of whom had been sidelined for weeks and months on end due to infrequent mishaps on the ice.

Locals around Jackson Hole called her the Wyoming Legend, after she and Paul won the gold medal in the World Championships the year before. That was great. It was the biggest rush of her life. But she'd lost her chance to be a true legend in figure skating. The thought of Olympic gold haunted her, even now, even with the fear of the ice.

Once, she'd loved going to practice. Just putting on her skates, lacing them up, feeling the ice under her sharp blades was exciting. But now, she was just a normal woman of twenty-three, using her real name, Karina Miranda Carter—not the stage name of Miranda Tanner, under which she'd skated for so long. It was her mother's maiden name, Tanner, and her own middle name. It gave her some anonymity which her mother, a former Olympic gold medalist in women's figure skating, said that she might need one day when she started winning medals. Famous athletes lived in a goldfish bowl. That was true. She thought of how her mother had encouraged her, delighted in even that eighth place in the Olympics three years ago. Her mother had injuries over the years. She'd always gotten right back onto the ice. Karina wasn't that confident.

Her gold medal notwithstanding, Karina was a nobody in Catelow, Wyoming, where she hoped to get the job she'd applied for, as a live-in babysitter for a wealthy widowed rancher's young daughter. She loved children. She'd never thought about having them, because skating had been her whole life. She and her partner spent every day on the ice, practicing for hours on end, perfecting their technique with the German trainer who'd pushed them and coaxed them into fantasy routines. It was one of those that had gotten them the gold pairs medal at the Worlds. It had been a milestone in their lives, the realization of a dream. But with her accident, the dreams of Olympic gold were folded up and put away, like a special garment with sentimental value, treasured but never to be worn again.

She couldn't look back. She had to forge ahead. She would heal completely, her doctor said. It was just a matter of doing the daily exercises. But whether or not she would be able to skate again at her former level was suppositious. There had been major damage. At the very least, she was certain that the ankle would require support if she ever put on skates again. She wasn't sure that she even wanted to try. She remembered with horror the bad landing on the ice, during practice of all things, that had announced itself with a crunching sound. She fell and only then discovered that she was unable to put weight on the ankle. It was her landing foot, which made it all the more tragic and frightening. She thought that the ankle would never be as strong as before, even with her endless physical therapy. The doctor had insinuated as much. A broken mirror was never going to be whole. She was damaged goods. Useless.

She could, however, take care of one small child. She hoped. She'd done babysitting in high school. She'd taken care of Paul and Gerda's twins when they were on the road in competition. She knew CPR and how to handle small emergencies. She'd even done tutoring at a local grammar school as part of her college class work. Surely she could cope.

Besides all that, it was the only job going at the moment. It was October and she had no source of income, with her skating ability lost. All she had to do was convince the rancher, a man by the name of Torrance, that she was capable and responsible so that he'd hire her. The ad had given very little information, except that the applicant should be good with children and willing to live on a ranch. It hadn't even provided the first name of the rancher.

Karina had grown up on a small ranch outside Jackson Hole, Wyoming. She loved animals. So the isolation of the ranch wouldn't be a problem to her. In fact, she liked her own company. She didn't mix well with most people, and she was nervous around men. Any men. It was what kept her single.

Her partner, Paul, had been only a friend all their lives, and she had no social life to speak of. Easy relationships had never appealed to her. Raised by religious parents, she took innocence seriously. Not for her were the one-nighters that some of her colleagues enjoyed. If she ever settled down, she wanted marriage or nothing.

But marriage, commitment, had been the last thing on her mind. She was obsessed with skating. She spent all her free time at the rink. Her grades never suffered, but she was focused on the future. Her friends thought she was crazy. It was so hard to get a place in any competition in skating. Not only was it physically difficult, but there were other pitfalls, the least of which was the internal politics of skating itself. Judges could be biased. Other skaters could be brutal. It wasn't a sport for the weak of spirit.

But Karina's spirit was strong, as her mother's had been. She worked her way up, through divisional championships, all the way to Nationals. From the time she and Paul were kids, they'd focused on pairs figure skating, far more dangerous than ice dancing. Karina had loved the speed, the recklessness, even the risk. Now, here she was, washed up at twenty-three, with no future on the ice, and her hopes of employment based on the acceptance of a nine-year-old girl who might not even like her. Worse, it was the only job offering she might even remotely be able to handle.

Her little white sports car was several years old, purchased when she'd been earning a good living on the ice with her sponsors and public appearances that she and Paul made at various venues sanctioned by the United States Figure Skating Association. It was dutifully maintained, although she'd hit a tree with it recently and it had a dent on the front fender. She couldn't afford body work, but a mechanic had said it was safe to drive. So she drove it through the snow to the ranch, using the onboard navigation system to get her to her destination.

There was a guard at the front gate. That was surprising. She didn't understand why a ranch would need one. He came out of a small block building and smiled as he asked what she wanted.

"I'm applying for this job," she said and smiled back. Her pale gray eyes twinkled as she handed him the newspaper with the ad circled. "I phoned last night, and Mr. Torrance's foreman said that he'd expect me today by two. It's a long drive from Jackson Hole," she added with a laugh.

"I'll say, considering the snow," he replied. "May I see some identification? Sorry, but it's my job if I don't ask."

This Mr. Torrance must be some taskmaster, she thought privately, but she handed him her driver's license.

"Okay, that matches what I've got down here." He indicated a cell phone. "Mr. Torrance is expecting you. Main house is straight down this road about two miles. Keep to the main road, don't turn off on any of the side roads. You can park in front of the house, anywhere you like."

"Thanks."

"I'm Ted," he said.

She smiled. "I'm Karina."

"Nice to meet you. I hope you get the job."

"Thanks. Me, too." She hesitated before she powered the window up. "Are there a lot of candidates?" she wondered.

He shook his head and smiled ruefully. "One lady came up and when she saw how isolated the ranch was, she turned around and went home. Not much to do around here. They draw in the sidewalks at six every day."

She laughed. "It's my kind of place," she said. "I was born down in High Meadow, southeast of Jackson Hole. Not much to do there, either. I like the country. I never was much of a city girl," she added, not quite truthfully.

He laughed, too. "I know what you mean. I'd wither and die in a city. Go right in, miss."

He powered the metal gate open and she drove through with a wave.

THERE WERE FENCED pastures everywhere, and they were maintained well. She saw herds of red cattle all along the way, along with outbuildings, lean-to buildings that would give them shelter in the harsh winter weather.

Red Angus, unless she missed her guess. She'd read about the various cattle breeds that thrived in a Wyoming winter. Black and Red Angus were popular in this part of the country. She'd only been around cattle in a limited way. Her parents had a small ranch when she was a child. She'd grown up with her father's farm animals, including a small herd of Black

Baldies: Herefords mixed with Black Angus, that were beef cattle. She'd helped feed and water them, year-round, as part of her chores. There had been dogs and cats and ducks as well. It had been a lovely childhood, despite the misery of school. She'd never mixed well with the other students. Even then, ice skating had been her life. She'd spent hours at the local rink every day, practicing, while her mother tutored her. Her mother had been an Olympic ice skating champion, an Olympic gold medalist, and she'd trained her daughter well. Karina had always loved the sport. She'd thumbed through her mother's photo album on a daily basis, delighted at the medals and acclamation her mother had claimed in the sport and the photos of her mother together with many legends of ice skating whom she'd known as friends.

She wanted very badly to be part of that world. She was willing to do whatever it took. But that precluded any social life. Other students laughed at her dedication, at her naïveté. She wasn't pretty, but she had a lovely figure. Boys wanted to date her, but she was wary of them. She had only one real boyfriend all the way through school, and he dated her only because his girl had thrown him over. Karina was his comfort. She liked him very much, but she hadn't felt anything for him physically. She wondered sometimes if there was something wrong with her. She'd never felt those passionate urges she read about in her novels. There was a reason that she never really tried to have a relationship. But it left a bad taste in her mouth even to remember it. She'd pushed it to the back of her mind. She didn't really want a boyfriend. Her whole life was skating.

As she approached the ranch, she noted that the ranch house was a huge Victorian mansion, with gingerbread woodwork and black accents. It, like the fences, was quite well kept and sat on what must have been two acres of level terrain with a long paved driveway, automatic gates, and trees and shrubs placed decoratively around the open spaces. The front yard adjoining the house itself was paved as well. The front porch had a swing and chairs everywhere. There were many outbuildings. It looked more like a modern complex than a ranch, and it was obvious that the owner was rolling in cash. Karina had seen properties like this listed online, and they sold for millions of dollars. A traditional small cattle ranch, it was not.

There was a big black-faced German shepherd sitting on the wide front porch when she parked next to it. She hesitated about getting out. She knew that dogs, especially guard dogs, could be ferocious if a stranger approached them.

A small girl came out onto the porch and petted the shepherd. He laid his head against her. She grinned and motioned for Karina to come out.

Karina slid her purse strap onto her shoulder and got out slowly. "Is he friendly?" she asked.

"Sure! He only attacks if Daddy says a word in German," she assured the newcomer. "Are you the lady who's going to take care of me?" she added.

"I hope so," Karina replied gently.

The little girl was petite, with long jet-black hair

in a ponytail, and pale blue eyes in a rounded, pretty face. "I'm Janey," she said. "Who are you?"

"I'm Karina," she replied, smiling.

"It's nice to meet you. My daddy had to go down to the barn. One of the bulls stepped on Billy Joe Smith."

Karina raised her eyebrows and smiled. "Billy Joe?"

She laughed. "He's from Georgia. He says lots of men have two first names down there. He's nice. He raises our German shepherds. They're famous!"

"That one is very handsome," Karina said, eyeing the dog.

"He's Dietrich," Janey replied. "Go say hello, Dietrich!"

The dog ambled over to Karina and sniffed her. She put out a hand to let him smell her, and when he looked up, she ruffled the fur on his neck. "Hello, handsome," she said softly. "You're a gorgeous boy!"

He laid his head against her and drank in the affection.

"You like dogs, don't you?" Janey asked.

"I love them. We had a Siberian husky when I was little. He was named Mukluk and he was an escape artist. He was always getting away. Dad spent so much time hunting him," she laughed.

"I like huskies, but we have lots of cats," Janey sighed, "so we can't have huskies. Daddy says that a lot of them are dangerous to little animals."

"Mukluk certainly was," Karina said with a smile.

"We had to keep our cat in a room of his own, when Mukluk came inside. Mukluk loved to chase him."

"Dietrich just licks our cats," Janey chuckled. "He's a sweetheart."

The sound of an engine diverted them. A big black truck drove up and parked next to Karina's car. A man got out. A big man, with a light olive complexion and jet-black hair under a wide-brimmed Stetson, husky and somber, with dark brown eyes and an attitude that stuck out a mile. He was wearing a fringed leather jacket with black beadwork that emphasized wide shoulders on a body like a wrestler. He glared at Karina.

"Who the hell are you?" he asked.

She was taken aback by the sudden, sharp words.

"She's Karina," the little girl said, smiling and unafraid of the big man and his bad attitude. "She's going to be my companion."

The big man moved a step closer. Karina moved a step back. He was intimidating. "I'm Karina. Karina Carter." She put out an unsteady hand. "It's nice to meet you, Mr...." She searched her memory, addled by his confrontational approach, "Mr. Torrance."

He cocked his head and deep brown eyes narrowed as he surveyed her. Light blond hair that was probably very long, pinned up in a bun on the back of her head. Pale gray eyes. Medium height, slight build, comfortable clothing that looked as if it came from a high-ticket store, sturdy shoes, one foot in a support boot. She was leaning on a cane.

"How can you take care of a child if you can't even walk?" he asked shortly.

"Sir, your daughter hardly looks as if she'd run from anything, even me," she replied with faint humor.

He made a sound, deep in his throat. "No. She doesn't run from much." His eyes narrowed, glittery. "Why do you want this job?"

"Because I'm about to be broke," she said honestly.

A faint smile touched chiseled, very masculine lips. "What do you think, Janey?" he asked the child.

Janey smiled. "I like her," she said simply.

He hesitated, only for a moment. "I run background checks on anyone who comes to work here." He raised his eyebrows when she looked faintly concerned. "Only surface stuff. I don't care if you cheated on a math test in sixth grade," he added, insinuating that the probe wouldn't dig deep. It relieved her. She didn't want him to know what she'd been. She'd lost her whole life.

"I never cheated on a test," she said softly.

"Why am I not surprised?" he mused. "You'll live in," he added. He stated a figure that raised both eyebrows. She'd been used to traveling first class while she and Paul were at the top of the tree in pairs figure skating. But that was a princely salary.

"Isn't that too much, just for babysitting?" she asked, trying to be fair.

"She's a handful," he replied, surprised by the

would-be employee's comment. Nobody had ever said he overpaid his people.

"Yes, I am," Janey said.

"She's obsessed with ice skating, too," he said with a heavy sigh. "I can't cure her, so you'll be required to go to the rink with her every day after school."

"I want to be famous one day," Janey said simply and grinned. "He says I can get a coach this fall, if I practice and prove I'm committed." She frowned. "Committed?" she asked her father.

"Sure. Committed. What you weren't when you said you had to have piano lessons and you stopped after two months," he replied.

Janey sighed. "It was too much time indoors," she said. "I like being outside."

Karina smiled. "I took piano for six years," she said. "I loved it, but I..." She started to say, *I loved skating more*. But she wasn't saying that. "I sort of grew away from it," she said finally.

In the back of her mind, she hoped the child didn't follow the Olympics. But she and Paul had been in Olympic competition only once, three years ago, and the World Championship they'd won was almost a year ago. Besides, they shied away from a lot of publicity. They were private people, in a very public sport. And Karina was known professionally as Miranda Tanner. It would be all right. She hoped.

"She never misses ice skating competitions on TV," her father said. "A whole two months of it," he muttered at his daughter, who grinned. Karina relaxed. The girl was just starting, not a longtime fan. It was unlikely that she'd even recognize Karina as she was now.

"And now we have ice skating at the local rink daily. A woman who used to be an Olympic trainer bought it and put it in good repair. There's a skating club that I enrolled her in. But I don't have time to take her back and forth, and I don't trust any man to do it," he emphasized in a curious way. "So that's going to be your job from now on."

Her heart skipped, not only at the thought of an Olympic trainer who might recognize her, but what he'd said about driving Janey being her job now. "You mean, I'm hired?"

"You're hired. Can you start right now, or do you need time to pack at your home?"

"It's an apartment down in Jackson Hole," she said. "I don't have anything with me..."

"Go home and get it. Come inside for a minute first," he added, noting her worried expression.

Janey danced up to her, with Dietrich still at her side. Her eyes were bright. "We'll have so much fun!" she said. "Do you like skating?"

"I haven't done much of it lately," Karina said. That wasn't a lie. She hadn't.

Janey looked at the support boot on her left foot and grimaced. "Gosh, I guess not. But you'll get better, right?"

"I'll get better," she said softly, and with a smile.

"How did that happen?" Torrance asked.

"I slipped on some wet leaves and fell down a

bank," she lied, not meeting his eyes. "The doctor said it would take about six months to heal completely, and it will be six months next week. I have exercises that I must do daily, so that it doesn't lose function."

"Can you skate now?" he asked, going into an adjoining room.

She swallowed, hard. "Theoretically," she prevaricated. Surely she could just watch Janey from the stands. She didn't want to put skates on ever again.

He came back with a checkbook. "I'm giving you an advance. You'll need gas money at least." He wrote out a check and handed it to her.

She was shocked at the amount, but he didn't comment.

"Don't be long," he added.

"I'll need a few hours, that's all," she stammered.

"If you need someone to drive you, I'll have one of the men do it," he added, looking pointedly at her ankle.

"I can drive okay," she said. "It's my left foot that had the broken ankle."

"All right. We'll expect you back before dark," he added.

"Why? Do you turn into a vampire after the sun sets?" she blurted out and then flushed because it sounded forward.

He suppressed a smile. "No, but these roads get treacherous after dark, and not just because of the snow. Wolves run in these woods." He nodded toward the surrounding countryside. "We protect them, but they're in packs and some aren't people-friendly."

"I'll be in a car. Not walking."

"Cars break down," he returned. "Yours would look right at home in a junkyard."

"It's a nice little car," she shot back, exasperated. "How would you like it if you had a few years more on you, and they said you belonged in a people junkyard?"

His thick eyebrows levered up. "Cars aren't pets."

"Well, mine is," she said haughtily. "I wash and wax it myself and I buy it things."

"Is it a boy car, then?" he mused.

She shifted restlessly, putting her weight on her good leg. "Sort of."

He chuckled. "Okay. Go get your stuff and come back."

She smiled. "I'll do that." She looked at Janey with real affection. "And I won't mind going with you to the ice rink."

"Thanks! Skating is my whole life," the child said with enthusiasm.

She reminded Karina of herself, when she was that age. How quickly the years had passed.

"Before dark," Torrance emphasized. "In addition to wolves, we have deer, lots of them, and they run out in front of cars. My foreman hit one just last week and we had to replace the truck he was in. Tore the front end right out."

She put her hand over her heart. "I shall return, either with my shield or on it," she said solemnly.

He chuckled. "You read about the Spartans, do you?"

She smiled. "I love ancient history. I spend hours reading it on my iPhone."

"Me, too."

As he spoke, his own phone rang. He pulled it out of the carrier on his wide leather belt. "What?" he asked curtly.

There was a pause. "Damn," he muttered. He glanced at Karina. "Well, get going, then."

"Yes, sir." She winked at Janey, climbed into her car and groaned when it backfired first thing. She just knew that Mr. Torrance was watching and laughing. It would only reinforce his bad opinion of her nice little car.

THERE WAS A rigid learning curve on the ranch. Torrance didn't keep regular hours. He seemed to be a night owl as well. On her first night at the ranch, she heard him pacing at three in the morning. She wondered what kept him up. She heard heavy footsteps going past her door, down the staircase, and a rough voice along with an apologetic one.

It wasn't until the next morning that she learned what had happened. A heifer, one of the first-time mothers, had gone into labor and Torrance had gone out with one of his cowboys to help deliver it with a calf pull.

"We had a milk cow whose calf was a breech birth," she commented after Torrance detailed the activities of the night before at breakfast. "Dad and one of the cowboys managed to get him turned without hurting the cow. The vet was about forty miles away, so they had to work fast."

"You lived on a ranch?" he asked.

She nodded. "It wasn't a big one, but my father was fond of Red Angus. We had those, and several Black Baldies."

He smiled. Black Baldies. Beef cattle. "I'll bet you named every one of them," he said slyly.

She flushed. "Well, yes," she confessed, noting Janey's amusement. "I only did it a few times before I learned why the cattle trucks came and took them away. It was a hard lesson. Dad actually told me that they were going to other homes as pets."

"Shame on him," Torrance said quietly. "You do a child no favors by lying."

"He loved me," she said simply, and with a sad smile. "He and my mother sugarcoated everything when I was little. Mama said that the world wouldn't cherish me, so they were going to, until I grew up."

He frowned. "Do they still have the ranch?"

Her face tautened. "They died together in a plane crash, three years ago," she said sadly. "I lost everything at once."

"Damn."

"They say air travel is safe, and I suppose it usually is," she replied. "But I hate airplanes."

"I love them," he said. "I have two. I use one for herding cattle during roundup. The other is a twin-engine Cessna that I use for long flights."

"Airplanes, on a ranch?" she asked, surprised.

He nodded as he finished the scrambled eggs and bacon the cook had brought in earlier. "This is a hell of a big ranch. I have oil interests as well. I do a lot of traveling, which is why you're here."

"Lindy offered to keep me," Janey piped in. She made a face. "I said bad things and got my TV privileges taken away."

"Lindy isn't used to kids," he said, glowering at his daughter. "But you'd better get used to her. She's going to be around for a long time."

Janey just sighed.

Torrance noted Karina's curiosity. "Lindy is my fiancée," he told her. "You'll meet her, in time."

She smiled. "Okay."

He didn't spot any disappointment that he was committed, which relaxed his face. He didn't know this woman. He hoped she hadn't wanted the job because he was wealthy and she saw him as a mark. It wouldn't be the first time it had happened.

"Lindy skated professionally," he continued, missing Karina's start of surprise. "She won a medal at district competition."

"A bronze, and only because two of the contestants dropped out," Janey muttered.

"Stop that," Torrance muttered.

"Well, she keeps trying to tell me how to skate, and I don't think what she says is right," Janey argued. "I have all sorts of books on figure skating. Her jumps are wobbly because she kicks off wrong…"

"Nine, and you're an expert," her father laughed.

"You listen to Lindy. She just wants you to be good on the ice."

"Yes, sir," Janey said, but with a mutinous look.

"You'll be late. I hear an engine idling at the door. Billy Joe's driving you this morning."

"Oh, boy!" she exclaimed.

Torrance sighed. "She loves Billy Joe," he explained. "He's teaching her how to train dogs. As if learning to skate isn't enough for her. And she's found a YouTube channel that teaches Gaelic, so she's fascinated with that as well."

"Cimar a tha sibh," Janey babbled, grinning. It sounded like *chimera a HAH shiv* to Janey.

"And what's that?" her long-suffering parent asked.

"Hello," Janey said brightly.

"Go to school," he groaned.

"Aww, Daddy, don't you want me to be smart?" she asked plaintively.

He got up and kissed the top of her head. "Yes, I do. But not too smart. Not yet."

"I'll take a stupid pill before I leave," the child said pertly.

He chuckled, turning to Karina. "See what you'll have to put up with?" he asked.

Karina was laughing. "Janey, you're an absolute joy," she said softly, and watched the child's blue eyes light up.

"He says I'm a pest." Janey pointed at her father.

"A very nice pest," he amended.

She grinned and went to her room to get her book bag.

A burly man with thick black hair under a wide-brimmed hat, wearing a heavy coat and denim jeans and boots, stuck his head in the door. "Hey, Big Mike," he called. "Is she coming or not?"

"She's on her way," Torrance said.

The man looked at Karina and smiled. "Who are you?"

"She's the new babysitter, and hands off," he told the man. "We're keeping this one."

The man made a face. "Spoilsport." His pale eyes twinkled. "Want to learn how to train dogs?" he asked.

Torrance glowered. "That only works on obsessed nine-year-old girls," he pointed out.

"Can't blame a man for trying," the newcomer chuckled.

"Hey, Billy Joe!" Janey called. "Here I am. See you after school, Daddy!" she added as she and the man went out into the falling snow.

Karina looked at the rancher with open curiosity. "Big Mike?" she wondered.

"Nickname," he said, getting up. "My first name is Micah, and I'm large. Hence the nickname they stuck me with. I'll see you later."

"What do you want me to do, while Janey's at school?" she asked.

"Read a book. Learn French. Watch YouTube to see how you attract aliens and capture Bigfoot."

"Oh."

"We're not rigid about schedules. Clocks have no place on a working ranch. Have a good day."

"You, too," she began, but he was already shouldering into his coat. He grabbed his hat and never looked back. All that, by the time she started the second word.

CHAPTER TWO

KARINA WAS SITTING on the leather sofa, reading a book on her iPhone, when the front door opened suddenly and a woman walked in. She had short blond hair and pale blue eyes, and she was dressed like someone on a Fortune 500 list.

"Where's Micah?" she asked.

Karina just stared at her for a minute, stunned. "Oh! You mean Mr. Torrance. I'm sorry. I don't know. I just started working here yesterday."

"Who are you?" the woman demanded.

Karina hesitated, but if the woman felt comfortable just walking in the door without an invitation, she must belong here. "I'm Karina Carter," she said. "Mr. Torrance hired me to take care of his daughter."

"Oh. You're the babysitter."

Karina smiled. "Yes."

"I'm Lindy Blair," the woman replied.

"Mr. Torrance's fiancée," Karina nodded, realizing who she was. "I'm very glad to meet you."

The other woman stared at her for a long moment, sizing her up. Then she seemed to relax, as if she didn't find anything threatening about the new employee. "He's supposed to fly me to LA later today. I have a business meeting."

Karina didn't know what to say, so she just nodded.

"Well, I'll go look for him," Lindy said. "He'll be out with those smelly cattle in the barn, I expect." She made a face. "All that money, and he helps pull calves. I don't know what the world's coming to..."

She walked out, still muttering.

So that was the fiancée, Karina thought. She seemed very intelligent, and apparently she was a businesswoman. It was what she'd expect of a rich man's future wife. She was also very pretty, and had a nice figure. But Janey didn't seem to like her. Perhaps she was less friendly with children than she'd been with Karina. It was pretty obvious that she wasn't fond of other women. But at least she didn't seem to think of Karina as a threat.

Fat chance, she thought to herself. Mr. Torrance was nice looking, but Karina knew nothing about men and she wasn't here to fall in love with the boss. She just wanted to take care of Janey and figure out what she was going to do later, when her foot healed.

THERE WAS AN injured calf in the barn. Karina had discovered the animals during her first week on the job. The livestock foreman, Danny something, had been welcoming when she asked if she could see what they kept in the barn besides the heavy equipment that was used to carry feed to the animals and check the pastures.

"We use that one to haul those big circular bales of hay you see." He indicated them in the distance. "We truck them out to the cattle. We use that one—" he indicated an odd-looking short-bed truck "—to help herd them and to go out looking for strays."

"I thought ranchers had cowboys who rode horses for that," she said.

"We do, and they do. But we use a lot of different methods to keep up with the herds," he chuckled. "It's not the boss's favorite thing, anyway. He's an oil man before he's a rancher. He inherited the ranch. He learned to love it, but it took time. He misses the city. You can tell. That's where he lived before his father died and left him this place. He was going to sell it, but there was a delegation."

"A delegation?"

"All the cowboys and the foremen and the vet and the farrier and even the townspeople came over in a group to beg him to keep the ranch in the family. See, the community grew up around the ranch. We all depend on it for our livelihood. Not many good jobs going in a place this remote, so the ranch keeps food on the table. Once he understood that, he backed off from the sale. He's been here ever since. That was ten years ago. He's somewhat settled." He made a face. "Of course, he's marrying that high-maintenance blonde. She'll probably bankrupt him in a year. Her last husband ended up on a Caribbean island, working as a tour guide. She got everything in the divorce. Had a really good attorney," he added on a chuckle.

"She seems very nice," Karina faltered.

"From a distance, so does a cobra," he returned. He grimaced. "Don't mention that I said that, would you? It's really hard to find work with winter coming on."

She laughed. "I won't sell you out. I'm in the same position. I'd have a problem finding something else, too."

"Don't mind the isolation?" he wondered as he walked her down the paved aisle past several small stalls.

"Not at all," she lied. "It's pretty here."

She missed the bright lights, too, but hers were in competition skating rinks all over the world. She missed them terribly. Lights and applause and music, always music…!

"We've got a little steer over here," he interrupted her thoughts. "His mama walked off and left him, so he's a bottle calf. We're keeping him inside and feeding him by hand until he's ready to go out into the corral."

"Oh, he's so cute!" she exclaimed. He had a black-and-white coat and big eyes that stared at the newcomer. "Can I pet him?" she asked.

"Sure. He's gotten pretty tame since he's been here."

She glanced at him with a mischievous smile. "What's his name?"

He flushed a little and cleared his throat. "Clarence. Don't tell the boss. He hates it when we name one of the beef cattle."

"Beef. Oh." She winced.

"We might start a delegation," he began.

She laughed out loud.

SHE SETTLED INTO the hay next to the little guy and ran her hand over his head. He laid his head in her lap and ate up the attention.

Meanwhile, Micah Torrance had come home and missed his newest hire. His cook and handyman, Burt, had just come back from a buying trip for the kitchen and noticed the new employee headed out back. He chuckled and pointed the boss toward the barn. Danny was outside, headed to his truck.

"Have you seen the babysitter?" he asked Danny.

"Sure. She's in there with Clarence." He stopped and bit his lip at his employer's amused expression.

"Clarence. For God's sake, we're not running a petting zoo here," he said shortly.

"I know that, sir."

"Clarence," he scoffed.

He passed Danny, who rushed to his truck before the boss could take a second bite out of him, and went into the barn. His footsteps didn't echo as he went down the bricked aisle. There, in the last stall, was Karina, sitting in the hay, talking to a beef steer. She was running her hands over his little head and telling him how sweet he was.

For some reason, the sight of her like that made him irritable.

"Do you work here?" he asked curtly.

She gasped, put the calf aside, and jumped up,

brushing hay off her jeans. "Mr. Torrance! I'm so sorry! I just wanted to see what was in the barn..." She stopped, flushed.

His dark eyes went over her like searching hands. The jeans fit in all the right places. They were conservative, but they did nothing to hide the exquisite figure they contained. Neither did that green sweater, which emphasized the pert, firm little breasts under it. He got an uncomfortable reaction to them, which caused him to turn away.

"Janey's just home from school," he said shortly. "She wants to go to the skating rink."

"Yes, sir!"

She followed him out of the barn, embarrassed that she'd forgotten the time. He was such an impatient man. She hoped she could get used to that. He reminded her of a skating coach she and Paul had signed on with four years ago, a man who was lauded as the best coach in skating, but he turned out to have a terminal bad attitude. He rode them mercilessly, made them both nervous and then chided them for mistakes they made because of it. They'd taken almost two years of his abuse because they were too nervous about replacing him. But they'd become acquainted with a Danish coach through another pairs skater. He seemed very nice and he didn't yell. So she and Paul coaxed him into training them. In fact, he was the one who'd helped them win the Worlds with his choreography. She still recalled how difficult it was to tell their old coach they were leaving. He'd been vicious and even more abusive. It had been a difficult parting. But you didn't go to a new coach until you'd informed the old one you were quitting him. There were firm rules about that sort of thing.

Still, the experience had left scars. Torrance reminded her of the man they'd fired. He was just as impatient, just as snarky. Yes, that was the word.

"Snarky," she muttered under her breath as they trudged through the cold wind to the front porch.

He turned, glaring down at her from under the brim of his hat. "Snarky?"

She turned red. "I was…thinking to myself," she blurted out.

He raised both eyebrows. "Snarky." He made a huffing sound, turned, and walked to the front door. "Why aren't you wearing a coat?" he asked.

She grimaced. "I don't like coats," she said. "I hardly ever feel the cold."

She reminded him of a figure carved from ice. She was poised and graceful and full of surprises. But her elegance—yes, that was the word—seemed as natural as if she'd been born of royalty. And she was like an ice princess, cool and unyielding. Odd, that he'd consider her in that light. She could still blush. How old had she said she was? Twenty-three. Were there any innocent women that age in the world? Then he wondered why he was entertaining such thoughts. He had a fiancée who was all heat inside, although she presented a cool and businesslike image to the world. He shouldn't be looking at other women in the first place.

His interest in her made him bad-tempered. "The

ice rink is just outside town. They're only open until 9:00 p.m. so make sure you're headed back soon after that," he instructed. "You have a cell phone, right?"

"Yes, sir."

"Is it charged?" he asked, turning, and his eyes shimmered.

It was as if he knew. She colored again. "I have a car charger for it."

"Use it," he snapped. "I hope you keep blankets and a shovel and water in that highway-going coffin you call a car."

She drew in a breath. "I'll get some."

"Have Billy Joe round some up for you," he said. "If you ever get stuck when it snows—and don't kid yourself, we get snow in early October—you call the ranch. Somebody will come and find you. Charge that phone." He looked at his watch. It was a Rolex. Karina had seen enough of them to recognize it. "I have to pick up Lindy and get to the airport. We've got meetings in LA. Take good care of my daughter."

"Always, sir."

He made another gruff sound, deep in his chest, and walked into the house.

"Hi, Daddy!" Janey called. She hugged him. "You're off again, I guess?" she asked with a wistful sigh.

"If I don't work, we don't eat," he pointed out. "Not to mention having to keep Billy Joe well fed. Without him, Dietrich will fall into bad habits and eat us in our sleep."

Janey laughed. "He never would. Would you,

sweet boy?" she asked the big dog, who was almost always at her side.

"Be good for what's-her-name," he told the child and glanced at Karina to make sure she knew that he didn't care enough to remember her name.

She got the message. She was office furniture. She just grinned. "Have a safe trip, sir."

"You're hoping I'll trip over my big feet and go headfirst into the dirt," he said with gleeful malice. "But I won't. I'll see you both when I get back. Probably next week sometime. Lindy wants to catch a show at that new nightclub in downtown LA."

"Bye, Daddy."

He smiled at her, glanced with studied disinterest at Karina, and went out the door.

"Are you ready to go?" Janey asked excitedly when her father had gone. "I can't wait to get to the rink!"

"You said earlier that you didn't have a coach yet?" Karina asked absently.

She sighed. "Not yet. But Lindy trains me sometimes," she said. She didn't look as if she enjoyed that at all.

Karina turned and smiled at her. "You need a coach in order to learn the basics. Has she run you through the preliminaries? Inside and outside edges, chassés, toe loops…?" She stopped because Janey was looking at her as if she were speaking Greek. "None of those?"

Janey grimaced. "She makes me do figure eights. What are inside and outside edges?"

Oh, boy, Karina was thinking. The district competition–winning skater was just running Janey through the old-time basics. Not bad, but it wouldn't prepare her for even the easiest pre-preliminary competitions. Perhaps Lindy thought, as Janey's father did, that she was only playing at it and wasn't serious enough for a trainer.

Janey's face fell at Karina's expression. "I'm not learning the right things, am I?" she asked plaintively.

"You're learning what used to be compulsories back in the '90s. They aren't used anymore. It's not a bad thing," she added firmly. "They teach patience and control. Are you learning to use both the outside edge and the inside edge?"

"What are outside and inside edges again?" Janey asked.

Karina made a whistling sound. "Okay. I'll teach you what I can. But you need a full-time coach if you really want to compete." She hesitated, her eyes quiet and soft as she smiled at the child. "Figure skating isn't a pastime, it's a career. It obsesses people who do it. They're on the ice every free minute, practicing. It really is a full-time commitment. Once you start, you won't have much of a social life," she concluded.

Janey sighed. "I don't have much of a social life already," she said heavily. "Nobody likes me except Bess. She's overweight and they pick on her, too."

She frowned. "Why do they pick on you?"

The young girl looked up at her with sad eyes. "I'm clumsy," she said. "I fall all the time, and they think it's funny. Once I fell right in front of the principal and tripped him and he went headfirst into the cleaning guy's bucket. It was full of dirty water." She drew in a long audible breath. "So I'm sort of the class joke."

That reminded Karina of her own childhood. She, too, had been clumsy and the other kids made fun of her. Karina moved closer. "There will always be bullies," she said gently. "Even when you're grown. You'll learn how to handle them. This is just a stage in your life, the hard part. When you're older, it will get better. Honest, it will."

"Were you picked on, in school?" Janey wanted to know.

Karina smiled. "Always. I had a hobby," she said. "I was obsessed with it, and my classmates thought I was stupid. I had to learn to balance what I did after school with what I was supposed to do in school. I made an effort to study every night, and brought my grades up."

"A hobby?"

"Yes. A silly one," she added, to keep Janey from asking questions. "We should go."

"Okay." She grabbed her skating bag and looked up at Janey. "You know about figure skating."

Karina nodded. "My mother used to be in competition," she said. She didn't add that her mother was a two-time gold medalist in the Olympics.

"You do skate, don't you, when you can, I mean," Janey amended, looking at Karina's foot in the boot.

"When I can."

"I wish you could skate with me. You wouldn't yell if I made a mistake, would you?" she asked with a resigned smile.

Obviously, Lindy did. It wasn't the way to teach. You had to be gentle and explicit and able to translate what you knew into words that a novice could understand. "I never yell," Karina replied.

"I guess I could pester Dad again about a coach, when he's home," she added quietly as they got into Karina's car and started down the long driveway to the highway. "He's never home, though."

"It's a big ranch," Karina said.

"Sure it is, and he has lots of stock in oil and oil refineries," Janey said. "But I'd rather he made less money and stayed home more."

"I'm sure he wishes he could," she replied.

"At least I have you, Karina," Janey said with a smile. "We're going to be great pals, I can already tell."

That lifted Karina's heart, and she smiled.

THE RINK WAS almost empty. Well, it was a school night, after all, and many children would be home doing work for the next day. Karina's own parents had insisted that she do her homework every night, even if it meant missing a few hours' practice when she had a lot of homework.

But this was bad for business. The rink needed to attract a lot of skaters in order to keep the doors open. It would be a shame if it had to close down for lack of patrons.

Karina frowned. There was no music. Apparently, there were no rental skates, either. She'd left her skates behind at her apartment, which was paid for a year in advance when she still had money. She couldn't afford to get rid of it, in case she lost this job and had to find another. It was great foresight, she thought, that she'd been wise enough to do that.

But she didn't have skates with her. Just as well. She was too afraid to get onto the ice, afraid of causing the ankle to break again.

She'd used the cane and the boot as a defensive mechanism, a way to convince herself that she was unable to get back on the ice. But her therapist had said that she could skate, that she was hiding behind a healed injury. She only had to conquer the fear, he insisted. She let out a long sigh."I wish you could skate with me," Janey said when Karina had helped her lace up her skates. "That's not how Lindy laces them," she added, frowning.

Karina frowned. She didn't like the skates Janey was using. They were hockey skates, not figure skates. It was a bad start.

"Why do you have hockey skates?" she asked the girl.

Both eyebrows rose. "Hockey skates?" She looked at the skates Karina was lacing up for her.

"Yes. Those don't have toe picks. You can't do jumps in them." She felt guilty when she saw the child's face fall. "Sorry. I probably shouldn't have mentioned it."

"Lindy said they were all I'd need, because I

wouldn't be able to learn anyway," Janey said with a long sigh.

Karina felt her temper rise. She fought it. "Anyone can learn to skate. It's just a matter of practice."

"I'm clumsy," the girl reminded her. "I fall a lot."

Karina finished the lacing. "Do you know how to fall properly, so that you don't break your wrists?"

She shook her head.

Karina stood up and demonstrated the correct way to fall, drawing in the arms and the chin. "You try to fall sideways if it's possible, so that you don't break your wrist trying to break your fall," she explained. "And you lean forward, so that you won't slip and fall back on the ice and hit your head." She hesitated. "Really, you should be wearing a helmet while you're learning."

Janey made a face. "Nobody wears helmets around here," she protested.

"Well, we can talk about that later," Karina compromised.

"THIS IS HOW you get up on the ice," she continued. She put herself down on the floor, pulled one leg up and propped both hands on it, then pulled up her other leg and stood up, keeping her weight on the bended knee.

"Wow," Janey said. "That's amazing!"

Karina smiled, loving the child's enthusiasm. That was how she'd felt when her mother first put her on ice skates at the age of three.

"Always remember to put the pads on your feet

before you put on your skates. It's how you keep your ankles from getting sore and blistered," Karina replied, with her long knowledge of skates and their idiosyncrasies. "I'm glad to see you have pads, at least."

"Lindy said I'd get blisters if I didn't wear them."

"These skates are very stiff. Did you get them new?"

"Yes," Janey said.

"There are heat molds that can shape them to your foot. I don't know if they have such a machine here, but I know they have one at the rink in Jackson Hole."

"Dad would never have time to take me so far," the young girl said with a sigh. "It's business, all the time."

"We'll see what we can do. Meantime, we'll try breaking in your skates slowly. It also helps if you exercise your ankles before you even put the skates on."

"You know a lot."

She smiled. "My mom knew all this stuff. She taught me."

"I don't know anything. I can just barely stay on skates. At first, I couldn't even stand up on them. But Lindy taught me to spread my legs apart with my ankles turned out. It feels good to stand that way."

"It's dangerous," Karina corrected. "You must always stand straight on your skates, with your feet together. Can you do swizzles and crossovers?"

"Can you speak English?" Janey teased.

Karina laughed. "See that girl over there, the one in the black outfit? She's doing backward swizzles."

Janey watched. "Gosh, I can't even skate backward at all!"

Obviously, Lindy wasn't interested in tutoring the girl. It was a shame.

"Get out there and skate for a bit. Hold on to the barrier and just walk along the ice near it. Feet together, weight forward, hold on to the barrier. I'll be back in a minute. I want to talk to the owner of the rink. They say she's a former coach."

"One of the older girls at school has lessons with her. She's German," she added. "The girl says she's nice and very patient."

"I'll just have a word with her. Go slowly," she added. "Stand straight, feet together, knees slightly bent, body slightly bent forward, but not too far. Feet with heels together and toes turned out. Walk like a penguin. Hold on to the barrier."

"That's so much to remember!"

"Just give it a try," she said. "How did you learn Gaelic?"

"By repeating the phrases over and over again until I knew them by heart."

"Skating is exactly the same. We learn by repetition. I'll go find the owner."

"Okay. Thanks, Karina!"

She smiled. "You're most welcome."

JANEY WENT GINGERLY onto the ice while Karina, with her cane, made her way to the office. It was a huge building. Walking tired her.

She was out of shape, she told herself, because she

was winded by the time she reached the owner's office and tapped on the door.

"Come in," came a very German-accented voice from the other side.

Karina went in, closing the door behind her, and gasped when she saw the woman's face.

"Mrs. Meyer!" she exclaimed, stunned.

Hilde Meyer lifted her eyes from her computer screen and recognition brought a beaming smile to her own lips. "Karina!" she exclaimed, rushing around the desk to hug Karina close. "Oh, my sweet girl, I'm so sorry for what happened to you!"

Karina fought tears. "The doctor at the rink where I fell said I should give up trying to ever skate again!"

Mrs. Meyer drew back. "Most doctors tell everyone that who breaks a bone," she scoffed. "One told me that, the last year I was in competition. I ignored him. I won the silver at the Worlds a month later," she chuckled. "But you, what are you doing here?"

"I'm babysitting a nine-year-old girl whose father owns a ranch. Please don't tell anyone about me," she added gently. "I don't want anyone to know."

"You're a legend down around Jackson Hole, you know," the owner teased. "Everyone was so proud when you and Paul won the Worlds."

Karina sighed. "Paul's trying out a new partner for the competitions this year. He didn't want to do it. We'll lose the Envelope, you see. But I told him that he has to have a partner to compete and I'm not sure I want to skate again. Ever." She sighed. "I miss Paul. We were good together."

"Good enough for Olympic gold, in my opinion," Mrs. Meyer replied. She winced as she looked down at the protective boot on Karina's foot. "You had a very bad fall. I hope you're keeping up with the physical therapy. And you should get back on the ice as soon as you're able," she added firmly. "The longer you wait, the harder it will be."

"I'm afraid to skate again," Karina confessed shamefully. "I actually heard the bones break, and it was on my landing foot, where the damage was done."

"We all have had accidents that put us out of competition, sometimes for a year, sometimes two," she was told. "But a true champion won't let herself be discouraged by an accident. And truthfully, Karina, you have been most fortunate over the years. This was your first bad fall. Most of us have had several."

Karina smiled sadly. "Maybe if I'd had more than bruises, I'd know how to handle being out of competition for so long. I don't know that I can go back to it. I told our coach that I was through with ice skating."

Mrs. Meyer just nodded. "It's early days yet. The accident is still fresh in your mind, and you must cope with the recuperation period. But you will. If I can help in any way, I will be happy to. I was a coach, you know, after my career on the ice ended. I like to think that I was a good one. I was told that my ideas for choreography were too old-fashioned and silly. I lost so many students to the more modern coaches that I just gave up," she confessed sadly. "I heard this rink was available on the market, and I had saved religiously while I was earning big money." She looked around and spread her arms. "So here I am," she said, forcing a smile.

"Your choreography was magnificent," Karina corrected. "You coached two Olympic-winning figure skating teams," Karina recalled. "Their routines were a little like the ones Paul and I did. Only, much better," she teased.

"I know your coach. He's good. But he isn't demanding enough."

Karina laughed. "That's what Paul said, after we placed eighth at the Olympics last time."

"I watched your performance," Mrs. Meyer replied. "There were a few things I would have changed about it."

"Our coach was involved with a skater at the time," she chuckled. "His mind was more on her than our choreography."

"Such a shame. You had the talent, you know, to go all the way. And Paul! Such grace, such athletic ability. He did the lifts with you as if you weighed nothing at all. He's trying out the Garner girl over in Colorado, yes?" She shook her head. "She's good on the jumps, she's a good athlete. But she has no grace, no elegance, and she's overburdened with piercings and tattoos and carnival-colored hair. She has an attitude problem that will make Paul uncomfortable. He's like you, sweetheart, he doesn't like confrontational people."

Karina smiled. "No, I don't like them either."

"Nor is she elegant. You were blessed with that

from the beginning. I remember your mother," she added with a sad smile. "She was so proud of you!"

"I miss her, still. I miss my dad, too. They made such sacrifices to keep me on the ice." She didn't add that she was still having nightmares about the way they died, three years after the fact. She kept that to herself.

"Parents do sacrifice, when they love their children. I was never so fortunate as to have them with my late husband. So I have adopted many skaters," she added with a grin. "I formed a skating club here, also, so that we can get a coach to help the beginners who want to learn through the Learn to Skate endeavor sponsored by the U.S. Figure Skating Association."

"That's a step in the right direction," Karina said. "Do you have a coach in mind?"

"Yes. He's coming next week to talk to me. He placed high in world competition and he was tenth in Olympic men's figure skating at the last Olympics."

Karina nodded. She wasn't really that interested in the coach. She sighed. "I miss being on the ice." She looked down at her boot. "The doctor said I could begin to skate this month. I didn't even bring my ice skates up here. You don't have any for rent at all, do you?" she added.

"It seemed a useless expense when I bought the rink," came the reply.

Karina cocked her head. "A lot of people won't go to the expense of buying skates and all the accessories that go with them," she said. "Casual skaters, especially. Rental skates would bring in a lot more business."

"You think so?" Mrs. Meyer asked.

"I do. I believe the rentals would boost your revenue. More people would be more inclined to hire a coach if they didn't have to spend money to buy skates."

Mrs. Meyer's eyes brightened. "I will consider it, quite seriously."

"One other thing," she began, and hesitated. "I'm sorry, I'm sticking my nose in..."

"What was the other one thing?" the coach interrupted, interested.

"Well, it's the music."

"There is no music," Mrs. Meyer said, frowning.

"I know. That's the other thing. Most rinks have it, especially where there are young skaters. It helps to have a variety, but it's nice to skate by. The rinks also have announcers who vary the free skate period by calling out men and women and pairs skates."

"Music. An announcer." She pondered that. "I have not considered music, although the wiring and the speakers are there to permit it. Perhaps a mix of classical and pop," she added thoughtfully.

Karina grinned. "Thanks for not being offended. I don't mean to criticize," she added quickly.

"Helpful suggestions are not criticisms. I would very much like the business to operate in the black," she added wistfully. "The attendance is not what I expected when I bought the business."

"I think with a few changes, you can make it pay

very well, even in a small town like Catelow. There aren't a lot of rinks north of Jackson Hole. You could make this one into a very profitable business. You might also consider advertising the rink in weekly newspapers around the area, along with the skating club. It will encourage people to sign up, since joining the club will entitle them to enter into competition and take tests to level up."

Mrs. Meyer caught her breath. "What a marvelous idea. Karina, you are amazing!"

Karina chuckled. "No, I'm not. I'm just observant. I very much want you to succeed. There must be many aspiring skaters who would be disappointed if they had to drive all the way to Jackson Hole to skate."

"I must agree. That was one reason I bought the property." She nodded. "I will consider the changes. If you will consider getting back on the ice," she added.

Karina let out a breath. "It's going to be very hard."

"Most worthwhile things are. You have a wonderful gift, that poise and grace on the ice. I would hate to see you forfeit it, out of fear."

"Perhaps you're right." She hesitated. "It was another matter I actually came by to discuss. I'm working with a young girl. Her father hired me to be a live-in babysitter because he's out of town so much. She wants to learn to skate. Her father's fiancée has been teaching her the old compulsory figures. She knows none of the preliminaries that she'll need to be able to do in competition, if she sticks with it. She needs a coach. I can show her the moves, but I'm not really good at training anyone else."

Mrs. Meyer laughed. "So it's a very good thing that my coach candidate comes next week, *ja*?"

Karina smiled. "Yes. Then all I have to do is talk her father into paying for lessons. But that won't be much of a problem, he's wealthy."

"A good thing, if the child truly wants to go into competition."

"Tell me about it," Karina sighed. "When Paul and I went to the World Championships, we were paying over $150,000 a year for equipment and travel expenses and skates and costumes. It's so expensive in the higher levels of competition. My parents took out a second mortgage to pay my way when I was rising with Paul into senior championship and then Nationals. Even with the Envelope, it's a sport that costs far more than most people can pay."

"This is true," came the reply. "But as to coaching the child, who better than a world champion to teach her, really? At least, until my coach is working here."

Karina was troubled. "I'd have to get on the ice to do it. And Mr. Torrance's fiancée might resent my interference."

"The child is Janey Torrance, yes?" the owner asked quietly. "Yes, I know her. Her father's fiancée started bringing her here two months ago. They only come one day a week." She shook her head. "She yells at the child for any mistake. It is not the way to teach. And what she teaches her, also not good," she added. “The child has had several falls because of the so-called instruction.”

“I’ll see what I can do to teach her correctly,” Karina said. “She loves the sport, but not everyone is cut out for it. I want to see what she can do before I encourage her. If she really has the talent, and the drive, I’d be happy to work with her temporarily.” She grimaced. “But I’ve never coached anyone.”

“It’s only for a week or so,” Mrs. Meyer said with twinkling eyes. “Then you can turn her instruction over to the coach.”

Karina sighed and smiled. “Okay, then.”

And just like that, she made the decision.

IT REQUIRED HER to drive back down to Jackson to get her own skates. She’d watched Janey on the ice during her tedious first few swizzles. The child did fairly well going forward. Backward was another matter. Karina had to teach from the sidelines, something that was very difficult at best.

She waited until Mr. Torrance came back from his business trip and asked for a few hours off.

“What for?” he asked curtly. “Bored already?” he added in a snarly tone.

“I have to go to my apartment to get my ice skates,” she said. “The local rink doesn’t rent them.”

His eyebrows went up. “How does she expect to stay in business without offering rentals?” he wanted to know.

“I asked. She says she’s thinking of doing that.”

“I hope she can make the business pay. The last

owner just let it slide. This new one doesn't seem to understand how to run it."

"It's a learning curve," Karina said. She hesitated. "Janey wants to learn, but if she's serious about skating, she'll need a coach. Mrs. Meyer is interviewing one next week and she thinks he'll do." She looked up at him with soft, patient eyes and felt a jolt as he looked back at her. She lowered her eyes at once, shocked to feel her heartbeat going into high gear. "If Janey really wants to compete, she'll have to belong to the ice skating club at the rink. They won't let you take the tests unless you belong to a club. She also needs membership in the United States Figure Skating Association. It gives great benefits to members."

"They don't have a coach at the rink," he said curtly, ignoring the other comments. "I asked. That's why Lindy's trying to teach her."

She grimaced.

He moved a step closer. "Spill it," he said shortly.

She bit her lower lip.

"Okay, obviously Lindy's doing something you don't like, but you're afraid to tell me in case I blow up and fire you."

Her eyes widened. "Are you psychic?" she blurted out.

He shrugged. "I never lose a hand in poker. Maybe so. Spill it. What's Lindy doing wrong?"

"She's teaching Janey how to do compulsory figures," she said. "That hasn't been part of competition since the late '90s. It's not required anymore. Not that it's a bad thing to teach. It's good for discipline.

But if Janey wants to compete at all, she needs to learn swizzles and crossovers and loops and flips…"

"Obviously you know something about skating," he said.

"I've been skating all my life," she replied simply. "I had a friend who competed," she lied.

"So why can't you teach her?" he wanted to know.

She looked up at him with all her insecurities visible.

"You broke your ankle and now you're afraid to go back on the ice," he said.

She flushed.

"When you fall off a horse, you get right back on or you'll never lose the fear," he said. "You'll never ride again. When I was six, I took a bad tumble. A horse threw me during the summer, when I was home from boarding school, and I broke my collarbone. I was scared to get back on a horse at all, but this is a working ranch and everybody who lived here had jobs to do. Even at the age of six, I was expected to do my part. My father was a hard taskmaster. He put me back on my horse the minute my doctor released me and sent me out to help keep the branding irons hot while the cowboys branded cattle." He smiled wistfully. "So I learned what to do about fear. It was a hard lesson, at the time. Fear must be faced. There's nowhere to run that you can get away from it."

"I guess so." She looked down at her foot. "I'll go get my skates and I'll try to teach her, if your fiancée won't mind."

"She won't," he replied. "She's not really good with kids and she's impatient. Janey came home from practice one day crying because Lindy yelled at her."

Inside, Karina was grinding her teeth. "It's not a good way to teach."

"I know that. You never yell, do you?" he asked gently, and his brown eyes twinkled as he smiled at her.

She laughed. "No. I never yell."

"I'll make it right with Lindy," he said. "It's not really her fault. I talked her into it, because Janey was so determined to skate. Lindy did win a medal in a regional championship, after all. She knows skating inside out."

Karina could have argued about that, but she wasn't going to blow her cover. She didn't want anyone to know how well known she'd been before. She was tired of questions. Reporters had been persistent when the accident first happened, and some were cruel. She was done with all that.

"No comment?" he asked.

"Sorry. I drifted away," she replied. She looked up into his soft, dark eyes curiously. "Why doesn't she like children?" she asked impulsively.

"She's a businesswoman," he said. "We get along well because we're not together much." He chuckled. "I suppose she'll mellow when we get married. I'd like more children, but she's not into that. I guess one will have to do."

"That's a shame," she said gently. She was thinking that he looked the sort of man who would welcome a houseful of children. She smiled, thinking about her own experience with little kids at the skating rinks where she'd practiced. "I'd like to have children one day. Lots of them."

He frowned. "You're what, twenty-three? Why aren't you married or living with somebody?"

She just stared at him, surprised by the question. She didn't quite know how to answer it. She wasn't comfortable telling him why.

CHAPTER THREE

MICAH STARED DOWN into Karina's soft gray eyes and got lost in them. That was a first. Even Lindy, as hot as she was behind closed doors, didn't have that tenderness about her. Lindy was demanding, aggressive, passionate. But she wasn't a nurturing woman, and she didn't want babies.

This woman had a tenderness he'd rarely seen in his life. He'd married his late wife, Anabelle, on a whim, because she was great in bed and her family's wealth equaled that of his own. It had been more a merger than a marriage, despite the unexpected and delightful event of Janey's birth. Anabelle hadn't wanted a child, but Micah had wanted the child badly when he knew his wife was pregnant. She'd tried to talk him into a termination, but he'd said that he'd take care of the child. She'd only have to carry it for nine months and he'd handle everything afterward.

So Anabelle had gone through the pregnancy, not happily, and they had a little girl. Janey was a joy to Micah from the minute she was born. He'd taken care of her, as he'd promised, with the help of a live-in nurse for the first few months while he took care of business. Anabelle had barely noticed the child. She went overseas on cruises with her friends and never seemed to care that she had a baby at home who needed two parents.

Not many years passed, there had been a catastrophe and Anabelle had been killed. Micah felt the guilt of her death. It haunted him. After the tragedy, his daughter became his great joy. He had a housekeeper, Burt, an older man of about sixty, who helped with her as she grew. But as his business prospered, and Janey became more interested in after-school activities, she got a little too much for the older man, who kept house and cooked for the family. It was difficult for him to manage the household and be required to drive Janey so many places, especially in winter, when the snow made driving difficult. Winter was coming on fast. He'd asked for help. So Micah had advertised and Karina had become Janey's new caretaker.

He wasn't sure he'd done the right thing when he saw the new babysitter in person. Karina was nursing an injury and she walked with a cane. Janey liked her. That was the important thing. But he was still concerned about having his daughter in an ice rink alone. People skated wildly sometimes, without considering that a child, new to skating, might be too unsteady on her skates to avoid collisions. Falls could do great damage. He knew that from Lindy, who'd told him stories about fellow skaters being badly cut by their own blades, much less someone else's. Falls could result in bruising or even broken bones. He stared pointedly at Karina's ankle. That injury was proof to him that the woman should never get on skates in the first place. Did she even know how to skate?

Karina grimaced when she saw where he was looking. She took a deep breath. "Mr. Torrance," she said softly, "I know I don't look competent enough to watch out for a child at a skating rink. But I can skate…sort of," she amended, because she dreaded even the thought of going on the ice after the accident. "I'll go out into the rink with her," she added, gritting her teeth, because she was afraid. "I promise, I'll take care of her."

"Your injury," he began gruffly.

"It's almost healed," she said quietly, hating to admit that. It had given her an excuse to avoid putting on skates again. "It will bear weight. I do my exercises and physical therapy every single day. The boot is a habit," she confessed, lowering her eyes. "The cane helps stabilize me. But I can skate. My mother taught me how, years ago. I'll be fine on the ice." *I think*, she added mentally.

He knew she was prevaricating. She probably needed the job. His keen eyes registered that her clothing came from midlevel stores. Apparently that high-ticket outfit she'd worn on the day she applied was her best. Now she kicked around in jeans and sweaters. Her car, although well kept, was several years old. She wouldn't be here if she could do something more than take care of a child. He could at least give her a chance, he told himself.

"All right," he said after a minute. "But if you

don't feel capable of watching her at the rink, let me know. I'll arrange for Lindy to go with her."

Over my dead body, Karina was thinking. The last thing the child needed was someone yelling at her at every mistake. There would be lots of mistakes for a beginner, just learning the art. But she smiled and forced the words out. "Yes, sir. I will."

"Headed out to the store," Burt called from the kitchen. "Anybody need anything?"

"Not me," Karina said, smiling.

"Me, either," Torrance replied. "Be careful. There's several inches of snow out there from last night. You'll slide all over hell and gone in the snow."

Burt made a face. "I'll stay in the ruts," he promised, and threw up a hand on his way out.

Karina liked him. She'd learned that Burt was the live-in jack-of-all-trades. A great cook, a chess master, a poet, he'd been the mainstay of the house for years. It was a big house. Once a week, a local company sent out people to make things spotless. They scrubbed and polished and cleaned. Burt kept the bed linen changed, the meals cooked and answered the phone, which rang incessantly. Between them all, the household was efficient.

Micah was still staring at her boot, as if considering another query.

"There's one other thing," Karina continued after Burt was gone, averting her eyes and hoping to distract the boss from more probing personal questions.

"What now?" he asked with resignation.

"It's Janey's skates. They're hockey skates."

"So?"

She looked up. "Mr. Torrance, if she's going to learn figure skating, she needs skates with a toe pick. You have to have them to do jumps. She also needs to be professionally fitted, even if she's only going to skate casually. The wrong skates can damage her feet. The new skates need to be heat molded so that they won't make so many blisters when she's on the ice."

His lips made a thin line. "Well, according to you, we've done nothing right, have we?"

She flushed. Her eyes shot down to his broad chest. "Sorry," she bit off. "I wasn't criticizing. It's just..."

"Lindy was in competition," he pointed out. "She placed high in Regionals. I think she knows more about skates than you do, Miss...?"

She swallowed. Hard. He made her nervous. She shifted to her good foot. "Carter," she answered.

"Miss Carter," he obliged. He drew in a short breath. "I don't have time to go running all over creation for hobby skates," he muttered.

She clenched her teeth. She'd told him all she was going to. If he was that hostile, she wondered how she was going to hang on here.

"All right, damn it," he snapped, infuriated by her lack of spirit. He was used to people who fought back. The girl's attitude made him feel guilty and he didn't like it. "I'll take her to Jackson this weekend and buy her a pair of skates."

She swallowed. "Thank you, sir."

"If you're going to Jackson, you'd better get moving," he bit off.

"Yes, sir."

She felt that she should salute, but she kept her cool. She went into her room, got her coat and purse and headed slowly for the front door, leaning heavily on the cane.

"And just how the hell are you going to skate with that?" he demanded, pointing to the boot on her foot.

"I don't know," she said honestly. "But I'll find a way," she added with a hint of the steely determination that had seen her win a World figure skating gold medal with Paul Maurice.

That light of battle in her pale gray eyes made them sparkle like silver. She was pretty in a temper. It was the first show of antagonism she'd let past that cool control that hallmarked her personality.

"It's your leg," he said. "But if you injure it again..." He let the sentence trail away.

Chills ran down her spine. What would happen if she broke her ankle again? She didn't dare consider that. She drew in a breath. "I won't."

"The roads are slippery between here and Jackson, and it's mountainous," he said, hating his own concern. "Be careful."

"I won't be long," she promised.

"You'd better not be," he returned. "I can't hang around here more than a few hours. I've got meetings scheduled in Los Angeles."

"I'll hurry," she promised.

"Skates. Heat molds. God, this little hobby of

Janey's is turning into my worst nightmare!" he muttered, stalking off before she went out the door.

Karina actually let out a sigh of relief when she was safely in her car and away from him. The longer he was away from home, the happier it made her!

KARINA WALKED INTO her apartment and went to her closet to bring out the skates she'd worn in the last competition, the one that had cost her a shot at competitions with Paul. She'd missed a jump when Paul threw her. It wasn't even a hard one. But she'd landed wrong and broken her ankle.

She remembered another break, in her leg, the same leg, three years ago. It had been a nightmare. She couldn't get the pictures of her parents out of her mind, except for small spaces of time. They haunted her nightmares. Two kind, sweet, loving people. To die like that!

She forced herself not to think about it. She had a job. The job involved helping a young girl do well on the ice, as she'd done long before she was Janey's age. The girl's enthusiasm had fired something inside her, made her hungry to put on skates again, to feel the blades slicing through the ice again.

She pulled them up and looked at them. They needed cleaning. They had a little wear. But they were comfortable, and well broken in. They wouldn't be rough on her ankles and feet. If she could conquer her fear, she might be able to skate again. It was frightening. But she wanted it so badly.

Her parents had cheered her on. You lost this time,

they told her and Paul, but you have plenty of time to prepare for the Olympics. Practice, win those competitions that get you to the next Olympics, make us proud!

She'd done that. Paul and Gerda had taken her in and given her a home while she dealt with the aftermath of the loss of her parents. The farm was sold, but so much was owed on it, that not a great deal was left over. There was enough for a small apartment in Jackson, and enough over for groceries and skating necessities. Paul and his wife had been more than supportive after the tragedy. With the help of the Envelope, and contributions from a private sponsor, she and Paul had managed the expenses and gone on to win almost every competition they faced, ending in a World Championship.

Then, after three years of competition, this had happened, this fall. It wasn't Paul's fault, but he'd blamed himself. Karina and Gerda, Paul's wife, had finally convinced him that it was simply an accident, that he hadn't caused it. Gerda and their twin sons had helped lift him out of his depression. He was still reluctant to go with another partner, but Karina didn't want him to miss the chance of that Olympic gold, even if she couldn't compete. She'd known at the outset that it would take her months to recover, and even more time to accomplish the simplest jumps again. She wasn't sure she had the nerve to try it again.

Skating had been her life since she was a toddler. She'd done solo competitions only as a child. Paul, who lived nearby, was equally fascinated with skating, and they'd first tried skating together when they were only ten. It was a magical combination. Paul was like the brother she'd never had. She adored him, although she could never feel romantic about him. They were wonderful on the ice. Even Karina's mother, super critical about the sport to which she'd devoted her life, applauded for them.

Dreams. Dreams gone to ashes. Paul was gone, guilt ridden but driven, trying to work up to competing with a prospective new partner and a new coach. And here was Karina, babysitting. She'd given up on her career because a doctor had said she shouldn't go back on the ice.

She'd taken his word for it because fear ruled her. She didn't want to risk another, even more serious, injury. She'd seen skaters who'd taken falls that led to concussion, to scars from skates that sliced through flesh. She'd seen nightmarish falls, even in practice, as hers had happened.

But sooner or later she'd have to try. Just as well to get her skates and step out onto the ice, to see if she could balance, if she could even skate at all.

She drew out her skating bag, with all her accessories, and tucked her skates into it. She had three other pair of skates, one of which had several signatures in black magic marker. She'd worn those skates at Sochi, in Olympic competition. Those signatures were the highlight of her Olympic appearance with Paul. The skaters were a who's who of the best competitors in the world. Several gold medalists from years ago had been at Sochi, and her mother knew most of them. It had been an honor just to meet them. Having her skates signed by them had been an experience she would never forget.

She read the names and smiled as she put them back in the closet. Janey likely wouldn't recognize most of those names in black marker, but Lindy might. It wasn't worth taking the chance. Besides, the skates she was taking back to Catelow were just as good.

She locked the apartment and drove back to the ranch.

"YOU'VE GOT A skating bag just like mine," Janey said excitedly, when she saw Karina putting it up in her room.

Karina smiled. "We all have to have bags for our stuff," she teased.

"Except yours is prettier than mine," she sighed. "I would have liked soft pink with sparkles. It's got bling," she added, laughing.

Karina sighed. "It does, at that."

"What sort of skates do you have?"

They sat down on the carpeted floor and Karina pulled them out to show them to Janey.

"Wow," she said softly. "They're really good ones, aren't they?"

"They are. But best of all, they're broken in," she laughed. "No blisters."

"I wish I could say the same," Janey said plaintively.

Karina almost blurted out that her dad was going to take Janey down to Jackson Hole for new skates, but she kept that to herself. Maybe Mr. Torrance meant it to be a surprise.

"You won't be doing any jumps right away," Karina told her softly. "So it's not urgent. We'll run you through the basics first, and they're mostly learning how to go forward and backward and how to stop."

"The how to stop part would be nice," Janey sighed. "I run into the barrier all the time."

"I'll teach you," she said. "You'll do fine."

"Well, we can hope so, can't we?" she laughed.

"I'm sorry you had to miss practice today," Karina said after she'd put her skating bag away. "But it's a long drive down to Jackson, and I needed my skates."

"Do you live there, when you're not working?"

Karina nodded. "I have an apartment. It's not much, but I like it."

"I'm glad Daddy hired you," Janey said. "You're not at all like I was afraid you'd be. I mean, Daddy likes women like Lindy," she added with a drawn down mouth. "They're all like her, sharp and smart and snarky."

Karina's eyebrows went up. "You stole my word," she accused. "Snarky's my own, personal word. You stole it."

Janey made a face. "I did not," she returned. "You can't own a word."

"I can so. I'll copyright it," Karina said with dancing gray eyes.

Janey just laughed.

MICAH TORRANCE, JUST walking into the house, heard his daughter laughing. It was a rare sound. She was depressed about school, where she was bullied so much. He wouldn't go and fight her battles for her. He couldn't. He'd make it impossible for her to defend herself when she grew up. She had to learn the lessons of how to fit in society. The school of hard knocks was the only way to manage that.

It hurt him to see her cry, but it was the same lesson he'd had to learn at her age. His father had been fairly brutal. Micah, like Janey, was an only child. His father had been a military officer, so Micah was raised like a little soldier. He was still used to that routine, and he lived it. He regimented everyone around him. Even Janey.

But that was for her own good, he reasoned. A child needed structure. It had been good for him. It would be good for Janey, too.

He paused at Karina's door and frowned. "Why are you two sitting on the carpet?" he asked curtly.

"I don't have chairs," Karina blurted out, indicating the bed and chest of drawers and television stand. There wasn't a single chair in the room.

He made a rumbling sound in his throat and turned quickly away, before the amused grin was visible. "Burt!" he called. "When's supper? I'm starving!"

"Go shoot a bear. I'm making venison stew. Don't interrupt me or I'll burn something," the older man teased.

"What would be unusual about that?" Micah murmured.

"I'll throw something at you," Burt threatened, his silver hair gleaming in the overhead light as it was reflected there, above his amused dark eyes.

"If you hit me, I'll scream. So help me."

Burt laughed and turned back to his chores, while Micah went into his office to check his email and return phone calls.

Karina had to smother a laugh. She hadn't credited her new, crusty boss with a sense of humor, but he seemed to have one, even if it wasn't displayed very often. Janey grinned at her.

"First thing Monday, after school, okay?" Karina asked. She wasn't going to tell the child about Micah's surprise: the trip to Jackson to buy new skates. She only hoped he wouldn't forget.

Janey grimaced. "Okay," she said reluctantly.

"It will be worth waiting for. I promise," Karina said and patted her skating bag. She hoped it was a promise she could fulfill.

THERE WAS A quiet routine to the ranch that turned to pandemonium when Micah was home. He kept everyone on their toes. Karina was a little afraid of him. He was formidable, like a tank.

She tried to keep out of his way. It wasn't hard. He was gone a lot since Karina came. After the first few days, he seemed to trust her. Not too far, but enough.

Micah, true to his word, did take an excited Janey to Jackson Hole to get fitted for figure skates, and to have the heat molding that would help prevent the usual blisters from new skates. He grumbled, but not too much, when he saw the light in the child's eyes.

"Aren't they beautiful?" Janey enthused that night, displaying them for Karina just before bedtime.

"They truly are," she replied, recalling her own joy at her first pair of real figure skates with toe picks. However, Karina's had come far earlier than the age of nine. She wasn't sharing that.

"I can't wait until Monday!" the child sighed.

Karina smiled. Inside, she grimaced. The fear was a living, breathing thing. What if she skated and broke the ankle again? What if she broke her leg? What if she fell…

She forced herself to put the fear aside, until she had to deal with it. And that wasn't easy.

Monday after school, at the ice rink, Karina put on her skates for the first time since her accident and tried not to remember the cheers of the crowd, the flashing lights, the music, the sound of her skates as she sped along with Paul and he hurled her into the air to do Lutzes and toe loops and Salchows.

Janey had been so excited about her new skates that she couldn't wait to get onto the ice. It seemed to take forever, she remarked. Karina had laced Janey's skates before she started on her own. Now, Janey watched Karina go through the long process of lacing up her own skates. "I didn't know that it was so important, how you laced them," she said.

"It can mean the difference between landing a jump and falling," she replied. "I always take time to do it right." She smiled at Janey. "We won't do much today," she added, indicating Janey's new skates. "You'll have to break those in a bit more. The heat molding will help, though." They'd already placed the pads in both their skates to help keep down blisters. Karina had ankle supports in hers as well.

Janey sighed. "So many things to learn," she said.

"And this is all just the very beginning," Karina replied gently. "You sure you want to do this? It's harder than you might realize."

Janey nodded. "I'm very sure. There's nothing like the feel of skates on the ice," she said, trying to put into words a feeling that was sheer exhilaration. "I've never loved anything so much!"

Karina saw herself in the child. "It was like that for me, the first time my mother laced me into ice skates."

"How old were you?"

"Three," Karina said.

Janey's lips opened on an indrawn breath. "Three?"

She nodded. "I was doing compulsory figures by the time I was four."

"They don't do those in competition anymore," Janey began, displaying her knowledge of the sport.

"No, they don't. But that's one thing your father's fiancée is right about: they should," came the firm reply. "They teach discipline and technique, learning to use your edges properly. That's why my mother taught me to do them first, before anything else."

"I didn't even know that skates had inside and outside edges," Janey said.

Karina frowned. "You didn't?"

Janey made a face. "Lindy just yelled when I didn't do something right," she said miserably. "If I asked a question, she made fun of me. I don't even think she's that good on skates," she added with unexpected rancor. "She stands with her ankles skewed, not straight up. I watched this video on YouTube by a trainer who said you never did that, because it was sloppy and taught bad habits."

"It does," Karina said, recalling that Janey had remarked about it before. "But don't you mention that to Lindy. Okay?"

Janey laughed. "Okay."

Karina finished lacing up her skates and took a deep breath as she slowly stood up, the edges of her skates encased in the guards that kept them from scoring the wooden floor. She looked toward the ice rink dubiously. There were a lot of people out there. One section was awkwardly roped off where a parent was working with three preschool children. Out on the ice, people were wobbling or skating recklessly or attempting jumps without regard to other skaters.

One skater fell and put his hands flat on the ice to push himself up. Karina groaned.

He barely avoided having his hand sliced open by a skater who almost ran over it when he fell.

"You never put your hands flat on the ice like that to get up," Karina said, turning to Janey.

"How are you supposed to?"

"I'll show you again. There's a correct way to fall as well. The important thing is to keep your feet under you, close together. Bend your knees and keep your chin tucked, and lean slightly forward as you go. You never want to flail about with your arms and get off balance so that you fall backward."

"This is all very complicated," Janey said.

Karina nodded. "Very. But it's fun, too."

She took a breath and started walking on her blades toward the entrance to the rink, holding on to the barrier with one hand as she got to the ice. It looked frightening, after the accident that had sidelined her. But she was going to have to conquer the fear, or she could lose her job.

Micah Torrance was right. It would be very dangerous for Janey to go on the ice alone, without supervision or training. Karina would have to conquer her own fear to teach the girl how to skate.

"You're scared, aren't you?" Janey asked gently. "It will be all right. I'll catch you if you fall."

Karina laughed. The girl was so sweet. "I'll be fine," she promised. "We'll take it very slowly. You know how to get onto the ice?"

"You just skate out there. That's what Lindy did."

"No. You do it like this."

Karina showed her. She took off the guards and put them aside. Holding gently onto the barrier, she put first one foot on the ice and then, slowly, the other, keeping her feet together. She bent her knees and began to walk forward, with her feet in a V shape, using the barrier for support.

"Like this," she told Janey. "See?"

"Oh. That's easier," the girl agreed. She followed

in Karina's footsteps and laughed. "This isn't so hard."

"Keep your knees bent. Weight forward. Tuck your chin. Just walk, as if you were marching."

"Okay!"

EVEN JUST WALKING was fun. Karina felt the wonder of being on the ice again, remembering with bittersweet pleasure times like this with her mother, when she was just learning to skate.

She glanced behind. "Doing okay?" she asked Janey.

The child laughed. "Yes! This is fun. And I don't fall so much."

"Keep going. Once you feel more secure, we'll try something else."

"Fine!"

They marched around the rink, stopping at the roped-off area, turned, and walked back again. They'd both been holding on to the barrier with one hand. But as the ice became familiar and they gained confidence, they turned loose from it and just walked.

"You see, with your toes in a V formation, you can grip the ice," Karina told her. "It gives you more traction."

"I noticed...oh, great," she muttered under her breath.

Janey held on tight to the smooth wood of the barrier. Karina followed suit as Mr. Torrance walked down to the rink with Lindy at his side.

Lindy started laughing. “Good Lord, can’t you get out into the rink? Why are you walking around like penguins?”

“It’s the best way for a beginner to gain confidence,” Karina said quietly, flushing at the criticism.

“I had her skating the first day,” Lindy scoffed.

Janey didn’t mention how many times she fell that first day in the clumsy skates Lindy had bought her.

“Seems better to start slow,” Torrance replied. “It’s less risky.”

Lindy made a face at him. “I was a champion skater,” she said haughtily, brushing back her blond hair. “I think I know how to teach people to do it. Janey’s just clumsy. She doesn’t listen.”

“She’s done very well today,” Karina said.

Janey beamed.

Lindy glared at the other woman. “Walking on the ice,” she nodded. “Wonderful. I can see you really know how to teach.”

“Let’s go,” Torrance said curtly. He glanced at Janey. He smiled. “I think you’re doing it the right way, sweetheart,” he said gently. “We were on the way to Denver to a business meeting. I wanted to stop by and see how things were going.”

“They’re going fine, Dad,” Janey said, grinning. “I love my new skates.”

“What new skates?” Lindy asked curtly. She glared at the white boots on Janey’s feet. “She doesn’t need figure skates, for heaven’s sake! She’s just going to skate. She’d only need those to do jumps!”

“I want to learn to do jumps,” Janey replied, holding on to her temper with difficulty. "Karina's going to teach me."

"On a broken foot," she chided. "Sure, she is!"

"Lindy, suppose you wait in the car?" Torrance said icily.

She let out a huffy sigh. "Oh, all right!" She glared at Karina and Janey and stormed off toward the exit.

"She's in one of her moods," Torrance said carelessly. "Both of you be careful on the ice." He looked out onto the rink, where one skater was knocking down others. "That boy is dangerous."

Karina glanced at him. She noticed the former coach who owned the rink, Hilde Meyer, calling the boy to the barrier. She laughed. "He's about to get his walking papers, I think," Karina said.

Sure enough, the owner said somcthing to him. He argued. She indicated the area behind the barrier and made a firm gesture. He skated off the ice and went with the owner to her officc.

"He's in trouble," Janey said with a grin. "The lady who owns the rink doesn't like people being reckless. She'll probably make him leave for good."

"I hope she does," Torrance said coldly. "People like that should be barred permanently." He looked back at Karina. "How's the ankle?"

"It's good," she said. "I was a little nervous, but Janey's helping me get my nerve back."

The child beamed at her. "That's not true, but thanks."

"You're really good," Karina replied. "You listen to advice."

"You're nice, too," Janey said. "You don't yell at me."

"I never yell," Karina smiled. "It doesn't help."

"I'll say!"

"Well, I'll get going. I may be late," Micah added.

"Okay, Dad," Janey said.

"Don't overdo," he cautioned Karina. "Make progress slowly."

"I will." His concern made her feel warm inside. She looked up into his brown eyes and felt their impact way down in her stomach.

He smiled slowly. "I'll see you two later."

"Bye, Dad!"

He threw up a hand and walked out the exit.

"Lindy was really mean," Janey said.

"A lot of skaters are good on the ice, but they aren't so good at teaching," Karina said kindly. "Besides, she's right. We do look silly walking around the rink. But this is the first step. You need to learn to skate the right way. It will serve you well, if you really want to try to do jumps."

"I do. I really do!"

"Then we'll keep this up for a while, and progress to forward skating. Okay?"

Janey grinned. "Okay!"

JANEY FOLLOWED KARINA'S LEAD. She learned to skate backward by spreading her legs out and bringing them back in a repeating motion. She learned how to fall, how to get up safely, how to keep from pitching backward and getting concussed.

"It's very complicated," Janey remarked, smiling up at Karina.

"And you're doing very well," Karina replied, returning the smile. "Now. Want to learn how to do the hockey stop? It's called a snowplow."

"Yes!"

"You keep your feet close together, throw all your weight to one side, twisting your upper body, with your knees bent, and your feet close together. Then you dig in with your blades. If you do it right, you'll spray snow when you stop."

"I've seen skaters do that," Janey said.

"Knowing how to stop is very important. It will spare you some bad falls. So you go like this." She demonstrated, bending her knees slightly as she skated forward. Then she shifted, so that her feet were facing forward, threw her weight to the side with a little jump that shifted her direction and sprayed snow like mad.

She laughed with pure exhilaration. It brought back so many memories. Sad ones. Happy ones.

"That looked amazing!" Janey enthused.

Karina laughed. "You'll be doing it like that in no time," she promised. "Follow my lead," she added. "Keep your feet together with your toes facing out, knees slightly bent, chin tucked. Skate forward, like we practiced. Then, do this." She demonstrated again.

It took several tries, but Janey finally managed a little spray of snow when she stopped.

She laughed. So did Karina. The girl really did have talent. “Nice. Very nice!”

“Thanks!”

They skated for another hour. Karina longed to go out into the rink and do what she’d done since she was three. She wanted to fly on the ice, feel it beneath her feet as she gained speed for the jumps. She closed her eyes for a few seconds and she could almost hear the applause of the crowd in Sochi, the excitement of skating a perfect program, only to lose to a team that skated a better one. It had been a crushing disappointment to place eighth in the Olympics.

But her mother had been very supportive. She was certain that Karina and Paul had the ability to win that gold medal. They skated perfect programs. They had speed and grace, and the choreography was both creative and athletic. They had all they needed to go all the way.

So soon that dream had died. Karina’s leg, broken in the crash three years ago, had put her on the sidelines for months while she worked with her doctor and her therapist to get function back in the leg. She and Paul had gone on to win a World Championship in figure skating.

But this latest break was worrisome. What if there had been more damage than anyone realized from the first break, when her parents died? What if it caused a permanent weakness in the leg, one that had led to the broken ankle several months ago?

She was insecure. She was frightened. But the ice felt good. She loved the sound of her blades slicing through it, she loved being on skates again. She smiled, and then she laughed, with pure delight.

She was turning unconsciously while she dreamed, into a perfect layback, the elegant and graceful one that her coach had taught her years ago. She wasn't aware of other skaters watching her, or Janey, who was breathless at what she saw.

Karina came back to the present abruptly when Janey skated slowly up to her and laughed.

"Oh, gosh, I'll never be as good as you!" she exclaimed. "That was…just beautiful!"

Karina stopped, with guilt written all over her face.

"You do know how to skate," Janey said softly. "You know how to skate very well."

Karina drew in a breath. "I can, sort of," she said, embarrassed. "But this is just between you and me, okay?" She had a nightmare vision of the child telling her father just how well Karina skated. She didn't want to be found out. Not yet. She wasn't sure that she could go back to competition. Right now, she only wanted to heal a little more and make progress slowly.

Janey didn't realize how much skill was involved in that layback. But Lindy would. She might start asking questions that Karina didn't want to answer. She wasn't doing anything illegal or immoral. She just wanted privacy. Only that.

"It's okay," Janey said quickly. "I won't tell a soul. Honest."

Karina managed a smile. "Okay. Thanks."

"I can't afford to lose my coach," Janey returned, tongue-in-cheek.

"Oh, is that it?" Karina teased.

"Yes, it is. So can you teach me chassés?" Janey added. "I've been watching those kids do it." She indicated the small group in the roped off area. "It looks complicated."

"It just takes practice, that's all." She glanced at her watch and grimaced. "We need to get back home."

"Awwww," Janey moaned.

"We'll come back tomorrow. I promise."

"That's okay, then," the child replied.

They headed slowly toward the barrier.

CHAPTER FOUR

MICAH WAS HOME very late. Janey was in her room. Karina was in hers when he came in. She heard his heavy footsteps slow as he opened his own door, down the hall, and went inside.

Karina had enjoyed her first skate with Janey. They'd progressed easily to forward skating and backward skating and the snowplow stop that Janey loved so much. Later would come chassés and flips and crossovers and toe loops. But for the time being, Janey was doing well.

The excitement of being on skates again made Karina's spirit soar. It was less scary than she'd thought. Yes, there might be a weakness in a leg that had suffered a fracture, followed three years later by a broken ankle. But both injuries had healed, and Karina felt no pain or impairment. She'd keep up the exercises, and, on her next day off, she'd go to Jackson and see her sports therapist.

She drifted off to sleep amid memories of flashing lights and speed and skating with Paul to their signature tune, Rachmaninoff's *Rhapsody on a Theme of Paganini*. She could close her eyes and see the beautiful fantasy composition of the last time they'd competed. Their performance had been flawless, earning high marks. World gold medalists, they skated perfectly most of the time. Until Karina's accident. Paul had tossed her in practice. She'd twirled, but landed awkwardly on her left foot. The accident had left her in tears, almost hysteria. She knew immediately what it meant. It was the end of her career, the end of the partnership, at least for several months. She'd never experienced such an injury while skating. It broke her heart. It broke her spirit. After the doctor examined her, treated her, he advised her to keep off the ice forever, citing the broken leg previously in addition to the broken bones in her ankle. It was an unnecessary risk that might leave her handicapped for the rest of her life.

Karina, frightened and traumatized by the accident, had believed him. She was certain that she'd never skate again.

Now, months later, here she was, going tenuously back onto the ice with this sweet little girl, who was encouraging her, when it should be the other way around. Janey seemed to sense Karina's fear. She reacted to it with gentle smiles and assurances that Karina could do anything she wanted to. It was a kind of partnership. It amused, and delighted, Karina.

She drifted to sleep. But sometime in the night, a loud voice woke her. A man was shouting. There was horror in his voice. Belatedly, she recognized the voice. It was her boss.

She got up and wrapped herself in a thick chenille robe that dropped to her ankles. Her hair had come loose from its high bun and was draping around her shoulders in a wavy pale gold mantle. She didn't take time to put it back up. She went out into the hall, hesitating halfway toward the boss's door.

He was still yelling. She knocked on the door. "Mr. Torrance?" she called loudly. She wasn't about to go into the room. Sheltered and virginal, Karina had never seen a nude man. She certainly wasn't anxious to see her boss that way, in case he didn't wear pajamas!

The yelling only increased. She knocked again. "Boss?" she called. "Are you okay?"

There was no reply. He sounded as if he was in terrible pain.

She went to the stationary phone in the living room and punched in Burt's extension.

He answered drowsily. "What?"

"Burt, I think Mr. Torrance is having a nightmare. I can't go in there. Can you come see about him, please?"

"Nightmares again?" he wondered. "I thought he was getting over them. Sure. Be right there."

She waited. A minute or two later, Burt appeared in his own pajamas and robe. Karina, on bare feet, was still at Micah's door, worried and uncertain what else to do.

"It's okay," Burt said gently. "I'll see about him."

"Thanks."

He opened the door, walked in, closed it. Minutes passed. Burt's voice. Another voice, shocked and angry. The door opened. Burt came out, closed the door, grimaced at Karina, and beat a path back down the hall.

That seemed ominous. Karina was about to go back to her room when the door jerked open. Micah was wearing long plaid pajama bottoms and nothing else. His broad hair-roughened chest was bare. His shoulders were broad, his arms muscular without being overstated. He was absolutely gorgeous like that, with his thick straight black hair tousled and hanging down over his wide forehead.

The only thing that spoiled the picture was the murderous glare on his face and the glitter of his brown eyes.

"What the hell do you think you're doing, getting the household up in the middle of the damned night?" he demanded hotly.

"Sir, you were having a nightmare..."

"It's not a public event," he snapped, interrupting her. "You do this again and I'll send you back to Jackson in a knapsack, do you hear me? You keep your nose out of my business!"

"Yes, sir," she said, almost shivering at the bite in his voice. Tears stung her eyes. He sounded just like the abusive coach that she and Paul had finally fired. The abuse had broken Karina's spirit.

"Go the hell to bed!"

"Yes...yes, sir," she stammered. She ran down the hall to her room and closed the door, her eyes and cheeks wet.

She hated him. She was only concerned and trying to help. He was an ogre. She couldn't stay here.

She was leaving in the morning. She'd wash dishes in some restaurant if she had to, to manage her finances. Anything was better than this!

MICAH FELT GUILTY when he woke again. He whipped on a robe and went into the kitchen to get a cup of coffee. Burt was already there.

"She hasn't come to breakfast?" he asked Burt, nodding toward the hall.

"Came to get a cup of coffee. Looked like she'd been crying all night. You yell at her or something?"

Micah's lips compressed. "Or something."

"She's just a kid, Micah," Burt said softly. "Don't you remember being twenty-three and intimidated by forceful people?"

He laughed hollowly. "I was never intimidated by anyone. My dad was a general. He raised me to be fearless."

"Well, she wasn't raised by the military, from what I can see," Burt replied. He handed the boss a cup of black coffee. "Mentioned that she might be leaving today," he added.

Micah grimaced.

"Janey won't be happy about that. She loves the girl already. Doesn't yell at her when she does something wrong at the skating rink," he added with a chuckle. "She's come out of her shell since Karina's been here, too."

"I noticed that."

"You don't like crow, I guess," Burt mused.

The boss's thick eyebrows went up in a question.

"If I were you, I'd consider eating some. Bad move to let Karina leave."

Micah glowered at him. Burt just grinned.

"I'm making pancakes," Burt said.

"I'll get dressed and eat some." He sighed. "I hate crow."

He walked back to his room, coffee in hand, and went to dress.

KARINA CAME TO breakfast uneasy and sick at heart. She was going to leave. She couldn't stay in a place where people yelled at her. She'd had enough of that from the former coach that she and Paul had endured until they couldn't take any more. Intimidation never made life easier.

Janey noticed her companion's misery and grimaced. It was obvious that Karina had been crying, a lot. Her father came into the room all taciturn and glowering, and Janey had a pretty good idea that they'd argued.

"Morning," he said gruffly.

Karina didn't answer. She ate a pancake without ever looking up.

Micah filled his own plate. "You going to the rink today?" he asked Janey.

Janey glanced worriedly at Karina. "Are we?" she asked plaintively.

Karina looked up, so unhappy that she almost vibrated with it. "Janey, I…" she began.

"I yelled at her," Micah said tersely. He didn't look her way. "Didn't mean to. I'm sorry," he bit off.

Karina had the impression that he'd never apologized before, because Janey and Burt gaped at him.

She took a deep breath. "Mr. Torrance," she began, "I don't know that I'm the right person for this job…"

He looked at her, his dark eyes apologetic and soft. "Don't go," he said gently. "I know you meant well. I'm not used to concern. Well, not from women." He averted his eyes. "I overreacted."

She hesitated. He didn't seem to be hostile anymore. She really needed the job. She loved Janey already. The indecision was plain on her face, on the pale gray eyes she lifted to his.

His own dark eyes narrowed. "Scared of me?" he chided. "Want to run away?"

She swallowed, hard. Yes, she wanted to run. But he was chiding her. Why? Did he want her to stay?

"Please stay," Janey said softly, her eyes pleading.

Karina ground her teeth together. "Oh, all right," she muttered with faint exasperation. "I guess I can live with a timber wolf, if Janey can."

It took a minute for that to penetrate. He laughed. A real laugh, not a sarcastic one, that rolled around the room like gentle thunder.

"A timber wolf?" He smiled. "Okay. I get the point. Janey, pass me the syrup, honey, will you?"

"Yes, sir." Janey handed it over, grinning. She glanced at Karina, who was smiling faintly. "So, you're staying, right?"

Karina's eyes were soft on her face. "Yes. I'm staying."

"Woohoo!" Janey enthused. "Burt, these pancakes are great!"

"They're very good," Karina added.

Burt chuckled. "Thanks. Not usual for the cook to get much praise around here," he added, with a pointed look at Micah.

"Not usual for the cook to produce anything edible, either," Micah shot at him.

"Just for that, you'll get liver and onions for supper!" he huffed.

"I'll fire you!"

"I'll quit!"

"Don't mind them," Janey told Karina, who looked puzzled at the argument. "They do that all the time."

"Not all the time," Micah protested. "I remember a day last month when we got along for a whole day."

"Because I went hunting and you had to get Doris over here to cook for you, that's why," Burt said. "It was a great day. I didn't get yelled at once!"

Micah glared at him.

Burt just grinned and went back to the kitchen.

DIETRICH SLEPT IN a huge dog bed right beside Janey's bed, on the floor. It was amusing to watch him try to fit his huge body into the memory foam oval with its soft cover.

"He really is big," Karina commented, as she waited for Janey to get her skating bag. She smiled. "How much does he weigh, do you know?"

"Ninety-five pounds," Janey said, laughing. "He

could sleep at the foot of the bed, but he won't. He's scared of heights, aren't you, boy?" she asked.

The big dog lifted his head, blinked sleepily and lay right back down and closed his eyes.

"Sleepyhead," Janey teased, rubbing his head. "He likes to sleep late."

"He's so sweet," Karina said.

"I think so, too," came the soft reply.

"I guess we'd better get going," Karina said.

"Daddy isn't mean," Janey blurted out, lowering her voice. "He's sort of short with people sometimes. But he isn't mean."

"I never thought he was," Karina lied.

"So you have to stay," the child said gently. "Really. Just think, I might grow up to be a world class skater and you could say you taught me." She smiled broadly and wiggled her eyebrows.

Karina laughed heartily. "You character, you," she teased. "Okay. I'll tough it out."

"Thanks."

Karina already had her skating bag. She waited for Janey to remind Burt to walk Dietrich before they went to the rink.

JANEY WAS MAKING good progress. Even the rink's owner, Mrs. Meyer, encouraged her.

"I've seen champions come and go," she told the child. She smiled. "You have the makings of one. You're starting a little late, but you catch on to new things quickly and you have enthusiasm. You'll do fine."

Janey flushed with pleasure. "Thanks," she said. "I love skating so much." She paused, frowned. "I'm just nine. That's late? To start skating, I mean?"

"It is," the owner replied gently. "Most champions start at the age of two or three."

"Wow," Janey said. "I had no idea."

"Just take it slow at first," the older woman said. "Don't try to rush it. If you practice the basics, and perfect them, you'll have an edge over other skaters your age."

Janey grinned. "Thanks!"

"Besides that," she added, with an amused look at Karina, "you've got a great teacher."

"I know that! She's wonderful. And she never yells," Janey added heavily.

"I've seen my share of trainers who yelled," came the reply. "Sometimes it drives sensitive skaters right out of competition."

"I don't like people who yell," Janey said. She made a face. "My dad's marrying somebody who does." She looked up at her companions with a whimsical expression. "I have to grow up really fast so I can leave home." She grinned.

They laughed with her.

KARINA WAS WORRIED about Janey. She came home from school a few days later with a morose expression and she was almost in tears.

"What's wrong?" Karina asked softly.

A single tear worked out of Janey's eye, down her flushed cheek. "It's nothing..."

Karina went down on her knees and caught the child close, hugging her, rocking her. She remembered when she was nine and classmates had made her life miserable because she didn't mix well.

"You'll grow up and this will only be a bad memory, tucked away out of sight," Karina whispered softly. "Some people are cruel because they're really mean. Others are cruel because all they know is cruelty. They learn it at home."

Janey drew back, her eyes red, her cheeks wet. She rested her hands on Karina's shoulders. "Sally Miller said that I was stupid and backward because I don't hang around with boys, like she does."

Karina's eyebrows arched. "What? Hang around with boys at your age?" she exclaimed.

Janey drew in a shaky breath. "Sally's eleven," she said. "She goes off with boys and skips class. She… does things with them. Everybody knows. She said that I was dumb because I didn't do it."

Karina smoothed back Janey's hair. "I never did those things with boys when I was your age," she said, smiling. "In fact, I've never done those things," she whispered, wary of Burt overhearing her.

"You haven't?" Janey asked. "Not ever?"

"Not ever. I don't go with the crowd even now." She sighed. "I'm something of a misfit. I lived on the ice when I wasn't in school. It gave me an escape. I could skate and all my worries just vanished, like smoke in fog."

"Wow." Janey was impressed, and it showed. "They say that good girls don't make history."

"Joan of Arc made history," she replied softly. "She was a teenager, a country girl with no knowledge of politics or armies. She had a vision that led her to seek out the dauphin in France. He had one of his subordinates pretend to be him when Joan walked in, because he thought she was a fraud. She went right to the dauphin and told him that she'd had a vision, that she was to lead his armies in battle, that she would regain France for him and put the crown on his head."

Janey smiled. "Really?"

Karina nodded. "She actually led armies into battle, armed with nothing except her faith and a flag. She was never bothered by the soldiers, all men, and they followed her anywhere she led. She defeated the English, put the crown on the dauphin's head. And then she was captured by the English, declared a heretic and burned at the stake. It was a sad end for such an amazing person. She even foresaw that she would be killed. But centuries later, everybody knows her name." She smiled. "So no matter how bad things get at school, at least they can't burn you at the stake. Right?"

Janey laughed. She hugged Karina, who hugged her back.

"Thanks," the child said, drawing back. "There's not much hugging around here," she explained with a flushed face.

That wasn't surprising to Karina, who didn't see her taciturn boss as a nurturing person at all.

A door slammed. "What the hell are you doing

sitting on the floor?" Micah demanded curtly. "And don't tell me there are no chairs," he added, indicating them in both the dining room, where she was, and the living room beyond.

Karina thought quickly. "Gravity," she said. She nodded. "That's it. Gravity. Pulled me right down here."

He was silent for a minute, then he threw back his head and roared. "Well, whatever else you are, you're inventive, I'll give you that."

He looked past her at Janey, whose eyes were still red. The smile vanished, replaced by an angry frown. "All right, what happened?" he asked his daughter.

She sighed. "Other kids."

"Something a little more specific, please."

"We have this girl in our class, she's eleven." She hesitated to tell him, embarrassed.

"Go on," he said, his voice dropping softly.

"She...does things with boys. She said I was stupid because I didn't."

"She does things with boys at school?" he exclaimed.

"Yes. In the woods, behind the school. She skips class. She makes fun of me. They all know that I go to church and they think it's primitive and stupid."

His eyes narrowed. "What's this progressive child's name?"

She hesitated, but he looked as if he'd stand there all night until she gave it to him. "Her name's Sally Miller," she said reluctantly.

"You okay now?" he asked, having added up

Janey's wet face and Karina on her knees. The girl had been comforting Janey. He knew it without asking.

"I'm fine, Dad," Janey replied. "Honest."

He glanced at Karina. "Gravity letting up now?" he asked her.

She got to her feet quickly. "Yes, sir."

It bothered him that she was that formal with him. He'd been aggressive with her when she'd been concerned for him in the night. He was sorry about it. She had a quality of compassion that was so rare as to be almost nonexistent in his life. Lindy had none. His late wife had been the same. He wondered why he'd spent so much time with women who were hard as nails. But this wasn't the time to ponder it.

"Aren't you two due at the rink?" he asked, glancing at his watch.

"Overdue, I think," Karina said softly. She smiled at Janey. "Ready to go?"

"Yes! Let me get my skating bag."

She ran off.

Micah studied Karina closely. She had the same look of innocence that a child had. It was almost blatant. His eyes narrowed. "You never went with the crowd either, did you?" he asked abruptly.

"No, I didn't," she replied. She grimaced. "I got picked on, too, just like Janey."

"Did your parents go rushing up to the school to protect you?"

She drew in a long breath. "My parents said that I had to learn to fight my own battles. They never interfered, except once. I made an enemy when I was in tenth grade. She harassed me to the point that I stayed out of school sick. Mom spoke to the principal. The girl was quietly moved to another school in the district after that. Life was sweet, until I graduated. Then I had it consistently from other…people," she amended, almost blurting out "skaters." It had been fierce competition, those district and then national ones. Some skaters would do anything to win, even injure other skaters or make fun of them to lessen their confidence.

"I make Janey fight her own battles, too," he said. "But what she just described is different. The authorities need to be told."

"I think so, too," Karina replied. "She's such a sweet child. I hate the very idea of some overly sophisticated girl ridiculing her for being innocent."

There was such conviction in her voice. He liked her. He didn't want to. He was engaged. Lindy kept pushing for a date for the wedding, and he kept resisting. In fact, he didn't want to marry Lindy, and he'd just discovered that. Almost too late.

"How's the ankle?" he asked.

"It's much better," she said. "I do strap it, just in case. I've already had one break in that leg, three years ago, before this happened. I have to be careful. But I can skate. I just don't want to try to do jumps again yet."

"Jumps?" He was studying her. Odd, how familiar she looked, as if he'd seen her somewhere before. "Where are you from?"

"A little town outside Jackson Hole," she replied.

"My parents had a small ranch. Dad was good at genetics and he kept a small herd of Angus cattle. But when they were both gone, it was too much for me. I had to sell it." She smiled. "I cried for three days. It was all I had left of them."

"You mentioned earlier that they died together."

"Yes. We…they were on a small commuter plane in Russia. The plane went down. They were both killed." Her face lost color as she said it, her mind reliving the horror. She blinked and forced the terrible memories to the back of her mind.

Her slip of the tongue didn't get past him. She'd been on the flight with them. Presumably she'd seen them die. He felt even worse about shouting at her when she'd been concerned for him the night he was reliving his own trauma.

"My wife, Anabelle," he began. "She died in a plane crash as well." He ground his teeth together. "I was flying the plane."

She winced. "I'm so sorry," she said huskily, knowing what he'd probably seen once the plane was on the ground. She searched his dark eyes. "Sometimes it's worse to be a survivor than to die."

He nodded slowly. "Much worse." His eyes narrowed. "You saw them after the crash," he guessed.

She swallowed. Hard. She bit her lower lip and fought tears. "They didn't look human," she whispered in a shattered tone.

"Neither did my wife."

It was a shared moment of tragedy, of horror.

They'd both seen things no human being should ever be forced to see.

"How old were you?" he asked.

"Twenty."

"Did you have relatives who took you in?"

"No. Both my parents were only children. I was born late in their lives. All my grandparents were dead by then. A friend and his wife took me in until I was able to sell the farm and get an apartment. They were kindness itself. But they weren't my parents," she added sadly. "It was the worst tragedy of my life."

"Mine as well. I served overseas in the Army. I saw horrible things. But it's different when the victim is related to you, even just by marriage. She wasn't much of a wife, or a mother," he added under his breath, so that Janey wouldn't hear. "But you get used to people when you live with them. Besides that, there was the guilt."

"That you lived, and she didn't."

"Yes. But I was flying the plane."

"It sounds odd, but when it's your time to go, nothing will save you," she replied. "I had to think of it that way, or I could never have gotten over it. Well, I'm still not over it. But I didn't see a thing the pilot did wrong. The snow was very thick and the lead investigator told me that no pilot could have foreseen the storm that made the plane crash."

"That's what they told me, after my plane went down. It didn't really help much."

"No. It didn't bring them back."

They stared at one another for a long moment, sharing grief, sharing torment, sharing guilt.

Until he frowned. “What were your parents doing in Russia?”

She flushed. She couldn’t tell him the truth. Not yet. “We’d gone over to see the Olympics in Sochi,” she said simply. “They splurged for the trip. We were all crazy about the competition. They loved it. So did I, until afterward.”

“It’s bad to lose people that way.”

“It’s bad to lose them any way at all.”

“Okay! I’m ready when you are,” Janey said, coming into the room with her skating bag over one shoulder.

Karina smiled at her. “Let me get my bag and we’ll be off.”

“Okay!”

MICAH WATCHED THEM go with confused emotions. He’d learned a lot about his daughter’s babysitter in a very short length of time. She’d walked away from a plane crash. So had he. They both lived with guilt, although his was greater. He’d been flying the plane.

But maybe she had a point. There were such things as acts of God, freak accidents that took lives, plane crashes, automobile accidents. Boats sinking. If you weren’t fated to go until it was your time, then maybe people were simply tools to accomplish accidents when it actually was your time.

Thinking about it that way made it just a little

easier. While he was pondering those odd thoughts, his cell phone rang.

"Where the hell are you?" Lindy demanded. "I need to go to Denver to meet a client. Will you get a move on, please?"

He didn't speak. Her belligerent, aggressive attitude was suddenly unacceptable. He was tired of it, and he hadn't even realized it until Karina came to work for him. The contrast between his child's babysitter and Lindy was striking.

"I'll get there when I get there," he snapped back. "Don't presume to order me around. You won't like the result." And he hung up.

She rang back. He turned off the ringer.

Burt stuck his head around the corner. "Lindy giving you trouble again?" he wondered.

"Lindy always gives me trouble," he muttered.

"Sometimes a wedding band is more of a noose than a symbol of wedded bliss," Burt commented. "She's your business, but I've seen men broken by women who shouted and criticized constantly."

"So have I." He grimaced. "Well, I'm stuck with her."

"Not really," Burt replied.

He met the older man's eyes. "Been thinking about that."

"Better think quick," came the amused reply. "She wants to stampede you into that ceremony."

"Been thinking about that, too," he repeated.

"Nice kid, that babysitter," Burt replied. "She was on her knees hugging Janey and promising her that everything would be all right. Been a while since I saw that kid cry, or be as happy as she is now."

"Which reminds me," Micah murmured, and pulled up the home numbers for Janey's principal and her teacher.

The principal was shocked and couldn't hide it.

"She's barely eleven," she replied.

"Janey never lies," he returned. "If she says the girl is doing things with boys when she should be in class, the girl's doing them. I don't have to tell you what would happen if her parents knew she was sneaking off during school hours to mess around with boys."

"No, you don't," the principal said heavily. "Goodness, we'd be sued to the back teeth. And if the local press got wind of it… I'll do something. I'm not sure what, but I'll handle it. You have my word."

"Thanks. I was going to speak to my daughter's teacher as well. The girl is making school miserable for her. She comes home in tears every day." He hesitated. "I have my own attorneys, you know," he added softly.

There was an indrawn breath. Most people around Catelow knew that Micah Torrance was rich beyond the dreams of avarice. Wealth and power, combined with the protective instincts of a parent, could be formidable. "I'm aware of that. I'll get back to you when I've resolved the problem," she said. "I'm going to have to investigate, and that will take a little time."

"Take down this number," he said, and started calling it off.

"Why am I taking down a number?"

"Because I know who your school attorney is, and he doesn't have an investigator at present. I know this one. He's done investigations for people I know. He's discreet, but he can provide proof. Will you ask your school attorney to call him?"

There was a hesitation. A sigh. "Yes," she said finally. "I will. I can't deal with the child until I have verification of the charges."

"I know that. I want my daughter to enjoy school," he said simply. "We live in sad times," he added. "When I was a boy, we were far more interested in building forts and playing baseball than sneaking off with girls. Especially when we were her age."

"I know. Society has done a complete flip. I'll be in touch, Mr. Torrance. And I thank you for your help."

"I'll be keeping in touch," he replied quietly. "You can count on that."

"Yes. Of course." She sounded as if she were being strangled as she hung up.

He knew how the wheels of justice turned in places like schools. The principal was afraid of bad publicity, if word of the girl's behavior got out. But Micah was going to ensure that she did something about the situation, and didn't try to sweep it under the carpet to save face. If worse came to worst, he'd have his attorney contact the girl's parents and threaten litigation. More often than not, it worked.

Nobody was picking on his daughter the way that girl had, he promised himself. Janey could fight her own battles as a rule, but this situation was sordid and frankly threatening. He couldn't stand back and let it escalate.

He checked his watch. Lindy would be fuming. He found that he didn't give a damn.

CHAPTER FIVE

"THAT'S THE WAY!" Karina praised as Janey did her first flip. She laughed at the girl's joy and pride. "You're doing great!"

"This is really fun," Janey said. "When I'm skating, I just don't cvcn think about things that worry me."

"It's always been like that for me. I've lived on the ice since I was a toddler," she added. "It was my whole life." Sadness claimed her face for an instant.

Janey saw it. She skated up to Karina. "You'll get it all back," she said. "Skating, I mean. I read where lots of skaters got injured and came back. One couple in pairs figure skating sat out two years while one of them had a baby. They came back and won a silver in the Olympics."

Karina knew who the girl was talking about, but she couldn't admit it. She just smiled. "I've read that, too."

"I'm a fanatic," Janey laughed. "I read everything I can find on figure skating. I want to compete. I love this!"

Karina felt her joy. It mirrored the pleasure she'd felt as a child, except that she'd been in competition for years when she was Janey's age. "You heard what the rink owner said about you. She thinks you have what it takes to compete. So do I," she added softly. "You're amazing already."

Janey flushed. "Thanks," she said, laughing. "I'll work hard, I promise."

"All right then. Onward to forward chassés."

THE DAYS PASSED LAZILY. Hilde Meyer's coach had been delayed, but promised to arrive soon. Meanwhile, Karina mentored Janey at the rink and helped Burt in the house when Janey was in school. He fussed at first, but she reminded him that work was work, and she couldn't look after a child who wasn't home. He gave in. He enjoyed her company.

"I hear the skating rink owner's putting in rental skates," Burt said while they washed dishes after breakfast. He washed, Karina dried. There was no dishwasher. Apparently Micah Torrance didn't think they needed one.

"I heard that, too," she said, smiling. "It's a smart move. She'll do lots more business. Most people won't go out and buy skates just to go around the rink a time or two."

"No, they won't. Especially in this economy. They say she used to be a famous skating coach."

"She was," Karina replied. "People told her she was old-fashioned in the choreography she taught." She made a huffy sound. "Her style was beautiful. She was a world champion skater herself, you know, before she began coaching."

"Why didn't she go into one of those shows, where ice skaters perform?"

"It's a dying thing," Karina said sadly. "Audiences don't care so much about sports like ice skating anymore. Well, except for the Olympics, but that's only every fourth year. A lot of the ice skating revues have pretty much folded for lack of ticket sales. I guess it's going to be a thing of the past soon."

"You know, I used to love to watch figure skating, back in the eighties," Burt said, smiling wistfully. He laughed. "I used to say that if they could lock the Russian pairs figure skaters in a closet somewhere, our country might win a gold medal. Those Russians were really great skaters."

She smiled. "Yes, they were. But the United States had some awesome contenders, especially in women's figure skating. Peggy Fleming. Dorothy Hamill. Many others."

He nodded. "Back then, skating was elegant and graceful. I used to love the music. It was always classical." He shook his head. "Now it's these wild tunes, and skaters can't even win if they don't have impossible throws and acrobatics on the ice. Where's the grace in that? It was like watching ballet on ice before. Now it's," he hesitated, "now it's roller derby on blades!"

She burst out laughing. "It's not that bad!"

He laughed, too. "I guess not. But I've got DVDs of the older pairs champions. I just watch those."

She had some of her own. She couldn't tell him that she was named for two gold medalists, or that she knew a lot more about ice skating than he might realize.

"Janey really took to you," Burt said. "I'm glad. She's had it rough at school. Micah wanted to put her in boarding school, like the one his father sent him to. Janey refused to go. First time I ever saw the boss back down. I don't like the idea of a child that young being away from home, unless it's absolutely necessary."

"Neither do I," she said.

"Her dad's all she's got. No other family living, not even grandparents. And he's gone all the time." He shook his head. "It's nice to have an empire, but you sacrifice a lot for it. He's missing Janey's whole little life. She's nine. In another nine years, she'll be in college or out on her own."

"They grow up fast," she agreed.

"How's she really doing on ice skates?"

"She's doing great," she replied. "I wouldn't have believed how much progress she's made already. She does flips beautifully. Her toe loops need a little work, but that's just practice. And she's great at crossovers, even on her weak leg," she laughed.

"You know a lot about it, don't you?"

"My mother put me on skates when I was barely three. I've been skating ever since. It was my solace when I was Janey's age. I got picked on, too. I was clumsy and awkward, and I never seemed to fit in with any of the other kids except one." That had been Paul, but she wasn't going to mention that.

"Boss never had a problem when he was that age,"

he mused. "His dad was a general, you know. He was regimented at home and in boarding school, tough as nails. Most of the other kids walked wide of him, even then. A lot of men still do. He's got some rough edges."

"He has," she said. "But he's fair and honest and you always know where you stand with him."

He arched both eyebrows. "Well, didn't you learn a lot real fast?"

She laughed. "I guess I did."

"Pretty much summed him up, except for that black temper. I don't think anybody can cure that."

"My dad had a temper like that," she recalled fondly. "He got over things quickly, though. So did my mom. She was a great companion."

"It's hard to lose parents," he commented. "Mine have been gone for thirty years, and I still miss them."

"Nobody is ever as proud of things you do as a parent is," she replied.

The front door opened, interrupting them. Micah came in with a swirl of snow and slammed the door behind him. "There's a blizzard out there," he muttered. "I damned near ran the car up a lodgepole pine that came out of nowhere."

"It's been coming down for about an hour, sure enough," Burt agreed.

"They've closed school," Micah added, staring pointedly at Karina, who flushed.

"Oh, gosh, I'm sorry! We didn't have the radio on!"

"You couldn't look out a window?" he asked with a snarl in his voice.

She flushed even more. She took off the apron Burt had loaned her and draped it over the back of a kitchen chair. "I'll go right now and get Janey," she said, flustered.

Micah felt guilty when he saw her lack of composure and Burt's scowl.

"Hell!" he said shortly. "I'll go get her myself."

He shoved his hat back on his head and stormed out the front door. As an afterthought, he slammed it behind him.

"Oh, dear," Karina said uneasily.

"He has moods," Burt said without rancor. "Mostly Lindy provokes them. She's never satisfied with anything he does. She probably stoked the fire before he even got off the plane."

"She's very beautiful," she said, not liking to complain about the boss's fiancée.

"Like I said before, so are some reptiles, at a distance." He shook his head. "Janey can't stand her. Neither can I. The kindest thing she ever said about my cooking was that it might be fit for the dogs."

She grimaced. "I think you cook very nicely, Burt," she said gently.

He smiled. "Thanks."

There was a quick knock at the door and Billy Joe walked in with Dietrich at his heels. "Boss home yet?" he asked.

"Already came and left," Burt said. "What do you need?"

"Nothing. I just wanted to know if I could have Sunday afternoon off. Well, if the blizzard lets up," he added on a chuckle. "There's a dog show over in Cheyenne. I thought I'd take Dietrich over and humiliate the other working class dogs."

Burt howled. "The boss would love it, if you put it that way to him."

Billy Joe grinned. He cocked his head at Karina. "Do you like kids' movies?" he asked.

She blinked. "Excuse me?"

"Cartoon movies," he emphasized. "That new one, *CoCo*, is playing at the Catelow Rialto downtown."

"Oh, that one! Yes, I love that sort of movie."

"How about going to see it with me, if you're not tied up Saturday night?"

"I'm not tied up any Saturday night," she said, smiling. "I'd love to go. Thanks."

He flushed a little and chuckled. "Okay, then. It's a date. We'll go about six. We can stop at the fish place and have supper."

"I love fish," she replied.

"Okay." He tipped his hat, grinned and went back out into the snow with Dietrich.

Burt didn't say a word, but he was thinking hard. The boss was abrasive with Miss Carter here, and he didn't think it was because he disliked her. He wasn't sure why, but he was pretty certain the boss wasn't going to like this. Not one bit.

JANEY CAME RUNNING IN, her book bag covered with snow. "Gosh, we almost went over into the ditch! It's bad outside!"

"That means no skating today, too," Micah said gruffly. "The roads are almost impassible."

"Aw, gee, no skating," Janey said miserably.

"The snow will pass," Karina said gently. "You'll see."

"Well, it's Friday. We can go tomorrow afternoon, right? I mean, if the snow stops."

"Of course." Karina hesitated. "But we have to be back by six."

"Six? Why?"

"Billy Joe's taking me to a movie…oh!"

She jumped. Micah had dropped the boot he'd just taken off, and it hit the floor like a small bomb.

"What movie?" he asked, one foot in a sock and one in a boot.

"CoCo," she faltered.

"Cartoons."

"Well, there's nothing wrong with a cartoon movie," she protested. "It's certainly better than some of the smut that passes for entertainment these days!"

His eyes widened. "Close the theaters. Shut down the bars. Ban music!"

She glared at him. "I am not Cromwell and this is not England," she said huffily.

"You could pass for a Puritan," he countered.

She made a face.

"We'll only get to skate for a couple of hours," Janey said miserably. "But it's okay. I mean…"

"We could ask Billy Joe if you can come, too," she said softly, and she smiled. "It's supposed to be a very good movie."

There were shocked faces all around. Karina was blissfully unaware of them.

"But you're going on a date," Janey protested.

Karina shook her head. "I'm going to a movie."

"Oh."

Burt and Micah were exchanging complicated looks.

In the middle of it all, Billy Joe stuck his head back in the door and grimaced. "Listen," he told Karina miserably, "I really wanted to take you to that movie, but it's the second Saturday in the month," he added heavily. "See, we have a band, sort of, and we have standard gigs. We've got one tomorrow night and I clean forgot..." He glanced around at the odd expressions on their faces.

"That's okay," Karina said brightly. "Janey and I can spend more time at the skating rink. It will be fine. Honest."

His face relaxed. "Okay, then. Thanks! Rain check?"

"Sure," she said easily.

He tipped his hat, let Dietrich in the house and smiled as he closed the door.

"That went well," Micah said to nobody in particular. "And without any blood loss to speak of." With that enigmatic remark, he pulled off his other boot, threw it beside the one he'd already discarded and padded off to his room.

He closed his bedroom door and felt mild surprise that he'd wanted to toss Billy Joe headfirst into a waste lagoon. He shouldn't be feeling betrayed because his daughter's babysitter had wanted to go out with an eligible young man. After all, he was engaged. Or was he?

The more he compared Lindy to Karina, the worse he felt. He couldn't understand why he was even making comparisons. The thought made him so bad tempered that he avoided the other occupants of his home all night.

KARINA WAS AFRAID she'd done something to upset the boss, but she didn't know what. She gave Janey some more pointers on her toe loops and the chassés that challenged her weaker leg.

"This is so much fun," Janey sighed. "I love coming here with you."

"I love it, too," Karina said, smiling as they skated along together. "I was so afraid to skate again. My ankle is almost completely healed now, but I kept thinking about how it felt when it was broken."

"You have to go forward," Janey said with a grin. "But backward is fun, too!" She turned around and moving her legs in and out, skated alongside Karina, laughing.

"Not bad," Karina said.

"Can you show me the toe loop?" Janey asked. "And maybe that Lutz…?"

Karina took a deep breath. "Well, sooner or later I'll have to try it, I guess." She hesitated. A lot of skaters came to the rink on Saturday night, but there were other things going on in Catelow, so there were only a handful now.

Mrs. Meyer saw Karina looking around. She

smiled and changed the music. She put on Rachmaninoff's *Rhapsody on a Theme of Paganini*, Opus 42, variation VIII, and waited.

Karina caught her breath at the music. She was back in time, at the Worlds competition with Paul. That was their music. Without thinking too much about it, she started around the rink, gaining speed with each movement of her legs. Speed was the thing she and Paul were praised for most often. There was so much power and grace in their routines.

She smiled dreamily as she skated the old program, oblivious to the few other skaters going to the side of the rink to watch as she did Lutzes and toe loops, Salchows and camels and laybacks.

The music was in her blood, removing her from the world around her, so that she skated blindly, passionately, to the music that had almost belonged to her and Paul when they were on the ice together.

Her final move was a beautiful layback, followed by a sit spin. When she came back to herself, it was to thunderous applause. She flushed as she realized that she'd been skating with an audience.

She moved quickly back to Janey, smiling shyly at the other skaters.

"That was beautiful," Janey said, agog. "I've never seen anybody skate like that, except on TV!"

Karina took a deep breath. "I used to skate a lot," she said. "Before I broke my leg, and then my ankle. I was so afraid to do it again. Thank you."

"Me? What did I do?" Janey asked.

"You gave me the courage to skate again, that's

what you did," she said softly, and smiled at the little girl. "You inspired me to try. I don't think I'd have had the courage, if it hadn't been for you."

Janey grinned from ear to ear. "Will I ever get as good as you are?" she asked.

"Of course you will," she replied. "It's not so hard. It's just that you have to practice a lot. And fall a lot," she teased.

Mrs. Meyer came to the barrier. Karina skated over to her with Janey.

"Sorry," Hilde said, but she didn't really mean it. She was grinning. "I just wanted to see if I could inspire you."

Karina laughed. "You and Janey certainly have," she told the older woman. "Thanks," she added huskily. "That music is...well, I feel as if it belongs to me, in a way."

"I knew that. It's why I put it on," Hilde said. "You skate beautifully. I wish I'd been your coach."

"I wish it, too," Karina replied. She grimaced. "We had a coach who cowed us," she added, remembering Paul. "We put up with it for two years, until we had no egos left and we could barely skate at all. It took a lot of guts to tell him we were firing him."

"Who's we?" Janey asked.

Karina thought fast. "Some other skaters and I," she replied. "It was a long time ago, in Upstate New York."

"New York?" Janey exclaimed. "But I thought you lived near Jackson Hole."

"I did. You see, when you're moving up in skating competition, it means going where you're invited to skate. I had to live with other families in a lot of places when I competed. Skating people are kind, and very generous. I've lived all over the country, even in other countries…" She trailed off. This was more information than she wanted Janey to have.

Janey pursed her lips. "You're scared that I'll tell somebody. But I won't," she added solemnly. "I promise. You were in competition, weren't you?"

Karina drew in a breath. "Yes. I had a partner. When this happened," she indicated the injured foot, "he had to find someone else to skate with. It was a blow. We'd been together since we were children."

"Gosh, that's sad," Janey said.

"His partner just left him, too," Hilde remarked.

"What?" Karina exclaimed. "But Regionals and sectionals are this month! With a new partner, he'll have to do those!"

Hilde nodded. "He won't get to compete this year. Plus, his new coach just moved to Norway, where he has several new younger students to train. The coach says they'll be world champions very soon."

"Poor Paul," Karina said, grimacing.

"He isn't very sad about it," Hilde laughed. "He said his new partner was more concerned with her costume and her makeup and her nails than she was in landing triples. She wasn't much of a skater, apparently."

"I haven't talked to him lately," Karina said. "I should have kept in touch."

"He knows you're struggling." Hilde smiled. "I

told him you were back on the ice again. He was proud of you."

Karina beamed. "Did he say how Gerda and the boys were?"

"Doing fine. They're all in Jackson Hole now."

"I've been out of touch. I'll have to do something about that."

While they were talking, a boy several years older than Janey skated over. "That was great, what you did," he said to Karina, flushing a little. "Your triple Salchow was perfect! I can't do one. I'd love to be able to skate like that."

"It's just practice," Karina said modestly. "You have to put in several hours a day to get really good at it."

"I wish we had somebody to train us," he replied sadly.

Hilde brightened. "Actually, I have a young man who's willing to do that. He's coming for an interview next week."

"A real coach?" the boy asked.

"Yes. He'll be here at the rink."

"I have to tell my dad!" the boy exclaimed. "I want lessons really bad!"

Hilde grinned. "I'll make sure we have somebody to do that."

"Thanks!"

She nodded.

He gave them a shy smile and skated back to his friends.

"A coach is a really good idea," Karina said.

"I wish I could do it, but I'm sort of out of the game," Hilde said sadly. "They said I had no idea how to coach modern skaters, that I was living in the dark ages." She laughed. "Then my friend talked bad about me to the skaters I was coaching and they went over to him. So here I am."

"You were a great coach," Karina argued. "Your routines were as graceful as ballet, and just as beautiful. I loved watching your skaters."

"I miss it."

Karina smiled. "I miss competition." She looked down. "I can skate again. But it's so much hard work, to get back to where I was."

"Nothing worthwhile is ever easy," Hilde said.

"Well, that's true," the younger woman agreed.

"Will I ever be able to skate like you?" Janey asked Karina.

"Yes, you will," she replied. "When the trainer comes, we'll talk to your dad about real lessons. I can teach you the moves, but you need a coach, a good one, to run you through the various jumps, to train you to do them correctly. I'm a skater, not a coach," she added with a smile.

"I think you do fine," Janey said.

"Thanks. But if you want to go into competition, you need a real coach. It's a long, tiring progression from beginner even to the next level. There will be required movements and tests you'll have to pass to progress. It's a very long way from where you are even to regional competition. There are grades all the way up. You have to go through every one. There are no shortcuts, and it means a lot of practice. Hours a day. You also have to keep up with your school work while you're doing it," Karina added. "Because skating will not support you unless you win a gold at the Olympics."

"The Olympics are next February," Janey said. "In Pyeongchang. It's going to be great!"

"I imagine so," Karina said sadly. She and Paul had wanted so badly to have a shot at those Olympics.

Hilde was frowning. "You know," she said, "it's several months until the Olympics. I can still coach."

Karina's lips fell open. She could almost see what the woman was thinking. Paul didn't have a partner or a coach. Hilde was a coach. Karina was able to do jumps again.

"Do you think…?" she began.

"Do you know what time it is?" a deep, angry voice said from behind them.

Karina ground her teeth together. Micah had come up unexpectedly and she hadn't even seen him. She looked at her watch. "Oh, dear."

"Yes, oh, dear," he muttered. "It's time to go home. You can't live at the damned rink."

"But, Dad, I have to practice," Janey said miserably.

"You've been here for five hours," he pointed out.

"Yes, but…"

"You have homework for Monday," he added curtly. "If your grades drop, skating is out."

She sighed. "I know. Karina just told me that."

"She did?" he asked, glancing at the young woman.

"She said that I couldn't make a living at skating unless I won the Olympics, so it was important to keep my grades up and have a profession."

"Well," he exclaimed, impressed.

"I'll think about what you said," Karina told Hilde.

She smiled. "Please do. It might be a second chance for all of us." She nodded at Micah and went back toward her office.

"Janey, let's get our skates off."

A young woman who looked to be in her late teens skated up to Karina. "That was wonderful, what you did," she said. "Do you teach?"

Karina cringed inwardly at Micah's curious stare. "No, I'm sorry. But Mrs. Meyer is hiring a coach."

"That's great news. But I wish it was you. I've never seen anybody skate like that," she added breathlessly. "You're great."

"Thanks. But I'm just an amateur." And that was the truth. She'd never skated professionally.

The woman smiled and skated off again.

"What was she talking about?" Micah asked.

"I did some jumps," Karina said, heading off the questions. "I'd almost forgotten how."

"She did a triple Salchow!" Janey exclaimed.

Karina ground her teeth together and looked pained, but it seemed to go right over Micah's head. Janey looked guilty. Karina gave her a reassuring smile.

"Well, we'd better go. I'll follow you home," he told her.

She and Janey got off the rink and removed their skates, drying the blades with a chamois cloth that Karina had in her bag.

"Why aren't you just using paper towels for that?" Micah asked.

"Chamois absorbs water better," she explained. "If you don't get the moisture out, your blades will rust. And that reminds me, we need to find someone who can sharpen the blades. They get dull with use and they don't work as well. We have to have them sharpened every few weeks."

"Burt knows how to do that," Micah said.

"He does?"

"He used to skate semiprofessionally. Didn't he tell you?" he asked Karina sarcastically. "Or did you think he knew all about skating from watching it on television?"

She didn't understand why he was so antagonistic. It made her nervous. He made her nervous. "He didn't say," she replied, and kept her eyes down. He was a very abrasive sort of man. And far too masculine for her taste. She liked gentle men.

His eyes narrowed as he watched her dry the blades and then put fuzzy pink protectors on the blades before she returned the skates to their bags.

"You're pretty good with that," he remarked.

She smiled, still not looking at him. "I've been skating for a long time."

"How long?"

"Since I was three, actually."

His dark eyes narrowed on her face as she bent

over the bag. She had pale blond hair, in a topknot. It was very long when it was loosened. He remembered without wanting to how it had looked the night she got Burt to check on him, the night he'd yelled at her. He grimaced at the memory. He loved long hair. Lindy wore hers short.

Lindy. He was more disenchanted with her by the day. She loved to throw orders around. It irritated him. He snapped at her more these days than he'd ever done before. She wanted to move up the date for their marriage, and he was certain that he wanted to cancel the whole thing. Burt had been right. It was a bad match. He was going to have to talk to Lindy, and it would be very unpleasant. But it wasn't something he had to do right now. It could wait.

"Are you ready to go?" he asked Karina.

She looked up at him and he became lost in her pale gray eyes. They were like fog on the lake in the early morning, he thought absently. Her mouth was a soft pretty bow and he stared it for far too long, until he saw a blush run over her high cheekbones.

She averted her eyes, dragged them away from his. Her breath came quickly, and stuck in her chest. He was making her heart race with those probing dark eyes. She felt frightened, suddenly, of emotions she'd never felt before.

"Yes, I'm ready…oh!" She got up too fast, tripped over her skating bag, and would have fallen if Micah hadn't caught her.

His big hands tightened on her upper arms. He moved a step closer. "You okay?" he asked gruffly.

She could barely manage words. He smelled of some spicy, exotic, expensive cologne. He was warm and strong and she wanted to crawl into his arms and be held while she told him the story of her life.

It was unexpected, to feel like that with a man who was almost a stranger. Worse, she loved the feel of his hands on her bare arms.

"Your skin is cold," he remarked. "It's cold on the ice. Don't you wear a jacket when you skate?"

"It gets in the way," she said. "I'm used to the cold. It doesn't bother me."

His big hands smoothed over her arms. "If you say so."

She looked up as far as his chin. "I'll just…get my jacket," she said, her voice breaking. He was really having an effect on her.

He knew it. She caught the faintly arrogant look on his face as she tugged out of his grasp and picked up her down jacket. He moved closer and held it for her while she shrugged into it. His big hands on her shoulders felt warm and gentle. She was amazed at the sensations they caused.

He let her go and turned to his daughter. "Ready?" he asked with a smile.

"Ready. Dad, they're going to get a real coach here, to teach skating. Do you think…?"

He grimaced. "I thought Miss Carter was teaching you."

"I'm not a professional trainer," Karina remarked as they started out the door. "If Janey wants to compete, there are levels and tests and she'll need someone who's familiar with the various stages of competition to guide her. I just know how to skate. I can't teach."

"Not true," Janey said. "You're a great teacher!"

Karina laughed. "Thanks, sweetheart. I'm really not. I'm just sharing with you what my mother taught me."

"So, how about the coach?" Janey asked her father. "I really want to skate, Dad. It's the most important thing in my life right now. Please?"

He drew in a long breath. "We'll talk about it. But you have to keep your grades up."

"I promise I will!"

He just nodded. Which could mean anything. "I'll follow behind you," he told Karina. "Go slow. Snow's still coming down hard."

"I will," she said.

"I'll ride with you," Janey told Karina, "so you won't be nervous driving home."

"You doll," Karina said softly, and hugged her. "Okay, let's go!"

They ran to Karina's car. Micah, watching them, felt an unfamiliar warmth inside. Anabelle hadn't wanted a child. Janey was something of a wonderful accident. But Micah had wanted her, loved her, taken care of her. Lindy hated kids. But Karina loved his daughter. It was mutual. He'd never known Janey to laugh as much, or be as happy as she was in Karina's company.

But what would happen when Karina left? She was a young woman. She wasn't going to want to spend her life looking after a child, regardless of how fond she was of her. That was what worried him the most. What would come after.

He tumbled it over in his mind all the way home.

CHAPTER SIX

MICAH FOLLOWED THEM into the house. Burt was just putting up the dishes he'd washed.

"Janey's skates need sharpening," he told Burt. "Think you can do it?"

"Sure I can," Burt said, grinning. "I'll do yours, too, if they need it," he added to Karina.

"They probably do," she replied. "They've had a workout in the past few days."

"She landed a triple Salchow!" Janey exclaimed and then bit her lower lip, because she'd promised Karina she wouldn't talk about it.

Burt's eyebrows went up. "A triple?"

"I've been practicing," Karina said, bluffing it through. She laughed. "Janey's inspired me."

"A triple Salchow." Burt whistled. "Hard stuff, for a beginner," he added with a wise look toward Karina that nobody saw except her.

"Really hard," Karina agreed. "Well, I'm going to turn in."

"Me, too." Janey mouthed "I'm sorry!" at Karina.

Karina just smiled and nodded. Janey went into her room with her skate bag and closed the door.

"Burt, how about some coffee?" Micah asked.

"Sure. Coming right up."

"Want some?" Micah asked her gently.

She should go to bed. She should go right now! "Sure," she replied, and sat down at the table with him.

Burt poured coffee in thick mugs and placed condiments on the table. "Would you like some cheese and crackers?" he asked them.

Micah chuckled. "Yes, I would. Lindy and I had rabbit food for lunch." He made a face. "If I eat anything that isn't a vegetable, it starts a fight."

"That's sad," Karina said quietly as she picked up her mug, declining cream or sugar.

He lifted an eyebrow. "Sad?"

She flushed. "Sorry. Not my business."

"Sad?" he repeated, and stared at her.

She grimaced. "Well, if I go out to eat with anyone, I don't try to dictate their food choices."

His dark eyes softened. "We should frame you and hang you on the wall," he commented. "Not a lot of people keep their opinions to themselves in this day and age."

"They're too busy marching in the streets with placards."

"Shades of the sixties and seventies," Burt commented as he busied himself in the kitchen with saucers and a block of cheese.

"Were there protests back then, too?" Karina asked, surprised.

He laughed. "More than now. The Vietnam War was raging. The 'flower power' generation marched to get us out of it. There were riots on campuses, and a few tragedies with deaths involved," he said, remembering. "But in the end, they won. President Nixon got us out of Southeast Asia. He brought the troops home."

"He was impeached," she said. "I read about it in my history class."

"Always remember that there are two sides to every story," Burt added. "Nixon wasn't perfect, but he saved lives, a lot of lives, by getting us out of the conflict. My father's was one of them."

"People are good and bad," Micah agreed. "We need another Theodore Roosevelt."

Karina laughed. "He was my favorite President," she explained when both men looked at her. "He was sickly and weak as a child, an asthmatic as well, but it never got him down. He was tough as nails. They said when he took his volunteer unit to Cuba in the Spanish American War that he had Native Americans, Ivy League athletes, Buffalo Soldiers, Texas Rangers outlaws and French Foreign Legionnaires, Germans and all sorts of extraordinary men in the group. No one could accuse Teddy of being prejudiced against any group." Micah nodded. "He was a man ahead of his time. He was famous for trust-busting. That's what we need today, someone to break up those multinational corporations. A handful of them control the media. They decide what news you'll watch, and a good many of them slant it to a particular political viewpoint. Not news in my opinion. No objectivity."

"Besides that," Burt interjected, "you get a political message in almost every television program, every product ad, you name it. I watch television to be entertained, not to be indoctrinated."

Karina laughed. "It does feel like that, doesn't it? I don't really watch television. I live on the internet when I'm not working."

"Doing what?" Micah asked.

"Going to out-of-the-way landmarks all over the world," she said. "Mysterious places like the Inca ruins in Peru, the Aztec ruins in Mexico, the Mayan ruins in the Yucatan. Stuff like that."

"Archaeology," he mused.

"At Teotihuacan, those pyramids had a thick layer of mica between the levels," she recalled. "The only mica of that sort known was mined in South America. Imagine transporting that all the way to the Mayan pyramids in a primitive age." She glanced at Micah. "Nobody knows why they went to so much trouble to get it, or why it was placed in the pyramids centuries ago."

Burt pursed his lips. "It's a great conductor of electricity," he pointed out.

Micah gave him a droll look. "Maybe it was a primitive antenna. You know, so the Mayans could watch TV when they weren't carving stelae."

Karina laughed.

Burt just smiled. "Well, who knows?" he continued. "Those huge stone constructions, like at Machu Picchu, how were they made? Nobody knows. Nobody's been able to replicate that sort of building, even with all our modern tech."

"Maybe it was aliens?" Karina suggested with twinkling eyes.

They both glowered at her.

She laughed. "You know, some Native Americans believe that human beings have risen to the same level of civilization that we have today, several times in prehistory. They think catastrophes destroyed those civilizations, and scattered the people, so that they had to begin from the Stone Age all over again. In fact," she added, warming to the subject, "part of the United States was once under the ocean. They've even found sea shells on top of mountains back east."

"Conspiracy theorist," Micah jeered, but kindly.

She sighed. "I guess so. It's just that we really don't know all that much about the planet we live on. There's a lot of guesswork, because it's almost impossible to date ruins that don't have an organic component. Even so, determining exact age is tricky."

"They're coming up with new methods of dating stone all the time," Micah replied. "In fact…"

He was interrupted by his cell phone. He answered it curtly, impatient at the interruption.

He drew in a long breath, got up and picked up his coffee. "Yes," he said, moving toward his study. "All right, give me a minute."

He went into the room and closed the door.

"Business," Burt said. He shook his head as he

placed crackers, sliced cheese and saucers on the table. "That phone never stops ringing. He won't even cut it off at night."

"He should," she said softly. "Even a relatively young man can have a heart attack from too much stress."

"Maybe eating rabbit food is good for him," he returned with twinkling eyes.

She made a face. "Rabbit food's not so bad. But I still love steak," she confessed.

He laughed. "Me, too. I'll just warm that coffee for you."

"Thanks."

BUT BY THE time she finished her cheese and crackers, and the warmed coffee, Micah still hadn't returned. She was faintly disappointed. She loved to listen to his voice. It was like deep, rich velvet.

She got up and put her dishes in the sink, pausing to thank Burt for the treat. It was late and she was tired.

Her ankle was a little swollen from the skating, but that wasn't worrying. She was delighted to know that she could still do the moves that had won her and Paul that gold medal at the World Figure Skating Championships. She really needed to get in touch with him. She hadn't thought about going back into competition. She'd been too afraid to go on the ice after her injury.

But Janey and Hilde had turned her life around. She saw possibilities. She'd practice when Janey did, and see how it went. When she was confident enough, she'd call Paul and see if he wanted to get back together with her with a new coach and try for the Olympics next year in Pyeongchang.

She reminded herself that it would be a struggle. But, then, life was a struggle. You just had to take the first step and keep going.

SHE'D ALMOST MADE it to her door when Micah came out of the office.

"That was my attorney," he told Karina. "They've dealt with the girl who was giving Janey so much grief. She's been expelled, along with the boy she was being intimate with at school. Her parents, apparently, knew nothing about it. They were devastated."

"That's sad," Karina said. "But it will make poor Janey's life easier."

"I try not to interfere, unless I have to," he replied. "But this was a circumstance that she couldn't handle on her own." He chuckled. "My attorney was shocked, to say the least. He's Burt's age."

"Don't make that sound like I got off the *Titanic* in time," Burt said, glowering.

"You're not old, Burt. You're a fine, aged wine," Karina said.

He grinned. "Hear that?" he told Micah.

"You're moonshine whisky with wood alcohol in it," came the retort.

Burt glared. "You're getting liver and onions for supper tomorrow."

"Sadist," Micah accused.

Burt made a harrumphing sound. "On that note, I'm going to bed. Don't forget your cheese and crackers, boss. I reheated your coffee."

"Thanks."

"No problem. Good night."

Burt went down the hall into his room. But Micah didn't move. "Janey said earlier that you did a triple," Micah said when Karina started to turn away.

She flushed. Not much got past him. "Well, sort of..."

He moved a step closer. She barely came to his chin. She smelled of flowers. He could see her breathing change at the proximity. It flattered him that he was affecting her. Women had played up to him for years, aware of his wealth and eager for presents. Even Lindy wanted him for what he had, not what he was. But here was a woman who was excited by the man, not his checkbook.

His big hand went out and touched a wisp of hair that had come loose from the high bun that wealth of pale blond hair was confined in. "How long is your hair?" he asked.

She fought to get enough breath to answer him. "It's...to my waist," she faltered.

He moved another step closer, so that he could feel the warmth of her body. The scent of her filled his nostrils. "Is it?" He looked down at her mouth. He stared at it with visible curiosity.

She was shaking inside. She'd had the usual crushes on boys as she grew up, but there had been nothing really physical, unless you counted the close contact she had with Paul. But Paul was like a brother. This man was a forest fire waiting for kindling. He was big and tough and gentle, and she was drawn to him in ways she'd never been drawn to any other man.

He could see her reactions. She couldn't hide them. She was too young, of course; twenty-three to his thirty-four. She worked for him. There were about twenty more reasons that it was a bad idea to even think about getting involved with her.

Karina was fighting a losing battle as he stared at her mouth. He wanted it. She could tell. She wanted his, too, that sensuous mouth that looked as if it knew everything there was to know about kissing. He moved one more step closer, and both her icy hands went to the thick black-and-red plaid shirt that was unbuttoned just at the top. Thick, curling black hair peeked out of it there. Under her hands, she could feel hard muscle. His big hands went to her shoulders and lingered there, smoothing over the soft material of her sweater.

"This," he said roughly, "is a very bad idea."

She swallowed hard. "Yes. You're engaged."

He blinked, as if he'd just realized that. Worse, he realized what he was doing. He was making a move on his daughter's babysitter. There were whole volumes written about men who did that. Of course, she was a grown woman, not a teenager. Still, she was, she should be, off limits.

He moved back a step, dropping his hands from her shoulders. An awkward silence followed.

"It's my cologne," she blurted out.

He stared at her. "Excuse me?"

"The advertisement said that men would jump out of airplanes with parachutes on just to get to women who wear it."

"I'm not wearing a parachute," he pointed out.

"Oh, it's probably outside, hanging from the limb of a lodgepole pine," she added, and her pale eyes twinkled.

He chuckled. "Maybe it is."

"Good night, Mr. Torrance," she said.

"Good night, Miss Carter," he replied.

SHE CLOSED HER bedroom door and sat down hard on her bed. Her heart was going like a fast watch and she couldn't quite catch her breath. Heavens, he was sexy! She could see why he drew women. Money would have been the least of the reasons.

She was going to have to work at keeping some distance between them. She loved Janey already, and she liked this job. She couldn't afford to get involved, in any way, with the boss. Besides, as she'd already reminded him, he was engaged.

She thought about his fiancée and how she'd taunted Janey at the ice rink. She didn't like children. What sort of life would Janey have, if Mr. Torrance married that woman? Lindy didn't seem like the nurturing sort. It would be a miserable existence for both of them. Not to mention Burt, who didn't seem to get along with Lindy, either.

It was none of her business, she reminded herself. She'd do best to keep her nose out of it and let Mr. Torrance lead his own life.

She got into her nightgown and climbed under the covers. But it was a long time until she could sleep.

JANEY WAS GETTING better at skating. Saturday, despite the snow, they spent all day at the ice rink. While Hilde explained the first level of competition to Janey, and schooled her in it, Karina worked at getting back to her old proficiency.

She began as she always did, with simple movements. She'd made sure she stretched first, especially her ankles, to keep from doing any more damage. She was going to have to see her sports therapist next week and let him check to make sure she was ready for jumps. She'd worried about the swelling when she did the triple the day before.

She didn't attempt any more jumps of that sort. She practiced the routine moves, the ones she'd learned at the beginning of her skating career. Besides helping with the discipline of forms, it also helped to keep Janey from seeing more than she should. The child was astute. She knew that a triple was not a move for a beginner. Karina had also rambled on about living in many states while she was in competition. But she had a remedy for that. She'd just tell the child that she'd gone no further than district competition. That should head off any worrying questions that Janey might pose.

She loved the way Hilde was with the child. She was ever so patient. Karina remembered watching Hilde at World Championships with her own skaters, the ones who'd quit her after saying she was too old-fashioned in her training methods. Karina disagreed. Hilde had a genius for choreography.

While Janey practiced, she paused beside the older woman to watch.

"She's very good," Hilde said. "She just needs practice and discipline, and she could go all the way to the Worlds. Even the Olympics. Just like you," she added with a warm smile.

"If she keeps at it," Karina replied. "She has no idea how grueling it is to compete, or how mean some of the skaters and their parents can be."

"You coped. So will she."

"The routine that Paul and I did, at the Worlds. You saw it. What would you have changed about it?" she asked.

Hilde started. "It was very good."

"What would you have changed?" Karina persisted, and she smiled.

Hilde drew a long breath. "You know that I am a hopeless romantic."

"Yes. That's why I loved to watch the skaters you coached. It inspired Paul and me. When we got rid of our abusive coach, and went with Harmon, we suggested moves very like those you'd choreographed."

Hilde beamed. "I am very flattered."

"So tell me. What would you have changed?"

"For one thing, the costumes," she said. "To do a fantasy, you should look the part. Something with flowing lines, very conservative and feminine. For him, a tailored look, but with a fantasy component."

"A short cape," Janey mused.

She laughed. "Just the thing, and a red cummerbund, like a prince would wear in the old days."

"What else?" Janey asked dreamily.

"The combination moves. I would do them differently, to conform to the rhythm of Rachmaninoff's exquisite score."

And she explained what she'd seen, and what she'd have liked to see.

"That would fit better with the tempo," Karina agreed, picturing it in her mind.

"Something like this." Hilde moved out onto the ice and performed a series of jumps, ending in a beautiful layback, one that Karina had never seen before.

"That's new," she exclaimed. "I've never seen a layback so graceful!"

"Try it," Hilde invited.

Karina got up some speed and imitated the graceful moves the older skater had performed.

"Excellent," Hilde laughed. "You make me look clumsy."

"You could never be called clumsy," the younger woman argued. She smiled. "You know, I..."

She stopped, staring, as Micah Torrance came into the building with an annoyed Lindy at his side.

She wondered if something was wrong. He looked irritated.

He motioned to Janey. She skated over to him, but a little clumsily, because another skater cut across in front of her unexpectedly. Karina followed, hoping she wasn't in trouble. They were at the rink later than she'd planned. She lost track of time when she skated.

Lindy laughed as Janey approached, sparing a glare for Karina. "If that's what you're being taught, you're wasting your time," she told Janey. "You don't have the self-discipline for skating."

Karina had to bite her tongue to keep from shooting back a reply. Her eyes glittered at the other woman, though.

Micah saw that. He wasn't very pleased with Lindy's remark, either.

"I don't expect exhibition-quality skating of a beginner," he told his fiancée curtly.

Lindy shrugged. "Whatever. She's not serious about it, anyway. She never did anything right when I was teaching her."

Janey flushed.

"She does very well," Karina defended her.

"Oh, like you'd know," Lindy chided. "You skate like a beginner, too. I won a district competition," she reminded the other woman.

How many judges did you have to bribe? Karina thought wickedly. But she only smiled.

Janey started to open her mouth, and Karina was certain that the triple was going to come up.

She headed off trouble. "Are we late?" she asked Micah. "I'm so sorry. I was talking to Hi…to the owner of the rink," she amended. It wouldn't do to let Micah know how well she knew Hilde.

"That old has-been," Lindy said, bored. She riffled through her purse for a lipstick. "She lost all her skaters, so she's reduced to being the caretaker of this dumpy skating rink."

Micah frowned. "What did you do, eat razor blades for dinner?" he demanded. "For God's sake, Lindy!"

She seemed to realize finally that she'd put everyone's back up. Janey and Karina were openly glaring at her now, and Micah was plainly annoyed. She closed her purse. "I'm hungry. I didn't get dinner, yet," she said pointedly.

"Don't expect me to go to any restaurant tonight. I've got to fly to Billings for talks with the owner of a refinery I'm buying."

"I guess I can eat a bowl of cereal," she said, sounding pathetic.

It was an act. Karina saw right through it. Amazingly, Micah seemed to, as well. "I guess you can," he said curtly.

Lindy glared at all three of them. "I'll wait in the car," she said. "It's cold in here."

She turned and walked out. Even her stride was snippy, like her voice.

"Peace at last," Micah said under his breath. He looked down at his dejected daughter. "You can't skate like an Olympic champion when you've only been at it for a few weeks," he pointed out. "You're doing fine. Honest."

Janey's face lit up. "You really think so?"

"I do." He smiled tenderly. "But you have to learn self-confidence. Don't let a sarcastic person convince you that you're incompetent. You can do anything you want to do."

"Not really," Janey said.

He raised both eyebrows.

"I can't go to Mars."

He rolled his eyes. "I'm leaving. Lindy and I have to get to the airport. Listen, one of the cowboys saw a bear close to the house. You both stay inside, unless you're going to and from school or the ice rink. Don't take chances. Make sure you both have your cell phones, and that they're charged." He glanced at Karina, who was flushed. He held out his hand and stared at her.

She ground her teeth together as she pulled her cell phone out of her fanny pack and handed it to him.

"One bar," he muttered, giving it back. "Didn't you say that you have a car charger?"

"Yes, sir," she said with a heavy sigh. "I'll plug the phone in the minute we get to the car."

He nodded. "Snow's coming down again pretty heavily. You should go home."

"We'll pack up and leave right now," Karina promised.

He searched her soft gray eyes. "Drive slowly,"

he said, his voice deep with feeling. "Don't take chances."

"I won't," she promised.

"Make sure she does," he told his daughter and grinned at her.

Janey skated up to the barrier and stepped onto the wood floor, to hug her dad tight. "You be careful, too. Make sure the pilot's sober this time," she added in a loud whisper.

"We don't have that one anymore. I sent him to rehab," he assured her.

She laughed. "Okay, Dad."

"Both of you take care. I'll only be away a couple of days, with any luck."

"Okay," Karina replied.

He looked at her for a few seconds too long for politeness. She fought another blush and tried to breathe normally as he tweaked Janey's hair and walked out of the building.

"Honestly, that Lindy," Janey sighed as they took off their skates and dried the blades before putting the cozies on them and zipping them into their respective bags. "I don't know how Dad stands it. She's never happy."

"Some people never seem to be," Karina agreed.

"You always are."

Karina laughed. "I put on a very good front," she explained. "No sense making other people feel miserable when I do."

"And it takes fewer muscles to smile than it does to frown," Janey added with a laugh.

"Good point."

"Do you think we could come back tomorrow, if the weather's no worse?" Janey asked.

"We'll have to wait and see. I can drive in snow, but we're going through some very narrow roads, and they're mountain roads. You and I would make very sad pancakes."

It took Janey a minute to get that. She laughed. "Yes, I think we would. I'm so glad I have you for a friend," she added as they got to the car, having made a path to the car through newly fallen snow.

"I'm glad to have you for one as well," she told the child with a gentle smile.

"Mrs. Meyer said I had potential," Janey replied. She frowned as she put her bag in the back seat and got into the front seat beside Karina. "What's potential?"

"It means you have promise," Karina said as she started the car. "When you love a sport, you give more to it."

"I love skating."

"So do I." She glanced at her companion. "But school comes first."

Janey sighed. "Yes, I know. Okay. I have to earn skating with school. I get it."

Karina laughed. "That's one way of putting it," she agreed.

BURT HAD A late supper on the table when they walked in.

"Pancakes and sausage," he told them with a smile. "Just the thing for a cold, snowy night."

"I love sausages," Karina remarked.

"Me, too! And especially pancakes!" Janey seconded.

Burt just laughed. He knew that.

"I GOT DAD to order me some books on skating from Amazon," Janey told Karina as they finished supper. "You know, the basic stuff. And there's one on Olympic champions, too."

Karina sighed. "I used to wear out the pages on my books about skating. I think all of them eventually became loose paper. I was obsessed with it."

"Like me," Janey chuckled. "It's the most fun I've ever had in my life. When do you think Mrs. Meyer's going to get that coach for the rink?"

"Pretty soon, I imagine. We'll ask her when we go back—tomorrow, if the snow's not too deep."

"Oh, I hope it's not too deep," Janey said heavily. "I truly do!"

BUT IT WAS, much too deep for driving unless it was necessary. Dietrich begged to be let out the next morning. Karina was uncertain about that, because of the deep snow and the bear Micah had mentioned.

"He'll be all right," Burt assured her. "I'd hate to see anything that riled that dog."

"Me, too."

She opened the door. Dietrich hesitated. He whined. He was panting. It wasn't hot in the house.

"Burt, do you think he's all right? He's acting a little odd."

"I'll call Billy Joe and have him come up and take a look."

"I think that's a good idea. Do you have to go out?" she asked the dog, patting his head.

He took a breath, which seemed to be labored. But he walked out into the snow. Karina closed the door, against her better judgment. He wasn't acting normally.

Billy Joe had gone to town for essential supplies for the livestock. He promised Burt he'd come right up to the main house and check Dietrich as soon as he returned.

Janey was sleeping late. Burt was busy in the kitchen with breakfast. Karina got on her heavy coat and boots.

"I'm just going to go out and check on Dietrich," she called.

"Okay. Got your phone?"

She rolled her eyes. "You and Mr. Torrance," she laughed. She went back into her room and picked it up. She'd charged it overnight. "I've got it," she said, and waved as she went outside.

But Dietrich was nowhere in sight. She called to him. No answering bark.

She looked around for dog prints and found them. They led down to the edge of the lodgepole pines that flanked the winding stream behind the house. She was careful as she went downhill, because there were sometimes hidden pockets that could throw someone, if they were careless.

Just as she reached level ground, she heard a high-pitched bark. Followed, closely, by an unmistakable deep growl. The sort of growl that a big bear would make.

CHAPTER SEVEN

KARINA'S HEART STOPPED. She had no weapon, and it sounded as if the bear was after Dietrich.

She looked around her and found a big stick, part of a fallen limb. She grabbed it up with her gloved hand, stood on it and broke it off, to make a pointed end, and walked toward the sound of the commotion.

When she got through to the clearing, she saw Dietrich lying down, panting and yipping. He looked as if he couldn't get up, and standing over him was a brown bear the size of a small car.

It was, of course, insane to attack a bear. But she was fond of Dietrich, who was Janey's pet, and she wasn't letting him get savaged by a wild animal. She'd learned to bluff very well as she rose in skating ranks. Maybe she could bluff the bear if she didn't show fear and didn't back down. It might be the only chance the poor dog would have. He looked as if he couldn't get up, and he was still whining and panting, and appeared to be incapacitated. There was no blood, but if the bear had slapped him hard enough, he might have internal injuries.

She heard noises nearby, but she ignored them.

Her only focus was Dietrich and the bear. She had to save the dog.

"You leave him alone," she yelled. She waved the stick and suddenly broke into a run, as fast as she could manage in the deep snow, right at the bear, waving the stick back and forth and yelling all the way.

The bear, startled, turned and actually ran away. She caught her breath. Well, it worked, she thought, and laughed out loud.

"And if that isn't the damnedest thing I've ever seen in my whole life!" came an amazed voice from behind her.

It was one of the cowboys. He was lean and rangy, dressed in jeans and boots and a thick shepherd's coat, with a black Stetson tilted at an angle over his right eye. He was leading a horse by the reins.

"Something's wrong with Dietrich," she said at once. "The bear may have hit him..."

He went down on one knee beside the dog and felt his belly. He made a face. "Bloat. We need to get him to a vet right now."

"Bloat?" she exclaimed. "But isn't that something that horses and cattle get?"

"Them, and big dogs," he replied.

"He was lying down when I saw him with the bear," she said quickly. "I don't know if the bear hit him or not."

He shook his head. "I don't see any blood."

"Yes, but he could have internal injuries," she said worriedly.

"All too true. We'll hope for the best. I'll ride him back to the house. Billy Joe's on his way back from town, he can drive him to the vet."

"Oh, poor baby," she groaned, going on one knee to pet Dietrich. "Poor baby!"

"He'll be fine," he assured her. He bent and lifted the big dog as gently as he could. He had Karina hold the reins while he balanced Dietrich on the saddle, slid in behind him and then gently lifted the whining dog across his lap. "Not the best method of transport, but we use what we've got. And lucky for us that my horse doesn't mind extra weight," he laughed. "You stay close behind. That bear may come back."

She hefted her stick. "Let him try," she said angrily.

He chuckled.

BILLY JOE DROVE up to the steps just as the cowboy and Karina made it into the yard.

"Poor old fellow," he groaned. "What happened?"

"Bloat, I think," the cowboy said. "You need to get him to the vet right now."

The cowboy handed Dietrich down to him.

"Do you want me to go with you?" Karina asked Billy Joe worriedly.

"It would help, if you could sit in the back seat and hold him," the dog trainer replied, plainly worried.

She climbed into the back seat of Billy Joe's SUV and let him slide the dog in, so that his head was resting in her lap. "There, there, Dietrich, it will be okay."

Billy Joe closed the door and spoke briefly to the

cowboy, who nodded and went into the house, presumably to tell Burt what had happened.

"There was a bear," she said excitedly as Billy Joe got in under the wheel and cranked the vehicle. "I chased it off, but it may have slapped him. There wasn't any blood that we could see, but he could still have internal injuries."

"Sadly true," Billy Joe said worriedly.

"He has to be okay," she told Billy Joe as he turned the vehicle around and headed for the highway. "He just has to."

"We'll get him to the vet ASAP," he said quietly. "Bloat's tricky."

"He was fine until just a few minutes ago, when we let him out," she said.

"Good. Then maybe there's time."

He didn't spare the engine getting them into Catelow, to the local vet. He carried the dog in and explained the emergency. They got him back into a treatment room in seconds.

Karina sat down in a chair in the waiting room, worried.

"What's wrong with your dog?" a man holding a cocker spaniel asked gently.

She sighed. "Bloat," she said.

He grimaced. "Nasty stuff. But if they catch it soon enough, it can be treated."

She smiled. "He'd just started showing symptoms."

"I had a black Lab who got it, before I had this one," he indicated the old dog in his lap. "It was years ago. They tacked his stomach to his backbone and he lived a good while after. Nowadays, they attach the stomach to the stomach wall. Simpler and more effective."

She frowned. "Why?"

"Well, see, if they get bloat, the stomach turns over, cuts off the blood supply and tissue dies. Attach the stomach to the wall and it can't turn over. They can still get bloat. They just don't die from it."

She caught her breath. "They can die?" she asked, horrified.

"If it just started, he'll be fine," he assured her. "My daughter's a vet, over in Utah," he told her. He chuckled. "I learned a lot while she was in college."

She could imagine that he did. She forced a smile, but she was still uneasy. What would she tell Janey if the little girl came home from school to find out that her pet was dead? It was a tragedy in the making.

It was a few tense minutes until Billy Joe came back out. He stopped by the receptionist and left his cell phone number and the house number. They promised to call with updates.

"How is he?" Karina asked as they went back out to the SUV.

"We won't know until they operate. It could be a few hours," he added with a heavy sigh. "We'd better get back home."

"What do we tell Janey?" she worried.

"Nothing, until we have something to tell her." He managed a smile. "We'll just cross our fingers."

Karina nodded.

KARINA DROVE JANEY to school, keeping up a flow of small talk and smiling, so that the child didn't notice anything wrong. Later, when they had to tell her, they could, but no sense in spoiling her whole day when they weren't certain of the outcome.

Burt and Karina had a simple lunch, both morose. The boss walked in as they were having second cups of coffee. He had on an overcoat that draped to his ankles. He looked worn under his dress Stetson.

His heavy eyebrows lifted. "Who died?" he asked, scanning their sad faces.

"Dietrich's at the vet," Burt said quietly. "He's got bloat."

Some unprintable words slipped out. "How?"

"Nobody knows what causes it," Burt said, sadness in his tone. "Sometimes, it just happens."

"He's at the vet?"

"Yes," Burt replied. "Billy Joe and Karina took him over. They're operating now. They said it might be two or three hours before they'll have something to tell us."

"I'm going over there," Micah said gruffly. "I promised to take Lindy to Las Vegas tonight to a show. If she calls, tell her we may have to postpone it."

"Sure thing," Burt said.

Micah went back out the door.

"SHE WON'T LIKE IT," Burt said.

"What?"

"Having the dog put a stick in her spokes," he said whimsically. "She doesn't like animals very much."

"That's a shame," Karina replied. "I like some animals more than I like some people," she added with a wicked grin.

"Me, too. Dietrich's tough," he added. "I'd bet on him."

"So would I. I just hate the waiting," she added.

"Good time to put an edge on those skates of yours and Janey's," he said as he stood up and took the lunch dishes to the sink.

"How did you learn to do that?" she asked, following him to the back porch.

"What, sharpen skates?" He grinned. "Gets expensive when you have to have somebody do it for you."

"I guess so." She'd never given it much thought, because that service had been provided for her and Paul when they were in competition.

He got out his equipment and gave her a look. "The skates?" he suggested with a faint chuckle.

"Oh! The skates! Right."

SHE BROUGHT BACK both pairs, hers and Janey's, and sat down to watch him work. The spacious back porch was enclosed and heated. It wasn't so much a work space as a living space, but Burt had claimed a corner for his tools.

"Janey said you landed a triple," he reminded her.

She made a face. "It was a fluke. I didn't plan it..."

He gave her a wise look. "I don't know any beginners who can do a double, much less a triple, Karina."

She drew in a long breath. "Busted," she murmured.

"You skate in competition, don't you?"

"I did," she confessed, "until I fell in practice and broke my ankle. It was a little more complicated, because I broke my leg three years ago as well. My landing leg."

"The same leg, both times?"

"Yes."

He made a face. "Need to be very careful," he cautioned. "There has to be a weakness there, after so much damage, even if it's repaired properly."

"It was, both times. But one of the sports medicine doctors said that I should give up competition entirely." She looked down. "I can't. I just can't. Now that I'm back on the ice, it's like living the fantasy all over again. I can't quit. Not until I'm sure that I have to." She looked up. "Don't tell on me, please."

He cocked his head. "I don't carry tales," he assured her. He smiled. "Not that I'd ever be guilty of selling out Miranda Tanner," he added with pursed lips.

She caught her breath. "You know who I am!"

He nodded. "I was in Sochi for the last Olympics. I didn't compete, but I had a friend who did. Boss flew me over in the company jet, just for the event my friend was in. I thought the marks you and Paul got were grossly unfair. You skated a perfect program. Should have had the bronze, at least."

She laughed. "Thanks."

“Where is Paul?”

“He started out again with a new partner, but she quit in a huff. So now he’s got no partner, and he’s lost the chance to skate in world competition.”

“He’s got no partner, you’ve got no partner and Hilde Meyer is a coach with no skaters.” He lifted both eyebrows. “Are you thinking what I’m thinking?”

She burst out laughing. “Well, it would be quite a matchup. Hilde had beautiful choreography for her skaters. But they wanted something more modern, so they ditched her. She came here and bought the local rink, so downhearted by their defection that she said she wouldn’t coach again.”

“Olympics are next year,” he said. “Nationals in January. Plenty of time, with enough practice.”

“If Paul comes up here to skate with me, the boss would find out.”

“And what do you think he’d do, fire you?” he asked. “He’s a fair man. Besides, Janey loves you.”

She sighed. “Well, maybe Janey wouldn’t recognize Paul. I could tell her he’s a friend from grammar school. Which is true,” she added.

“And you could swear her to secrecy, at least until you and Paul get your mojo back.”

She laughed. “Burt, you make everything sound so simple.”

“Most things are, until people complicate them,” he said.

“Where did you compete?”

“Oh, I was small potatoes compared to you,” he replied. “I never got past Nationals, and I placed just out of the top five even there. But even so, better than Lindy," he added with a wicked smile. "She won a bronze in division, didn't even make it to Nationals. To hear her tell it, she was robbed. But I've seen her skate, and she wasn't." He shook his head. "Like watching a robot go through the motions." He looked up. "You, on the other hand, are poetry in motion. You and Paul together were magic. I'm sorry about the fall. But you're doing fine. You just go slow, take it easy. Don't overdo. And keep up with your appointments with your doctor. Make sure he approves, first."

"I'll go see him this weekend," she promised.

He lifted his head and frowned. "Isn't that the phone?" he asked.

"I'll go see."

It was the phone. Karina picked it up. "Hello, Torrance residence," she said.

"Where the hell is Micah?" Lindy demanded hotly. "We should be taking off at the airport right now or we're going to miss dinner and the show!"

"I'm so sorry. Dietrich has bloat. They're operating. He's at the vet's."

"What's so special about a stupid dog?" she demanded. "If he dies, they can get another one!"

She bit her tongue. "Dietrich is Janey's..."

"I don't give a damn who he belongs to, he's just a dog! Why won't Micah answer his damned phone?"

She drew in a calming breath. "There's a dead spot there, where cell phones don't work," she said, remembering Billy Joe say something of the sort.

"Then you drive over there and tell him to get off his butt and get over here right now!" She hung up.

Karina, shaken, went back out to Burt.

"What happened?" he asked, noting her expression.

"It was Lindy. She said Micah was late picking her up and that Dietrich was just a dog, if he died they could get another. She said for me to drive over there and tell him to pick her up right now so they didn't miss the show in Vegas."

He chuckled. "Love to see you do that," he commented. "The boss would have you for lunch and then he'd have Lindy for a snack."

"That's what I thought. So what do I do?"

"Nothing," he said. "Let her fume. She's the boss's problem, not ours."

She rubbed her arms. "Poor man," she said.

"He made his bed," he replied. "She sashayed up and played on his senses. She likes rich men. He knew what she was, but he let her lead him to a jeweler's to buy her an engagement ring. He'll get what he deserves for mixing up with a woman like that." He noted her frown. "Have to let people make their own mistakes and learn from them, kid. You can't take the licks for them."

She smiled. "Burt, you're a philosopher."

"Not quite, but I'm working on it." He finished with her skates and started on Janey's. "You should call Paul."

She sighed. "Yes. I guess I should."

She went back into her room and pulled up Paul's private number. She called it.

"Maurice," he answered, his voice sounding dull and heavy.

"Paul?"

"Karina!" he exclaimed. "I didn't look at the caller ID! How are you? How's the ankle?"

"It's mending nicely. I'm skating again. I did a triple this week!"

"C'est vrai? Magnifique!" he exclaimed.

"There's something else. Remember Hilde Meyer, who choreographed those exquisite routines for her skaters? They dumped her, so she came to Catelow and bought an ice skating rink. She's not coaching anyone."

"Oh, this is too good," Paul said with a long sigh. "Too good! My partner recovering, a coach without skaters, a rink for practice. What else do we need to win the Olympics, *ma belle amie*?" he chuckled.

She grinned. "Not much. Instant stardom, just add Paul."

"I'll pack up Gerda and the boys and we'll be residents by next week!"

She grimaced. "Paul, nobody knows who I am. Especially not my boss."

"Oh, dear," he said. "Then if I show up with my family, there will be questions, yes?"

"I'm afraid so."

"Well, it would be difficult. The boys are in pre-K, anyway, you know. It would mean taking them out. So I will work it out with Gerda. Perhaps I can rent a room for weekdays and come home for Sundays. Yes. That will work, I think."

"Tell Gerda I'm sorry. I've sort of put myself in a fix here, not telling people who I really am. I didn't want the attention, and at first, I wasn't sure I would ever skate again."

"So was I," he replied solemnly. "I know what the doctor told you."

"Hilde says he tells every skater that," she replied, laughing.

"Well, he might not be so far wrong, sometimes. But if your sports medicine doctor says it's okay, I'd trust him. We can try, *n'est-ce pas*?"

"We can win," she replied firmly. "That's all I ever really wanted, to win the gold just one time."

"Afterward, we can sign on with the TV networks to sit at a microphone and make rude comments about other skaters," he said mischievously.

"We'd be kind," she retorted.

"Mostly kind," he said. "I'll speak to Gerda. She'll be thrilled, and I mean that. She's been sad for me. I've been moping around making everybody miserable since my prospective new partner threw me over."

"This partner will never throw you over, and we're going to win the gold. Tell Gerda that."

He laughed. "I will. Later, *chérie*."

"Later."

SHE WENT BACK out to tell Burt.

"Now that's something to look forward to," he said. "Pyeongchang next year. And I'll be in the audience cheering you on."

She knew without saying that the boss and Janey

wouldn't be, because she couldn't afford to let the boss know about her ambitions. He hired her, not even knowing that she was so much as a casual skater, to look after his daughter. She'd be watching Janey and training for the Olympics at the same time. What if the boss recognized Paul? What if he found out who she was? Would he fire her? Without a job, she couldn't afford her doctor, her small apartment in Jackson, equipment, anything! She didn't dare tell him.

"Stop worrying yourself to death over what-ifs," Burt said wisely. "Just go with the flow."

She laughed. "Am I that obvious?"

"To an old guy like me, yes. Don't worry. I won't sell you out. Neither will Janey. For a nine-year-old, she's pretty good at keeping secrets."

"Well, except for the triple," she recalled.

"She slipped once. She won't do it again. She loves you."

"That feeling is entirely mutual," she replied.

He shook his head. "Lindy belittles her all the time. Boss doesn't even seem to notice. I guess he's used to her carping at him."

"She has a nasty temper."

"You haven't seen how nasty, just yet," Burt said. "If she comes into this house, I'm going out the back door and I won't come back. I can't live with her."

Her heart jumped. "Neither could I," she said. She bit her lower lip. "Have they set a date for the wedding?" she asked worriedly.

"Not just yet, thank God," he replied.

"Well, maybe there's hope."

"There's always hope. I just wish..."

The sound of an approaching SUV being driven hurriedly up the driveway stopped him in midsentence.

"That's the boss again," Burt said.

"I hope it's good news," she added. "I'll go see."

MICAH OPENED THE DOOR. He'd taken off the overcoat. He was wearing a suit and expensive boots with that top-of-the-line Stetson, cream colored and wide brimmed. He looked down at her and frowned.

"How is he?" she asked worriedly.

He drew in a breath. "He's out of surgery," he said. "Now we wait. But the doctor is cautiously optimistic."

"Oh, thank God! I was worried about Janey."

He scowled. "Janey is my problem, not yours. You just babysit. That's all you do."

He was back in boss mode, authoritative and combative. She lowered her eyes and tried not to look as intimidated as she felt. "Yes, sir."

He drew in a rough breath. Her submissive tone bothered him. He'd just had a call from Lindy and she was mad, furious that he'd cared more for a family pet than her desire to see a Las Vegas revue. Surely she was more important than a stupid old dog, she'd raged. They could get another dog if Dietrich died, so what was the problem?

To contrast that, here was Karina, soft and sweet and concerned for his daughter's feelings about the dog. Lindy was never concerned about Janey. She hated the child and made no secret of her desire to have the kid sent away to boarding school right after the wedding. It was their biggest point of contention.

He lifted his chin and studied Karina's dejected figure. He felt guilty and he didn't like it.

"Don't you have something to do?"

"Yes, sir." She went back out to where Burt was still working on Janey's skates and sat down.

Burt looked up past her to the boss, who was glaring after her. He went into his bedroom.

"You were lunch, I gather?" Burt mused.

She sighed. "I guess. I set him off by breathing."

He only smiled. He was getting some ideas about that. It wasn't like the boss to be unpleasant to any employee. If he was guessing, the boss was bothered by the babysitter, and felt things he didn't want to feel. Boss had a sense of honor, from that military upbringing. He wouldn't cheat on his fiancée. But that didn't stop him from being interested in their newest resident. Karina was pretty and sweet and she loved Janey. That made a tremendous contrast to Lindy, who was selfish and cold and hateful toward the child. Boss loved Janey more than anything. Trouble was brewing. It was just a matter of time.

KARINA WENT TO pick up Janey at school. She was afraid to tell the child about Dietrich, after what Micah had said, so she put on a happy face and they talked about school and skating all the way home.

Janey ran inside with her school bag and looked

around. "Where's Dietrich?" she asked. "Is he outside?"

Karina's face fell. She didn't know what to say. The boss's SUV was still there, surprising after Lindy's tirade. She just stood still.

Micah came to the door of his study when he heard the child. He opened it. Janey's curious expression and Karina's tortured one told him all he needed to know.

He went down on his knee and called the child to him.

"You have to be brave," he told her. "Chin up. Okay?"

"Dietrich is dead?" Janey exclaimed, her face contorting.

"No. He's not dead. He got bloat. The vet operated on him this afternoon, and he's holding his own."

Janey took a deep breath. "Do you think he'll get better?"

"I'd bet on him," he replied. "He's tough."

She relaxed. "Okay, Dad." She smiled. "Thanks."

"You might thank your babysitter as well," he added with an odd look as his eyes went to Karina. "She fought off a bear with a stick to keep him from getting mauled before he was taken to the vet."

"What?" Janey exclaimed, turning to Karina.

Karina winced. "Well, Dietrich was lying on the ground helpless and the bear was going to attack him. Nobody else was around. I had to do something!"

Micah studied her. Most women would have run away screaming from a bear. It took rare courage to go after one with a stick. His employee was full of surprises.

"Oh, Karina, you're so brave!" Janey ran to her and hugged her and hugged her. "Thank you!"

She hugged the child back. "I love Dietrich, too, you know. But I think it was the yell that made the bear run. Not the stick," she laughed. "I ran at him screaming. I had a tae kwon do instructor when I was small who taught us that a yell is sometimes as good as an attack."

"Tae kwon do," Micah mused.

"I liked athletics," she said. "My father taught me. He was a black belt."

He pursed his lips. "My, my." His brown eyes twinkled with something like affection.

"Weren't you supposed to go to...?" Karina began, and then bit her tongue. He was going to snap at her for butting into something that wasn't her business. She pressed her lips together tightly, waiting for the explosion.

"I told her to go by herself if she was so hell-bent on Vegas," he replied mildly. "I even offered her a ride in the company jet."

Janey looked confused.

"Lindy wanted to go see a show in Vegas," he told the child. "I said I had worries here, and I wasn't going." He made a face. "My ears are still ringing."

Janey laughed. She ran to her dad to be hugged again. "Dietrich has to be okay," she said. "He just has to."

"We'll have to wait and see about that," he replied,

not pulling his punches. He looked over her head at Karina. He smiled.

It was the sort of smile that kept her awake for hours. She didn't understand why it seemed so different.

The next morning, he was back to his normal, abrasive self. He was on the phone most of the day. The rest of it, he was giving Burt hell for anything he could think of. Karina stayed in her room, hoping to avoid being barbequed.

The one nice thing that came out of the night was a call from the vet, saying that Dietrich was holding his own.

PAUL DROVE UP on the weekend. He was at the rink, skating, when Karina and Janey came inside. He came off the rink and put the guards on his skates as they approached.

"Paul!" Karina exclaimed. She ran to hug him. "It's so good to see you." She pulled away and smiled at Janey. "This is Paul, my best friend from grammar school!" she said. "Paul, this is Janey. She's just learning to skate. I take care of her when her father's away. Oh, what a surprise to find you here!" she lied.

He laughed. "I had a day off from work and I wanted to see what Hilde was doing up here. A surprise to see you here, as well," he lied, smiling at Karina's approving glance. "She grew up near Jackson Hole," he told Janey. "I moved there with my parents from Quebec when I was eight. Karina and her family lived near enough to go to the rink every day. So she and I skated together after school until we graduated."

"Gosh, you're so tall!" Janey exclaimed.

He chuckled. "So I'm told."

Karina felt as if the world had grown golden again. She spotted Hilde, coming toward them.

"I'm going to visit with Hilde for a few minutes. Then we might skate…?" Paul asked Karina. "If your small friend doesn't mind."

Janey laughed. "I don't mind. Mrs. Meyer has a coach now who works with beginners. I can take lessons every day. Karina's free while I'm being taught!"

"Yes, I am," Karina said, smiling up at Paul.

"So I'll see you in a minute, then, when you get your skates laced up," he said, waving to Hilde.

He went to join her.

"Janey, let's get our skates on," Karina said.

Janey smiled. "Okay!" She sat down beside Karina. "I like your friend. He's nice. Do you like him?"

"As a friend, I truly do," Karina agreed. She smiled. "But he's more like the brother I never had. I was an only child. So was Paul. We were both lonely."

"Oh. So he's not a boyfriend or anything?"

"No," Karina said softly. "It was never like that. But we loved skating together. His parents and mine were interchangeable. I was at his house or he was at mine until we got out of school."

"He's really nice," the child said.

"And he can skate," Karina said. "You'll see."

HILDE AND PAUL spoke until Karina took Janey over to her new coach in a big roped-off area.

A minute later, Paul, on skates, came out into the rink.

"Ready?" he asked Karina.

She looked up at him affectionately. "Ready."

THERE WERE A lot of people, many of them beginning skaters, so it wasn't possible for Paul and Karina to practice their old routine. Mostly they just skated, with a few turns and easy loops. Camels and laybacks and sit spins were more comfortably done in the confined area they had for skating.

Karina's layback caught the attention of other skaters. It was graceful, beautiful, the most telling move she'd accomplished in her years of skating. Paul watched her with approval and a big smile.

In the doorway that led to the outside, a big man in a shepherd's coat, jeans and a battered black Stetson was glaring down at the rink with angry brown eyes. That is, until he saw Karina, and the layback that almost hypnotized him.

Who was she, he wondered, that she could perform a perfect, balletic move like that? She was no beginner, that was certain. But why was she willing to work for wages at his ranch, with skill like that? He was going to have to talk to her. Secrets made him angry.

While he was thinking that, he noticed the tall athletic blond man who moved to her side and took her hand, twirling her around gently on the ice. He had to contain a rage he hadn't felt in his life. He didn't like the blond man touching Karina. He didn't like it at all!

CHAPTER EIGHT

PAUL AND KARINA, oblivious to the angry man walking down the aisle, skated together, but apart, doing mirror moves. The last was dual sit spins, perfectly executed, as if they were held together by a string.

They paused by Janey, who was clapping, and both of them laughed at her enthusiasm.

"Gosh, you two are good!" she exclaimed. "I wish…uh-oh." She grimaced, looking past them.

Karina and Paul turned. Micah was standing by the barrier, both hands on his hips, glaring in their direction.

Karina flushed, which didn't help matters. She skated over to the boss, with a worried Janey by her side.

"You found someone to skate with, I gather?" Micah said with an icy glance at Paul.

The tall blond man chuckled. "*Oui*, a friend from grammar school. Karina and I have known each other for many years. I'm Paul. I heard that Hilde Meyer had bought an ice rink here and I came to talk to her about coaching me."

The boss seemed to relax. "I see." He didn't, but

it was a mental placeholder, to keep from trying to skewer the man, whom he didn't know. Yet.

"Paul lived with his parents in Jackson when I went to school there," Karina said with a warm smile at her partner. "We were both only children."

"You compete?" Micah asked Paul.

He made a face. "I try to," he said heavily. "My new prospective partner just tossed me over and walked off with a younger and more sophisticated man." He shrugged. "It was no great loss. I fail to see how many body piercings and tattoos and green hair would have helped in any real competition. Most of the judges are rather conservative."

Micah's dark eyes twinkled in spite of himself. "How old was she?"

"At a guess, fifteen," Paul said in a disgusted tone.

"How did you end up with her?"

"The skating coach, and I use the term facetiously, thought she would make up for my conservative approach to the ice."

Micah seemed to relax even more. "Who did she find to partner with?"

"Another American with many more body piercings than she had, blue hair and an attitude. I wish them joy of each other."

Micah burst out laughing.

"I'm Micah Torrance," he said, holding out a hand for the younger man to shake. "Karina works for me, babysitting Janey, my daughter."

"Dad, will you stop using that word?" Janey

asked, cringing. "Honestly. Babysitter? She's my companion!"

Micah rolled his eyes. "Kids."

"Hey, at least she doesn't have green hair and body piercings," Paul pointed out.

"Green hair. Yuck," Janey said. Her eyes twinkled. "I'd like pink!"

"Over my dead body," her father promised, glowering at her.

"How's Dietrich?" Janey asked suddenly. "Is he worse? Is that why you came down to the rink?"

"No. I came to tell you that the vet thinks he'll recover completely," he said, smiling. "It was news too good not to share."

Janey hugged her father, with tears of joy streaming down her cheeks. "Oh, thank goodness! I was so scared!"

"So was I," he confessed.

"Who is Dietrich, if you don't mind my asking?" Paul wondered.

"Our German shepherd," Janey said. "He got bloat!"

"Le pauvre!" Paul exclaimed. "I had an Alsatian who developed it. We were not so fortunate. We waited too late to take him to the vet and we lost him."

"He wouldn't eat for two days," Karina said, indicating Paul. "His mother cried for a solid week."

"As you did, when you lost that vicious Siamese cat you loved so much," he chuckled. "I still have the scars where he bit me!"

"You should never have tried to move him off his favorite chair," she chided.

He rolled his eyes. "Pets! How would we live without them?" he laughed.

"Dietrich had bloat, but he was facing down a bear in the woods and he was helpless to defend himself. She—" Micah indicated Karina "—went after the bear with a stick and scared it off. A grizzly bear, no less," he added with a look of such pride that Karina flushed.

Paul chuckled. It was odd to see his friend unsettled by a man. She was nervous around most men. Well, except for him, but Paul was like family.

Micah's phone rang. He checked the number, glared at it and put the phone back in its compartment on his belt. He looked very angry.

He was angry. It was Lindy again, and he was mad enough already. Her attitude toward Dietrich had sent him through the roof. The dog wasn't disposable, and he couldn't "just get another dog" if Dietrich died. He loved the dog. So did Janey. He was thinking more and more that he'd made a serious error in judgment, letting an experienced woman lead him around by his libido. Lindy was wearing thin.

"I'll get back to the house. I'm waiting for a conference call," Micah said. "You be careful driving home," he told Karina. "There are still some slick spots on the road."

"I will," she promised.

"Nice to meet you," Paul said.

Micah nodded. "Same. I'll see you later, honey," he told Janey with a smile.

"Okay, Dad."

"I'M SO GLAD Dietrich's going to be all right," Janey said as they skated. "I was really worried."

"So was I," Karina replied.

"You really fought a bear off with a stick?" Paul exclaimed, recalling what Janey's father had said.

She laughed. "I really did."

"Brave and foolhardy, my friend," Paul chided. "But exactly what I would expect of you. Always, you were braver than I."

"Don't you believe it," she told Janey. "He's the brave one."

They looked around the rink. It was getting near closing time. Skaters headed out to remove their skates and return rental ones to the counter. Hilde came out of her office as the last couple called good-night.

"We should go, too," Karina began.

"Not yet," Hilde said. "Wait."

She lifted her head. And the music began again. This time, with Rachmaninoff's *Rhapsody on a Theme of Paganini.*

Paul looked at Karina. "Shall we?" he asked.

She smiled and turned toward Janey. "Do you mind waiting just a little longer?"

"Heck, no," Janey said at once. "I'll go be your audience!"

Hilde just laughed. "I'll help her."

It was as if the last few months had never happened. Paul and Karina skated seamlessly into the routine that had almost placed them in the top three at the last Olympics. They skated as if joined by a thread.

The lifts were perfect. The jumps were perfect. Once or twice Karina landed a little prematurely, but she only fell once, and onto her padded hip. She laughed as she pulled herself up and went right back into her series of jumps.

Her leg wasn't bothering her. Well, not much. There was some residual soreness and she had to do a lot of exercises to limber up before she went on the ice. But the exhilaration of skating again, of performing again, lifted her heart as if it were floating on a cloud. She almost burst with joy. Paul's face held the same rapture of feeling, the joy of skating, the exquisite pleasure of perfect coordination.

They finished with a death spiral that was poetic in its beauty. Paul pulled her up effortlessly to his side and they ended with outstretched arms.

"Wow," was all Janey could manage. She wasn't stupid. She'd only ever seen people skate like that in high-level competition on YouTube videos. No beginners could have skated such a program, and she knew it.

Beside her, Hilde was almost in tears as she clapped along with Janey. "Magnificent," she said huskily. "Poetry!"

They skated up to the barrier, winded but still flushed and elated.

"Imagine, so good even after the terrible events of the past months," Paul remarked, catching his breath.

"You are unbeatable," Hilde said. "A few tweaks to the program here and there, much practice…"

Paul and Karina stared at her.

"Do you think…?" Karina asked.

She nodded. "I know."

Janey looked from one adult to the other. "What do we tell Dad?" she asked worriedly.

They all looked down at her.

"Oh, get real," she said with a wry smile. "I'm not that dumb that I can't see how good you two are. There were worse skaters at the Nationals this year! I watched them on YouTube! You two aren't amateurs like me," she concluded.

"We're…hopefuls," Paul said, finding a word that wouldn't incriminate them too much.

"Hopefuls," Karina agreed with a smile.

Janey sighed. "Well, I won't tell," she said. She grinned. "And if you win the Nationals, I'll never let Lindy forget it," she chuckled.

"Nobody can know. Not yet," Karina said.

"I won't tell," she repeated. She grimaced. "I slipped, about the triple. But I won't do it again. Honest."

Karina glanced at Paul and Hilde. "We try?"

They nodded and smiled.

She grinned. "Okay. We try!" She didn't add that it wasn't Nationals they would be trying for this time, but the Olympics. The less Janey knew, the better.

DIETRICH CAME HOME several days later, so exuberant that nobody would have noticed that he'd just come through major surgery. They kept him inside, spoiling him with new toys and organic treats while he mended. He slept beside Janey's bed every night in his own bed, as he always did, and was even more spoiled than before.

Billy Joe came up to see him often, although Burt teased Karina that he actually came to see her, instead of the dog. There had been another invitation to the movies, but now that Karina was practicing with Paul again there was no time for a social life. She let the dog trainer down easy, remarking that she was having some trouble with her ankle and had to rest it in between Janey's skating lessons.

She wondered if Billy Joe believed her. He seemed okay with it, but there were rumors that Karina was skating with an outsider down at the ice rink. Gossip said he was her boyfriend, so Billy Joe gave in gracefully and without bad feelings.

"He's sweet on you," Burt teased. "But people are talking about you and that blond feller down at the rink."

"Oh, dear," she said, worriedly. She and Burt were sharing lunch, in between her routine practice with Paul.

"Don't worry, it's harmless. Micah knows you and Paul are hoping to compete. He doesn't mind." That wasn't the whole truth. Micah didn't like Karina spending so much time with the other man and was making snarky remarks about it to Burt. He, too, had heard the gossip.

"Paul's married, you know."

"What?" Burt exclaimed.

"He doesn't advertise it, but he and Gerda have two little boys. I'm the children's godmother." She grinned. "They've been married for over six years. Paul's very mum about his private life. He's afraid for the boys if they realize how famous their father is. He wants them to fit in with other kids at school."

"An unusual attitude."

"Yes, it is. They're very private people, he and Gerda. Well, we all are. It's why I skated under another name. It was my mother's idea. She had two Olympic gold medals in women's figure skating. She used her own maiden name. She said she'd seen so many good skaters driven mad by the publicity, that she didn't want to give up her privacy for it. I didn't like the idea at first, but I came to see the sense of it as I grew in skating."

"Olympic gold?" he asked, impressed. "Who was your mother?"

She told him.

He caught his breath. "I remember her," he said, nodding. "She was poetry on the ice, one of the most graceful skaters I ever watched." He shook his head. "You remind me of her."

She smiled sadly. "Thanks."

"How's it coming? Practice?" he qualified.

"Hilde says we're improving by leaps and bounds. She had some beautiful concepts for the choreography, ones we hadn't even considered. We've altered our routines, added some new material and refined some old spins and jumps." She nodded. "I think we've got a shot at the Olympics."

"Oh, I imagine you'll make the team," he chuckled.

"We can hope."

"Lindy's coming down for the weekend."

She spilled coffee. "Oh, dear."

"I'll help head her off. She and Micah will go down to Vegas to see the shows, I'm sure. She won't be hanging around the skating rink."

"I hope you're right."

There was a plaintive whine from Janey's room.

"Oops. Forgot to let you back out, didn't I, old dear?" Burt asked as he opened Janey's door and Dietrich came out. The big dog licked him.

"Need me to walk him?" Karina asked.

"No. I don't mind. You'd better get back to the rink. Paul will be waiting."

She grinned. "Thanks for the sharpening job, by the way. Paul wants to give you a check for it."

"You can get me tickets for the pairs figure skating event at next year's Olympics. That's my check."

"I'll make sure of it," she promised. "If we get that far."

"Want to bet on that?" he teased. "I'll get Dietrich's leash. And maybe a stick. For bears," he added with a chuckle.

"I'd never be that brave again, I promise you," she laughed. "I'll see you later."

SHE AND PAUL got into a routine, using every spare minute to perfect their new routine.

"It was a good thing that I never actually told them we were splitting up, after you were injured," Paul remarked. "We're still in the Envelope," he added, referring to the financial help the United States Figure Skating Association gave to high-rated skaters. It wasn't a great deal of money, even so, but it helped.

"It truly is," she replied. "You never gave up on me, even when I tried to get you to take a new partner. I thought I'd never skate again," she confessed as they rested briefly. "The doctor really scared me."

"I felt guilty," he said quietly. "You fell because I tossed you too high, that last time we skated."

"I missed my landing," she returned. "It was an accident, Paul. I never blamed you."

"I blamed myself enough for both of us."

"But that's in the past," she replied. "And now we have so much to look forward to!"

"And plenty of time to get ready for the competitions."

"And if we're very lucky," she teased, "we'll make the Olympic team."

"I have no doubt about that," he replied with a warm smile.

She sighed. "Well, practice makes perfect."

"It does. When do you see the sports therapist?"

"Tomorrow morning in Jackson," she said. "I'd hitch a ride with you, but I have to come back to get Janey to practice at two," she added. She grimaced. "Boss's fiancée is spending the weekend with us."

"You don't like her."

"She's all right," she replied. "She's just very bossy. I don't like the way she treats Janey."

"You love the child."

Her face softened. "Very much. Janey's special. She's very sensitive, though, and Lindy isn't kind." She shook her head. "I don't understand what the boss sees in her."

He chuckled. "I don't imagine it's her cuddly personality that attracts him. Nice figure?"

"Nice figure, gorgeous face," she returned. "She must have something going for her, if he wants to marry her."

He lifted an eyebrow and pursed his lips. His eyes twinkled.

She laughed, getting the subtle message. "I expect she's cuddly with him, even if not with Janey," she conceded.

He drew in a long breath. "Things work out for the best, usually."

"I hope so."

THEY WENT BACK out onto the ice and ran over the new routine twice before it was time for Karina to pick up Janey at school and bring her back to the rink for her lesson.

"I'll get a bite to eat and meet you back here in a bit," Paul said.

"I'll have a sandwich at the house before I come," she agreed.

JANEY WAS TALKATIVE as they had an early supper before heading out to the rink. "Coach Barnes says that there's a competition in my beginner class coming up soon, in the Learn to Skate USA program that you had Dad sign me up for," she told Karina. "We're going to put in a lot of practice on the required elements, so I have a chance to move up a level. It's down in Jackson."

"You'll do fine," Karina assured her. "It's a forgiving program. One of the best," she added, smiling. "Competition can be brutal as you level up, though."

"I'll be very tough," the child promised with a grin. "You'll see."

"You're amazing on the ice," Karina told her, laughing as the little girl flushed at the compliment.

"Lindy said I was clumsy and stupid."

"You're neither. And when you win the Olympics, you can flaunt your medal at her," she said, chuckling.

Janey sighed. "Oh, roll on the day!" she replied. She finished her sandwich. "No school tomorrow, thank goodness, so we can stay late at the rink, can't we?"

"I'm not sure," Karina said worriedly. "Isn't your future mother coming tonight?"

Janey made a face. "Dad's future wife," she corrected. Her face fell. "Can you imagine Lindy here, all the time?" she asked miserably. "Suppose we run away to Siberia?"

"Why Siberia?" Karina asked.

"Well, it's cold and there's lots of ice," she said, smiling wickedly. "So we can skate all the time."

Karina gave her an affectionate hug. "You have to face your problems, not run from them," she said sagely. "If I could get back on the ice after my injury, you can cope with Lindy."

"If you say so."

THEY WERE BUNDLED UP, ready to leave for the rink with their skating bags, when Lindy and the boss walked in the door together.

They were both taciturn and unsmiling, and it looked as if they'd been arguing.

"Where are you off to?" Lindy asked belligerently.

"The ice rink," Karina said. "Janey has a lesson at six…"

"Lessons! What a waste of time! The kid can't skate," she added, glaring at Janey. "She's too clumsy."

"She's not clumsy," Micah snapped. "Stop running her down."

Lindy gave him a surprised glance, but she shut up.

"Have fun," Micah told his daughter, forcing a smile. "Don't stay too long," he added.

"But there's no school tomorrow," Janey protested.

"We're all going to Jackson for the day," he said, looking uncomfortable. "Shopping. You need some new school clothes."

"I need a skating dress, too, for the competition," Janey said excitedly.

"What competition?" Lindy asked huffily, glaring at Karina. "I suppose she talked you into it. Neither of you know enough about skating to compete in anything!"

"I'm taking lessons," Janey said tautly. "My coach says I'm good enough to compete at my level."

"Some coach," she scoffed. "A washed-up Olympic coach with no skaters!"

"It's not Hilde, it's Chad Barnes," Karina interjected, trying not to sound aggressive. "He's started coaching at the rink. He won silver at Nationals three years running in men's singles."

Lindy shrugged. "Whatever. It's a waste of money, however you look at it. The kid never sticks with anything. How about some coffee, Burt?" Lindy snapped at the older man in the kitchen. "I'm freezing! And don't make it so strong that I have to water it down again!"

"Coffee would be nice," Micah agreed.

"I'll put on a pot," Burt said, trying not to look as offended as he felt at the newcomer's demands.

"We won't be late," Karina promised as she herded Janey out the door.

"See that you aren't," Micah said coolly.

KARINA FELT THE words like blows. She wondered why Micah was so abrasive with her lately. He'd seemed less aggressive since her run-in with the bear, but now he was back to his old self.

She wasn't really afraid of him, but he made her very uncomfortable. She couldn't understand why.

"You're really quiet," Janey commented on the way to the rink.

"Just thinking about the new routine Paul and I are practicing, that's all," she prevaricated. "I'm excited about your first competition. You'll do great!"

"Thanks for defending me," Janey said. "Lindy makes me feel stupid."

"Well, you're not. You have to believe in yourself, in what you can do. Don't ever let anyone else shake your self-confidence. You can do whatever you think you can do."

Janey smiled. "Okay. Thanks."

Karina smiled back. "You're welcome."

PAUL WAS WAITING for them out on the ice. Karina skated over to Chad Barnes with Janey and left her with him for her lesson.

"You and Paul are looking good," Chad commented.

"Thanks," she said, smiling. "Paul's been in touch with the figure skating association. Since they use a varied criteria to choose the team for Nationals and the Olympics, we've got a good chance of getting in, thanks to that gold at the Worlds last year, and our record in international competition," she replied. "It depends on whether or not I can skate a difficult program and keep my skating consistent. It's a long road back from an injury."

"We all get them," he remarked. "I've had shin

splints and strains and pulled muscles. I had a concussion once and a fractured ankle another time. I always came back with therapy and practice. You will, too."

"It was hard to get back on the ice," she confessed. "But now that I'm skating again, it's the same old story." She grinned. "I'm in love with the sport."

"So am I," he chuckled.

PAUL AND KARINA worked on a jump sequence they were going to incorporate into Hilde's comprehensive dance routine for the long program. It was slow going. Not only did the jumps have to be performed flawlessly—landing consistently on either the inside or outside edge of the skates and not flubbing it—but they had to be synchronized, so that it looked as if they were joined by a long string. It took a lot of practice to get it just right.

They were panting for breath when they finished. Janey had long since gone through her lesson and was sitting out past the barrier, watching them.

"I never thought about how much energy it takes to skate a long program before I started skating myself," Janey remarked when they came off the ice. "It's really tiring, isn't it?"

"Very," Karina laughed, mopping her sweaty face with a handkerchief. "The rink is cold, but when you exercise so much, you get hot pretty fast."

"I see why they told us to layer our clothes and wear thin socks, too," Janey laughed. "Bulky clothes make it harder to skate."

"There's a lot to learn," Paul agreed. "What time are we leaving in the morning?" he asked Karina.

"It's a long drive. About nine?" she asked.

He nodded. "I'll follow you in my own car. I'd offer you a ride, but you have to come back and I don't," he chuckled.

She smiled. "That's okay. My car's doing really good so far."

"So, see you in the morning. *Bonne nuit*," he added after he'd taken off his skates and packed up to go back to the room Hilde rented him.

"You, too," Karina called.

"Night," Janey said. "What's *bonne*...whatever?" she asked after they were back in the car heading to the ranch.

"Bonne nuit," Karina replied, smiling. "It's French for good night."

"I guess you speak it, huh?"

She nodded. "Enough, at least. Paul taught me when we were about your age."

"A long time ago, huh?" the child teased.

Karina laughed. "Not nice!"

"At least you're not as old as Dad," she retorted. "He'll be thirty-four in August."

"Gosh. Ready for the retirement home," she teased. But she was thinking what an age difference there was. He was eleven years her senior. She hadn't thought much about his age. But there were those sparse silver hairs. She grimaced, wondering why it should matter to her. He was just her boss, and he was engaged.

"He's got a lot of good years left." Janey sighed. "I'm going straight to bed when we get home. Lindy will be up all night. She never sleeps. She just sits and smokes and watches movies and drinks black coffee."

"She smokes?" Karina asked worriedly. Her lungs wouldn't tolerate smoke.

"Oh, not in the house," Janey added. "Dad put his foot down. He doesn't like the smell."

"I don't like smoke," Karina replied. "Lungs are very important in ice skating. You have to have enough wind to get around the rink without collapsing."

"I believe it. She'll smoke outside. She hates that," she added with a smirk.

"You bad girl," Karina chided. But then she laughed.

WHEN THEY GOT to the house, Lindy was sitting alone on the sofa with her arms and legs tightly crossed, watching an audience participation show with the volume up. Burt was nowhere in sight. Neither was Micah.

"Well, there you are, finally," Lindy snapped as Janey and Karina walked in. "I thought you were going to spend the night!"

"We always stay later on Friday and Saturday night," Janey said, but in a faintly submissive tone. She hated confrontations.

"Stay as late as you like, you won't skate any better than you already do," the older woman ranted. "I couldn't teach you a thing. You're thick as a plank."

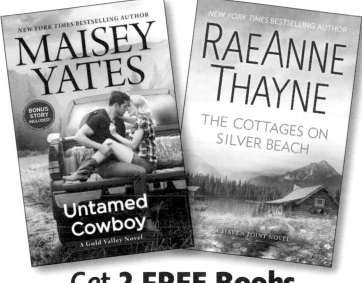

Dear Reader,

Since you are a lover of our books, your opinions are important to us... and so is your time.

That's why we made sure your **"FAST FIVE" READER SURVEY** can be completed in just a few minutes. Your answers to the five questions will help us remain at the forefront of women's fiction.

And, as a thank-you for participating, we'd like to send you **4 FREE THANK-YOU GIFTS!**

Enjoy your gifts with our appreciation,

Pam Powers

"I'm going to bed. Good night, Karina," Janey said, and beat a path to her room.

"Smart-mouth," Lindy said hotly. "She can't even be bothered to be polite to me. Your doing, I imagine," she glared at Karina.

The study door opened before she could say any more. Micah came through it, scowling when he saw Karina standing there.

"Where's Janey?" he asked.

"She's gone to bed," Karina said. "She was tired."

"Tired of skating, or tired of watching you and your new boyfriend play footsies at the ice rink?" Lindy said with a mean smile. "Everybody's talking about you."

Micah's face tautened. "Playing footsies?" he asked.

"We're just skating together," Karina said defensively. "He's my friend."

"Oh, sure, that's what they're saying, all right," Lindy added nastily. "You're there with him before daylight every day and all day when the kid's in school. Nobody practices that much. And the ice rink owner's renting him a room by the week, too, isn't she? That must come in handy for the two of you."

Micah was looked oddly murderous. Lindy was smiling, but it wasn't a nice smile.

Karina didn't feel like trying to defend herself. She was tired and her ankle was sore. "I have to drive to Jackson in the morning to see my therapist," she said. "Is it okay?"

"Therapist?" Lindy mused. "Do you have…mental challenges?"

Karina ignored her. "My sports therapist. He has to check my ankle."

"Is it giving you any trouble?" Micah asked.

She shrugged. "It just gets sore, that's all. He said last time that the break had healed very nicely."

"Will it continue healing with all this exercise?" he wanted to know.

She wasn't sure about that herself. The leg had a weakness from its former break as well as the ankle injury. She was aware of it, and worried about it. There was going to have to be a lot of training if she and Paul went to Nationals and were chosen for the Olympic team. Hours of practice every day, mostly all day, until the routine was set in stone. Would her ankle be all right, with so much stress?

She reminded herself that many Olympic athletes had come back from far worse injuries. It was a matter of exercise and proper stretching and medical attention when needed. But there was still that little nagging worry…

"I'll ask him," she said, aware that Micah was waiting for a reply. "Good night, boss."

"Good night."

"Honestly," Lindy muttered as the other woman left the room, "how much time does she have to devote to the kid if she's skating all day with that man?"

"I've been wondering that myself," he said tersely.

Karina heard that comment and it wounded her. She went into her room and closed the door, her face flaming, her heart racing. Did Micah think she'd been neglecting Janey with all this training? She realized that she probably was. It was going to be an issue, she could see that already. Lindy was fanning the flames of Micah's anger as well. The future didn't look very bright at the moment.

CHAPTER NINE

KARINA WOKE IN a cold sweat. She'd been dreaming again about the plane crash that had killed both her parents. It was a nightmare that never ended. She recalled all too vividly their faces, their torn bodies. She'd lain there in the snow all night long. The moon had been full. The bodies were vividly colored. Karina's leg had been broken and she couldn't move. The pain had made her pass out at first. Then it was a continual throb that almost blinded her to the two beloved dead people near her in the strewn wreckage of what had been an airplane.

The fuselage had survived the impact, although it had split. Her father had been in the pilot's seat. He was still strapped in, despite the crash, sitting up, stark dead. Her mother had been in the seat across from Karina. Her seat belt had snapped, like Karina's. The two of them had been thrown. Her mother's head was at an impossible angle, her body torn by the stressed and crumpled metal of the airplane's body.

Death. It had a smell, even in the numbing cold that was unmistakable. It had been late morning before search crews had found them. By then, Karina was going in and out of consciousness. She'd had blood loss from cuts on the broken leg and her torso, not life threatening, but weakening. Only her thick coat and boots and a blanket she'd had in her seat had kept her from getting frostbite. She'd spent several days in the hospital.

Paul and Gerda had come to see about her, to help with the red tape that would permit her to bring her parents' bodies home for burial. That chore had been nightmarish. The broken leg, the aftermath of the crash, the nightmares that had gone on and on and on.

Micah had guessed that she'd seen her parents' bodies. He didn't know that she'd been in the wreckage with them all night, or that she had constant nightmarcs for months afterward. Like tonight's.

She got out of bed, pulling a robe around her gowned body, and opened her door. She stood there, hesitating. She didn't want another confrontation with Lindy if she could help it. But, then, Lindy would be in the bedroom with Micah. Why did that hurt?

She went into the kitchen, relieved that nobody else was up. It was three o'clock in the morning. She put on a pot of coffee, leaning against the counter, trying to cope with the misery the nightmare had resurrected.

Her heart jumped when she heard a door open. Not Lindy, she prayed silently, please not Lindy…

She turned, guilt all over her face, flushed from sleep, in its frame of long waving pale blond hair that cascaded around her shoulders, to her waist in back. Her gray eyes found the boss and she relaxed, just a little.

He was wearing black pajama bottoms and nothing else. His black hair was tousled. His chest was thick with curling black hair over muscles that had the same light olive tan as the rest of him. He was magnificent to Karina's innocent eyes. But he looked irritated when he spotted her in the kitchen.

"What the hell are you doing up at this hour?" he asked curtly, glaring at her. The way she looked made him wild. She was exquisite like that, with her long hair down, her face soft from sleep, her eyes quiet and still, like mist in the early morning.

She drew in a quick breath. "Nightmare," she said tautly.

His chin lifted. His dark eyes slid down her exquisite figure, over her pert breasts, outlined sweetly by the flimsy robe, to the deep curve of her waist and hips. She was enticing. His body had refused to cooperate with Lindy, who'd finally stormed out of his bedroom into the guest room and locked the door. It wasn't uncooperative now.

The sight of Karina drew his big body as tense as if it had been slammed with a bat. He was aroused. Very aroused. She was too young and she worked for him. He shouldn't even be thinking of her in those terms. He was engaged. Lindy was insistent about setting a date. He didn't want to set a date.

He glared at Karina and went to the cabinet. He took down two mugs and placed them in front of the coffee pot. He was close. So close that she could feel the heat of his body, feel the quiet strength of it in ways that made her nervous.

He touched her long hair, gathered it into one big hand and used its light pressure to turn her toward him. It was wrong. He shouldn't... Even while he thought it, his mouth lowered to settle on hers.

"Mr....Torrance," she whispered, a faint protest that was suddenly smothered by the warm, hard pressure of his mouth on her soft lips.

He nipped her lower lip. "Open it," he said gruffly.

"Wha...?"

She gave him, involuntarily, the opening he was looking for. It galvanized him. Pleasure shot through him like a jolt of whiskey, drawing his powerful form taut, drowning him in urgent need.

"You...mustn't," she began in a choked, helpless tone. She was hungry for him. She hadn't realized it. Not until now, when she had no defenses whatsoever.

"Shh," he whispered into her mouth, and drew her completely against him.

The feel of her went to his head. He felt young again, drunk with need. She made him ache. Made his breath catch in his chest. He groaned softly as his big hands smoothed down her back, coaxing her close to the raging need that his body betrayed.

She'd never felt an aroused man. Not since long ago, during one of the many out-of-state events that she participated in while moving up the levels of ice skating before she and Paul had officially become a pair. An assistant coach had backed her into a wall after practice, the night before the event she'd come to do, and tried to force her. She'd fought, screamed. That had made him furious. He'd hit her, over and over again, tearing at her clothing, terrifying her.

Her father had come to pick her up, and worried that she wasn't outside waiting for him. He'd gone into the practice area just in time to save her from being overwhelmed by the angry, vicious man who was assaulting her.

She'd been in tears. Her father had called the police. There had been a minor scandal. The assistant coach had been fired, but he was liked and Karina came in for some angry taunting from fellow skaters that he'd coached. Some of them didn't believe that he'd really tried to rape her at all. They thought she was hungry for attention.

The assault had frightened her so much that she'd skated badly and placed far down in the competition. In the end, she'd given up ladies' singles and gone back to the skating club in Jackson to be Paul's partner in pairs. It had been a good decision, but the experience had left scars on her emotions. She'd avoided men, for the most part, ever since. She and Paul skated together, but aside from him she disliked being touched.

Or she had. Until now. She'd dated a little, mostly double dates with other girls who skated. But a few casual kisses hadn't done much for her, and she'd never been in the arms of an experienced man who knew what to do with a woman.

Micah knew what to do. She was on fire for the first time in her life, aching for something she'd never known, hungry for the hard mouth that was devouring hers.

She lifted closer to him, her arms around his neck, intoxicated, shivering with feeling.

One big hand went to the base of her spine and moved her roughly against the most male part of him. He groaned as he felt himself losing control completely. She worked for him. She was his daughter's companion. What the hell was he doing?

He jerked away from her, his dark eyes blazing as he looked down at the result of his ardor. She hung there, her gray eyes wide and soft, her mouth swollen from the force of his kisses. She was trembling. But she wasn't trying to get away.

He caught her by her upper arms and moved her back, his jaw going taut as he registered just how close he'd come to losing control of himself. That had never happened before. She was potent.

But for all that, she seemed oddly innocent. She just stared at him, as if she couldn't believe what had happened. She wasn't angry or offended. She was...spellbound.

He wondered briefly just how experienced she really was. She didn't behave like a woman who knew much about men. But, he reminded himself, some women perfected a technique like that, to draw in unsuspecting men. He wasn't one.

He put her away from him and went to pour coffee into two mugs. He handed hers to her, herded her back to her room, opened the door and put her inside without a word. He closed the door. Firmly.

Karina sat down on the edge of her bed and lifted the coffee to her mouth. Her hands were shaking. She almost spilled it. She still couldn't believe what had just happened. She'd had no sense of self-preservation whatsoever. Micah could have done anything to her, and she wouldn't have been able to stop him. She didn't want to stop him. She ached for him, even now. She felt cold, alone. How in the world had that happened? And how was she going to face him again, with the memory between them?

IN THE KITCHEN, Micah was wondering the same thing. He was ashamed of what he'd done. She was years younger than he was, a guest in his home, an employee. He had no right to touch her.

But it had been sweet. Sweeter than honey. It had been years since he felt so alive, so full of vigor. Even Lindy, with all her experience, had never aroused him to such a point.

He thought about going back to bed and satisfying the ache with her. But it seemed sordid. Indecent. He couldn't bear the thought of Lindy after the taste he'd had of Karina.

And Karina was involved with her so-called friend at the skating rink, he thought angrily. Was she playing the boss? He was rich. Her skating friend wasn't, judging by the casual clothes he wore.

He was more confused than ever. After finishing his coffee, he went back to bed. Beforehand, he looked in on Lindy, who was still asleep in the guest room. He didn't wake her. He would have to find some way out of the mess he'd landed himself in.

KARINA GOT UP before dawn. She'd never been able to go back to sleep after the emotional upset she'd endured. She dressed and went out to her car. She'd phoned Paul already. He was waiting for her at the rink to follow her down to Jackson to her sports doctor.

"Ready to go?" he asked with a bright smile.

"Yes, I am." She smiled back, acting for all she was worth. She didn't want anyone to know what had happened. She had to pretend that it was a dream, otherwise she'd never be able to go back to the ranch at all.

THE SPORTS THERAPIST checked her ankle and pronounced it healed. He recommended more exercises and more stretching before practice. He wasn't enthusiastic about the intense workouts she and Paul were doing, because they were going to stress that leg even more.

Karina knew herself that an injured joint usually developed arthritis, and she'd had some aching in the damaged ankle that wasn't just soreness. The therapist wrote her a prescription for anti-inflammatories, but cautioned her about taking them with food and not before practice. They would help her sleep, he added. She must not go overboard with practice, although he realized she couldn't slow down very much if she wanted a shot at the Olympics. He advised sleep and rest in between practices and emphasized the stretching and exercises to keep the joint limber.

She stopped by her apartment while she was in town and pulled out the skating dress that she'd worn at the last Olympic Games. It was still beautiful, but it came with tragic memories. It had been in her suitcase when the plane went down.

She tucked it back into a drawer. She'd have to have another for the upcoming competitions. She had an acquaintance at one of the skate shops who contracted with an up-and-coming designer to do custom costumes. Karina told her what she wanted, sketched it out, and the acquaintance promised to send it on to her by express at the ranch. She had money, at least, for that sort of expense. She and Paul were registering for Nationals in January. Their combined cumulative scores were more than adequate to get them that far. They wanted to make sure they had a chance to get on the US Olympic team.

Then she realized what it would mean. She couldn't possibly keep her job and manage all the travel she and Paul would have to endure, skating at so many venues. First would be Grenoble, France, then Lake Placid, New York, which were two of the international events they wanted to compete at, later in November just before Thanksgiving. Many figure skaters skipped the international competitions for lack of time, but Paul thought it would help them. It probably would. The thing was, she'd have to quit her job.

The thought of giving up Janey, not to mention

the boss, was torture. If she planned to continue with her career, she wouldn't have any choice about it. Paul gently reminded her that they couldn't sit here in Wyoming and let the world pass them by. If they wanted to go to Pyeongchang, they'd have to do the work. It was going to take a lot to get them back to their former status. The more they skated, the more confident they became, the easier the routine was to master.

She wanted that Olympic gold. She wanted it more than anything. It had been the dream of her mother's life, to see her daughter stand on the same podium where she'd stood to receive the coveted gold medal around her neck. Karina's parents had sacrificed so much to get her to this point. She couldn't just chuck it all because she had a flaming crush on her boss.

Her face burned as she remembered the heat of his embrace, the hunger of his hard mouth on hers. He'd looked guilty when he put her away, when he took her back to her own room and closed her up in it. He was already impatient with her. This, surely, would make things even worse.

Too, there was Lindy. He was engaged. The businesswoman wasn't about to stand aside for some other woman. It had already occurred to Karina that Lindy was as much in love with the boss's fortune as she was with him. If you could call it love. She didn't seem to care much for him. She was more interested in things. Possessions. Nights on the town.

Karina had loved the limelight, but she could take it or leave it. Money was nice to pay bills with, but apart from that, she wasn't overly concerned with it. She'd never understood the obsession some people had with things. People were far more important.

She hoped the boss wasn't going to be in an impossible mood when she got back. Would he blame her for what had happened? She hadn't known he was out of bed until it was too late, or she'd never have gone into the kitchen in the first place. But he wouldn't be aware of that. He might even think she was trying to play on his senses.

She ground her teeth together. Well, she'd have to try to keep her feelings hidden and not let on that she thought he was the most magnificent male she'd ever known. And meanwhile, she was going to practice and practice until she could perform the leaps and jumps of the new routine in her sleep.

She wished she felt better. She was a little queasy and she felt weak in the knees. There had been a virus going around the ranch. She hoped it wasn't terribly contagious, because practice was more important than ever, now. Paul wouldn't be back at the rink until Monday, but Karina could practice while Janey had her lesson.

KARINA PULLED ONTO the long winding ranch road, waving at the man inside the little block building who waved back. It had been a long drive to Jackson and back and she was tired. She hoped she wouldn't have to spend a lot of time with the boss and his girlfriend. She still had to get through the weekend. She wasn't looking forward to it at all.

But when she drove up next to the house and parked, Lindy wasn't anywhere in sight. She went inside, and noted that the occupants of the house, save Burt, were all gone. Then she remembered that they were all going shopping down in Jackson Hole today. She relaxed, just a little.

Burt was making lunch.

"Thank God," he murmured when he realized it was just Karina. "I was afraid you were Lindy," he added darkly. "Can't do a damned thing right, according to her. Eggs were overdone, toast wasn't brown enough, coffee was too strong…"

"There, there," she said gently. "This, too, shall pass away," she added, grinning.

He laughed through his irritation. "Okay."

She sat down at the table and watched him work. She drew in a long sigh as she recalled with painful clarity the night before, when Micah had kissed her so hungrily. It was hard to get the image out of her head.

"How's the ankle?" he asked.

"He said it's doing fine, but he emphasized that I mustn't overdo at practice." She traced a pattern on the table. "It's such a long, hard road to the Olympics," she added quietly. "My parents sacrificed so much, to make sure I had lessons and access to all the venues when I started moving up in figure skating. It's a very expensive sport."

"I know all about that." He glanced at her while he worked. "You started out in singles, didn't you?"

She nodded. "I thought it was what I wanted. But

I had a really bad experience with one of the assistant coaches at a venue back east, when I was in my early teens. I came back home to Wyoming with my parents and Paul talked me into doing pairs with him. That way he'd always be with me at practice, and he'd watch out for me. He's the brother I always wanted," she added with a tender smile. "He and Gerda and the boys are the only family I have left. I love them all very much."

"You look bad," he said abruptly. "Feel okay?"

She smiled wanly. "Not really. I'm sort of queasy and my knees feel weak. I think it may be that virus that's going around. Paul had it. Just a twenty-four-hour thing. I'll be fine."

"Stand close to Lindy, will you?" he murmured with a wicked glance. "In case it's contagious."

"You wicked man," she teased.

He shrugged. "A woman like that could make a man wicked. I don't know why the boss puts up with her." He grimaced. "Or maybe I do. She's pretty enough."

"She is that," she agreed, and wondered why it hurt so much to recall that the boss was going to marry the vicious woman. "Poor Janey," she added quietly.

He sighed. "Yes. Poor Janey." He shook his head. "Boss never seems to notice just how mean Lindy is to the kid. Well, he called her down last night," he added. "That was a first. He's usually too busy to notice. Phone rings all hours. He never turns it off."

"I'd hate that," she said.

"So would I. He's used to it. He told me once that he didn't think he could slow down. He lives for those adrenaline rushes."

She laughed. "I know the feeling."

He glanced at her as he finished the chicken dish's trimmings and stuck it in the oven. "Want some coffee?"

"I'd love a cup. The stronger the better," she added with a twinkle in her eyes.

He just laughed.

KARINA HAD JUST finished watching the news when car doors slammed outside. She ground her teeth together, expecting trouble.

Janey came running in. She had a shopping bag in her hands. "Karina, I got a costume to wear at my test!" she exclaimed. "Let me show you…"

"Costumes," Lindy scoffed angrily. "Unnecessary expense," she chided. "She'll never stick with it long enough to do a test. And she won't listen, so how is she going to learn enough to pass one?"

Janey winced.

Micah glared at his fiancée. "Why do you do that?" he asked shortly.

Her fine eyebrows arched. "Do what? Tell the truth? She's lazy," she said, indicating Janey. "She doesn't want to learn figures, she just wants to skate like a bat out of hell and terrorize the people at the rink!"

"Figures are no longer compulsory," Karina began.

"Oh, like you know what's compulsory or not," Lindy interrupted angrily. Her eyes spat at Karina.

"You don't know enough to teach someone how to skate! You told Mike she needed figure skates, but the hockey skates were fine for her little hobby. Another outrageous expense!"

"It's not your money," Janey said in an undertone.

"Well, it's not yours, either, is it?" she snapped at the child. "I'm going to lie down until supper. I hope it isn't something swimming in grease, like usual," she added, glaring at Burt as she went down the hall.

Janey was almost in tears. She'd been so excited about her costume.

Karina knelt beside her. "Aren't you going to show me the dress?" she asked gently, and smiled. "I'd really love to see it."

Janey wiped at her tears. "Okay."

She pulled it out of the bag. It was silver with metallic pink accents. It would go well with Janey's dark hair and light olive skin.

"This is lovely," Karina said. "You'll look wonderful in it."

"I really want to pass that test," she said. "It's really exciting. All of it. And I am going to stick with it," she added a little belligerently, glancing at her father.

But he wasn't listening. He was on the phone, already, making a call.

"Hold dinner for an hour," he told Burt on his way into his study. "I've got to take this call."

"Sure thing, boss."

"Go ahead and feed them so they can get to the rink," Micah added, indicating his daughter and

Karina without quite meeting Karina's eyes. He went into his office and closed the door.

"I'm not really hungry," Janey confessed, still miserable from Lindy's abusive words.

"I'm not either, really," Karina agreed. "Let's go skate for a while. If Burt doesn't mind heating it up when we get back…?"

"I don't mind at all," he said. He smiled at Janey. "Don't let her upset you," he lowered his voice, nodding toward the closed door of the guest room down the hall. "She enjoys it."

"I wish Karina and I could run away to Siberia," the child said with a stage sigh.

"Siberia?" Burt asked, all eyes.

"It's got lots of ice, so we could skate all the time," Karina laughed.

"I suppose it does. You be careful," he told Karina. "Sure you feel like going?"

"I'll be fine," Karina lied. She was feeling worse by the minute. But she'd rather be sick at the rink than stuck here with the resident shrew, especially at the dinner table. "We won't be too late."

"I'll heat it up when you get back," Burt promised.

KARINA LACED UP Janey's skates and deposited her with Chad for her lesson. She put on her own skates, but her heart wasn't in it. She felt even sicker.

In the end, she skated off the ice and sat on one of the benches with her head down. The world around her was spinning like a top and she was so hot. Burning up. Sweating. How in the world was she going to get Janey home when she could barely lift her head?

JANEY FINISHED HER lesson and came off the ice, concerned about her friend.

"Are you okay?" she asked worriedly. "You look awful."

"I'm sick to my stomach," Karina confessed. "I feel terrible. I'm so sorry..."

Janey hugged her. "It will be all right. You just sit still."

The child pulled her cell phone out of her skating bag and called the ranch.

KARINA WAS BARELY aware of what the child was saying, or what was said back to her.

Janey grimaced. "But, Daddy, she can't help being sick," the child was saying apologetically. "Please...? Okay. Thanks."

She hung up. "Daddy's coming to get us," she said. "He'll bring Burt so he can drive your car back to the house." She hesitated. "Lindy's coming with him," she muttered. "I can't think why."

It occurred to Karina that Lindy might be jealous of her. The boss had been alternately irritable with her and dismissive, all at once. Lindy wasn't dim. She might suspect that there was something between them. She'd want to break it up. She'd already been feeding the boss gossip about Karina and Paul. Karina wondered if she hadn't been embroidering that gossip as well, to make it look as if Karina was having some sordid affair with Paul.

She kept her head down. She really was sick.

"Can't I get you anything?" Janey asked worriedly.

"I'll be okay," came the smothered reply. "It's just that stomach virus, I imagine. Billy Joe had it. Paul had it, too."

"I know. Poor thing." Janey rubbed her back, frowning. She saw Mrs. Meyer looking their way.

The older woman came over to see about Karina.

"Can I do anything for you?" she asked Karina.

Karina managed to shake her head. "Thanks anyway, Hilde, but I think I just need to go to bed."

"A cold wet cloth might help. I will be right back."

She was, a minute later. She pressed the wet washcloth to Karina's feverish brow.

"Oh, that feels so good," Karina whispered, holding the cloth in place.

"I thought it might."

The outer door opened and Micah came in just ahead of Lindy and Burt. He wasn't smiling. His wide-brimmed Stetson was slanted across one eye, pulled low, and his eyes were glittery with feeling.

"What's wrong?" he asked without preamble.

"Virus, I think," Karina managed weakly. "I'm so sorry..."

"You should have stayed home in the first place," Lindy snapped. "Now we're going to miss the show in Jackson Hole because you were selfish!"

"That's enough," Micah said irritably. He felt

Karina's face. "You're burning up with fever," he said curtly, and he had the oddest protective feeling for her. She was vulnerable, fragile. She needed someone to take care of her. His face hardened. "Where's your new partner?" he chided.

"In Jackson for the weekend," she whispered.

"So we're stuck with taking care of you," Lindy said angrily.

"I'm taking her by the twenty-four-hour clinic," he said decisively. "Janey, you ride home with Burt in Karina's car. Keys?" he asked her.

She dug them out of her blue jeans and handed them to him.

"Here," he told Burt. "Take the skating bag, too."

"I am not wasting time sitting in some stupid clinic," Lindy said furiously.

Micah ignored her. He bent and lifted Karina into his arms, holding her tenderly against him. "It's okay," he said softly. "I'll take care of you."

Tears burst from her eyes. His voice was so tender, so gentle, that it made her ache for things she could never have.

"And now she's going to turn on the tears to impress you," the other woman scoffed.

"Go with Burt," he told Lindy.

"And do what, sit at the house until you finally come home?" she demanded. "I'm going back to Vegas tonight. Burt can drive me to the airfield and your pilot can get out there and fly me home!"

"Fine, then go the hell home!" Micah exploded. His eyes glittered at her. "And stay there, for all I care!" He turned from Lindy's shocked face to Burt's surprised one. "Burt, take care of that."

"Yes, sir! It will be a pleasure," Burt said, with enough enthusiasm to make Lindy's lips curl down even more.

"I won't come back!" Lindy threatened.

Micah didn't even look at her. "I'll be home when I can," he added, turning with Karina held close in his arms. He walked out the door toward his car without looking back once.

CHAPTER TEN

KARINA WAS BARELY aware of her surroundings, she was so sick. The nausea boiled out of her about half-way to the clinic. Micah pulled onto the side of the road. She spilled out onto the grassy edge of the road and lost her lunch.

He knelt beside her, wiping her face with the cold wet cloth Hilde had provided. "Better now?" he asked softly.

She bawled. "I'm so sorry!"

He kissed her pale hair. "You're sick, honey," he said tenderly. "There's no reason to be sorry. Feel better?"

She swallowed hard. "Yes. A little, thanks."

"It usually helps me, when I do that," he chuckled. "More room out than in."

"Yes." She managed a smile as he helped her back into the vehicle and closed the door.

THE CLINIC WAS BUSY. There were a lot of people in the waiting room, but Micah spoke to the receptionist and Karina was taken right back into a cubicle.

Micah went with her. He sat down in a chair beside the examination table that the nurse laid her out on. They waited for the doctor.

He came in very quickly. He examined Karina, who told him her symptoms. He smiled.

"Stomach virus," he mused. "It will wear itself out soon enough. Drink plenty of fluids. You can have Jell-O or soup, but nothing solid until the nausea passes. If you're not better by day after tomorrow, come back."

"Yes, sir," she said gently. "Thanks."

"You missed the last cattlemen's association meeting," Micah chided.

The doctor sighed. "I can treat patients or run cattle, it seems that I can't do both lately. I'll try to make next month's meeting." He made a face. "And you missed the last one."

"I know. I had to fly to Dallas and straighten out a little problem with an oil refinery."

"The one that's on strike?" the doctor asked.

Micah looked innocent. "It's not on strike anymore."

"Why am I not surprised? Well, take her home. Keep her warm. You know the drill. I treated Billy Joe for this last week." He frowned at Karina. "Have you been kissing Billy Joe, young lady?"

She flushed red. "I have not!" she burst out, laughing with embarrassment. "Actually, I think my skating partner passed it along. He had it the middle of the week."

"It's very contagious," the doctor agreed. He noticed that Micah's face had gone hard when the girl mentioned a skating partner. Micah was engaged to that Las Vegas businesswoman. But here he was acting protective, and even jealous, of the woman who was taking care of Janey. The doctor knew Micah Torrance very well. They'd been in the same class in college, years ago.

"Thanks so much," Karina repeated as she got to her feet.

"All in a day's work," he chuckled.

"See you," Micah told him.

He herded her back out the door to his car.

"But, the bill," she protested weakly.

"Taken care of. Here." He put her inside the car and went around to get in under the wheel. "I'll have Burt heat you up some of his homemade soup. It's the best I've ever tasted."

"I don't know if it will stay down," she worried.

He smiled. "You can have Jell-O to go with it."

She leaned her head back against the seat and covered her eyes with the cool damp cloth. "Okay," she said softly. "Thanks," she added huskily, and without looking at him.

He fastened her seat belt and then his own before he cranked the car. "Good babysitters are hard to find," he said noncommittally.

"Oh. Is that it?" she asked with a soft laugh.

"That's it." He was lying through his teeth. He glanced at her. She was more vulnerable than usual. It brought out strange, new feelings in him. He'd sent Lindy home and she'd threatened not to come back. He found that he really didn't care if she stayed in Vegas forever.

It was a revelation. He'd been putting up with

Lindy's bad attitude for a long time, passing over the way she treated Janey, because Lindy was hot and he'd wanted her badly. But it was a hunger that, once sated, seemed to die very quickly. They had nothing in common except his wealth and her love of possessions.

This little sunflower sitting beside him, however, wasn't overly interested in things. She loved skating. She was protective of Janey. In fact, she'd been defending Janey more than he had when Lindy cut loose on the child.

"Do you honestly think that Janey will stick with ice skating?"

"Yes," she said weakly.

"Why?"

She smiled and drew in a breath. She still felt nauseated. "Because when Lindy was so mean to her, she wanted to run away to Siberia."

He frowned. "Siberia?"

"Ice. Lots of ice. She said she could skate all the time there."

He chuckled softly. "I see."

"She works hard at the rink," she added. "Chad's a great instructor. He never yells, and he's up on all the programs. He'll take her to the next level, and if she continues, he'll coach her all the way to seniors."

"Your partner gave you the virus," he mentioned. He glowered. "Have you been kissing him?"

"Paul? Of course not," she said weakly. But the cloth was still over her eyes and she didn't see the angry look of distrust that he shot her.

He'd heard the gossip, just as Lindy had, about the amount of time Karina spent with her old friend at the skating rink. Sure, they were trying to practice enough to be able to compete, but it involved a lot of physical contact. Almost intimate contact, if the figure skating he saw on television was any indication. He was jealous. And he didn't want to be.

He shrugged. "Never mind."

She moved the cloth long enough to glance at him. "Paul's my partner," she said. "We have to have physical contact, especially with the throws. That's how I caught the virus."

"Throws?"

She nodded. "I get great height on the jumps when he tosses me. I have to be precise about which edge I come down on, and that takes a lot of practice. It was during practice that I broke my ankle. Paul felt so bad about it, but it was the way I landed that did the damage. I didn't quite get the rotation I was going for when I came down, and I wasn't in position."

"It's a dangerous sport," he replied. His eyes were on the road, but he glanced her way. "Why do you love it so much?"

"My mother loved it," she said. "She taught me from the time I was three years old. She was patient and gentle. She never pushed me. In fact, when I got into high school, she did try to dissuade me. She knew what a long, torturous process it would be. I had no social life at all. I just skated. I loved being on the ice. I still do."

"You're twenty-three," he remarked. "Don't you want to get married, have kids?"

She wrapped her arms around herself. "I love children," she said softly. "But I had a, well, a bad experience, in my teens, before Paul and I really settled into pairs figure skating. I was at a venue out of state. My father came to pick me up at the rink after practice, and when I wasn't waiting for him, he went inside to look for me." She hesitated. "An assistant coach was trying to force me," she added quietly. "I screamed and fought, but everyone had gone home except me." She drew in a breath, unaware of the silent rage in the man beside her. "My father taught martial arts. He put the coach on the floor and called the police. I had to testify. It was very messy and there was a scandal, because the man was liked locally. His friends said I was lying, because I wanted attention."

"What a piece of work he was," he muttered.

"He got probation, but I was too upset to skate my best, so I didn't even place in the singles competition. I came back home and Paul said we should do pairs together, so that he could watch out for me. He has, too. He's big enough that most men won't try him." She smiled. "Dad taught him martial arts, too. Paul has a black belt in tae kwon do." She didn't add that she had a brown. She'd trained in martial arts and ballet, because both taught balance and grace of movement. It helped when she and Paul were doing the long free skate programs at the various venues.

Micah didn't like the way she favored her blond

friend, even if he was just a skating partner. They spent a lot of time together. Maybe too much. He didn't understand how they could have been together so long and still not be involved. Or maybe they had been, and it didn't work out.

He put his torturous thoughts aside and just drove.

WHEN HE DROVE up in front of the ranch house, the front door opened and Janey came running out.

"Are you okay?" she asked, opening the door for Karina.

"I'm very contagious," Karina said gently. "So don't get too close, okay?"

"But you're going to be all right, aren't you?" she added worriedly.

Karina smiled. "Of course. It's just a virus, sweetheart. I'll be fine. Thanks for caring," she added softly.

Janey flushed. "You're my friend," she said. "I worry."

"Is Burt back yet?" Micah asked.

Janey made a face. "He hasn't left."

He scowled as he unfastened Karina's seat belt and lifted her easily out of the car in his strong arms, bumping the door shut with his hip. "Why?" he asked curtly.

She sighed. "Lindy said she wasn't leaving until you got home."

His lips made a thin line. He walked to the porch, waiting while Janey opened the door.

Lindy was sitting on the sofa with a smoking

cigarette in her hand and what looked like straight whiskey in a crystal glass, watching some audience participation show. She looked up, fuming.

"Well, so you're finally back! What did you do, park at lover's lane?" she demanded furiously.

"Put that damned thing out, and get it out of my house," he said angrily, indicating the cigarette. "You know you're not allowed to smoke in here!"

She cursed roundly, but she took the cigarette to the front door and pitched it out.

Micah carried Karina into her bedroom and put her gently on the bed, with Janey hovering.

"Help her get into a gown, honey, will you?" he asked Janey.

"Okay, Dad," Janey replied, with a sigh of relief. Apparently Lindy had already had a few bites out of her.

He smiled at Karina. "I'll get Burt to heat you up some soup, if you think it will stay down."

She hesitated. "I'm pretty queasy," she said hesitantly.

"Later, then. I'll check on you in a few minutes." He turned and left without looking back, closing the door firmly behind him.

Janey and Karina exchanged sad looks as the explosion went off in the living room. Lindy was cursing at the top of her lungs, questioning everything from Karina's ancestors to Janey's.

"She's been horrible," Janey said softly as Micah's deep voice snapped back. The voices receded, indicating that Micah had moved the argument to a quieter place, like his study. "Burt tried to take her to the airport and she said she wasn't leaving until Daddy brought you back home. She thinks Daddy's got feelings for you," she added with a grin. "She's furious."

Karina's heart leaped. Micah had been kind to her, but he would have been that way with anyone who was sick. He was a good man, with a big heart. He hid it under bad temper and bluster, but he was pretty much a marshmallow inside.

"I wish she'd go away and never come back," Janey said miserably. "She's so mean! She's even mean to Daddy. He stays so busy that he just ignores her. But I can't."

Karina rolled over on the bed to look at the little girl. "Things always work out," she said gently. "Even when you think they never will. It only needs time."

"It's been months," Janey said heavily. "Daddy tells her to go away, but she never leaves. She always bounces right back and he lets her stay."

A door slammed suddenly. There were more curses, in a high-pitched, furious tone. Footsteps dimmed. Another door slammed.

There was a tap at Karina's door. It opened. Micah had his hat on again, slanted over one eye, and he was absolutely furious. "I'm driving her to the airport," he said shortly. "I've got the company jet on the way to pick her up and take her to Vegas. I'll be right back."

"Drive carefully," Karina said weakly, because she could see how unsettled he was.

Those soft gray eyes, that gentle voice, melted him inside. Lindy had never cared about him. She cared about the things he could give her, the places he could take her. This quiet little sunflower just cared about him. It was…nice.

"I will. Get her into a gown," he told Janey again. "If you need anything, Burt's hiding in his room until we leave." A twinkle lit his dark eyes. "She threw a pot at him because he wouldn't fix her any supper. He locked himself in for the duration."

They both laughed softly.

He winked. "Back soon." He closed the door again.

Burt came out of hiding when he heard the car leave. He tapped on Karina's door and opened it.

"You need anything?" he asked her.

She smiled. "Thanks, Burt, but I'm too sick to eat anything."

"How about some orange juice?" he asked. "With lots of ice."

"Oh, that sounds wonderful!"

"I'll go fetch it." He made a face. "She threw my favorite saucepan at me and it dented when it hit the wall. Shrew." He glowered. "I hope she stays away this time."

"We could form a delegation," Karina murmured dryly, referring to the time Micah had planned to sell the ranch and the people who lived around it congregated to plead for him not to.

Burt laughed. "I'll think about that. Back in a jiffy."

After Burt brought the juice, Janey dug out one of Karina's silk gowns and helped her put it on.

"This is so pretty," she said, admiring the white lace panels in the royal blue gown that draped to Karina's ankles, held up by wide shoulder straps. It was demure for a gown. The bodice had a square top that didn't dip below her collar bone.

"You look pretty in blue," Janey said.

Karina managed a smile. "Thanks. I like blue. It's my favorite color."

"I like purple."

"I did notice," Karina murmured, having seen Janey's bedcover, which had purple flowers on a lavender background, with shams and even curtains to match.

Janey laughed. "Dad said I must have been touched by grapes, because I'm obsessed with the color."

"Maybe he's right."

"Do you need another wet cloth?" Janey asked.

"That would be very nice, if you don't mind. I'm still sick to my stomach."

"I don't mind."

The little girl jumped up and went into Karina's bathroom. She came back with a wet washcloth. She folded it and put it over Karina's forehead. She frowned. "You've got a fever, I think."

"I think so, too. Janey, you shouldn't be in here, you might catch it," she said worriedly.

Janey sat down beside her on the bed. "I never catch anything," she said brightly. "Not even the flu."

"I wish I could say that."

"If it's what Billy Joe had, you'll be better in no time," she replied. "His only lasted a day."

"I hope mine does," Karina said. "We'll miss skating at the rink tomorrow if I don't bounce back."

"That's all right," Janey said firmly. "You get well first. Skating can wait."

Karina peered out from under the washcloth. "I know how much your lessons mean to you..."

Janey looked sheepish. "Yes, well, you mean more," she said, and flushed. "You're my friend."

Karina fought tears. "You're my friend, too," she said softly.

Janey bit her lip. "I wish it was you instead of Lindy," she said miserably. "I don't understand why Daddy wants to marry her. She's just mean, all the time. She's so hateful to him."

"Nobody understands love," Karina said wisely.

"Have you ever been in love?" the little girl asked.

Karina laughed. "Not really. Unless it's with skating. It's been my whole life for a very long time."

"You and Paul are going to win the Olympics," she said. "I just know it."

"We have to make the team first," she replied. "There's a lot of work between now and then."

"It's mostly just practice, though, isn't it?" Janey asked. "And the way you two skate together is beautiful. It's like watching a fantasy movie."

"That's very nice. Thank you."

"Mrs. Meyer is really good at coaching."

"She is. She was an Olympic coach for years and years."

"But she quit?"

Karina nodded. "Her skaters didn't like classical music and what they thought of as old-fashioned choreography. So they jumped ship and went with younger coaches who liked contemporary music and uninhibited moves."

Janey made a face. "I don't like some of the new music. It's noise."

"I totally agree," Karina said. "I much prefer classical. But in the short program, everybody has to skate to a specific set of moves and corresponding music. It can be a real challenge."

"You don't get to choose your own music?"

"Well, for the free skate, we do. But the short program is geared to give everyone a flat playing field, so that everyone has to fit a routine into a certain style of music." She laughed weakly. "It's actually a lot of fun."

"If you say so."

"Chad thinks you're doing great," she added.

Janey smiled. "He said he thinks I can pass my first test. I'm really excited. I love the dress Daddy got me for the competition." She made a face. "Lindy said it looked awful and it was a waste of money."

"It looks beautiful and your father can certainly afford a skating outfit without going broke."

"Do you have one?" she asked. "A skating dress?"

"I have the one I wore in…" She hesitated. She didn't want to talk about the last Olympic Games, in which she and Paul had competed. "The one I wore in my last competition with Paul," she amended smoothly. "But I want a new one for the next venue, so I'm having one made."

"Is it expensive, having one made?"

"It is. But the dress sets the mood of the skating," she replied. "My mother used to make all my costumes." She smiled sadly. "She had such hopes for me. She'd have been at every event, cheering us on. She loved Paul. So did my dad."

"How did they…how did you lose them?" she asked.

"They died in an airplane crash. Together."

Janey winced. "That would have been awful. I mean, losing both of them at once. At least I still have Daddy."

"Your father loves you. He's a great parent," Karina said with genuine feeling.

"I think so, too. No matter how busy he is, if I'm in a program at school, he's always in the audience. So is Burt." She sighed. "Lindy never comes. She says it's a waste of valuable time." Her eyes twinkled. "So she stays here and watches those audience participation shows instead. Lame."

"I'm sure whatever you do at school is better than that," Karina said. "I like history and science programs."

Janey brightened. "I like nature shows, you know, like about wolves and bears." She caught her breath. "I still can't believe you attacked a grizzly bear to save Dietrich," she added, shaking her head. "Weren't you scared it would charge at you?"

"I was too worried about Dietrich to think of that. He was so sick." She grimaced. "I'm so glad he's okay."

"Me, too."

Karina frowned. "Where is he?"

"Billy Joe took him home with him tonight, because he thought we'd all be away until late."

Karina sighed. "We would have been. I messed it all up."

"Not really. Lindy went home. That made me and Burt very happy," she said mischievously.

Karina laughed. "Bad girl."

"She'll be back, though," Janey said sadly. "She worms her way back into Daddy's life, every time." She shook her head. "Maybe men like women who treat them like animals. Do you think?"

"I honestly don't know that much about men," Karina confessed.

"You know about Paul."

"Well, yes, but I've known him since we were kids."

"He's really nice."

"I think so, too..."

THE FRONT DOOR SLAMMED. Loudly. Janey got up from the bed just as her father knocked and then opened the door. He looked like ten miles of rough road. He was glowering.

"Feeling better?" he asked Karina.

"Yes, thanks, a little bit."

"You shouldn't be in here. In case it's contagious," he reminded his daughter.

"I've been nursing her," Janey said. "Somebody needs to."

He drew in a breath. He appeared very out of sorts. "I guess so." He noticed the orange juice. "Burt came out of hiding, did he?"

"Lindy threw his favorite pot at him and dented it," Janey said.

He grimaced. "We'll have burned eggs for a week. He'll swear the dent is why he can't fix them anymore."

"Eggs?" Karina asked.

"His favorite pan is the one he uses to scramble eggs," he explained. "It's from France. I bought it for him last Christmas. I swear to God, I think he'd sleep with it if he thought nobody would notice."

She laughed. "My mother had a cast iron griddle that had been in our family for generations. She made homemade rolls and biscuits and scones. That's what she used to bake them on. She swore than no other sort of cookware would produce the same results."

"Did she look like you?" he asked unexpectedly.

"Yes. But her hair was paler than mine and she had blue eyes."

He cocked his head, smiling oddly. "Do you favor your dad at all?"

She laughed. "Not really. He had dark hair and green eyes."

"I look like my daddy," Janey said proudly, smiling at the tall man.

He grinned at her. “Yes, you do.”

He pulled a pharmacy bag out of his pocket and put it on the bedside table. “Forgot to mention that I phoned Roger after we left his office and asked if you needed something for the nausea. He said this would do the trick. And he said to take Tylenol for the fever. Antibiotics don’t work on viruses unless there’s a secondary infection.”

She laughed. “I did know that. This isn’t my first experience with a stomach virus. I’ve had them in cities all over America.” She sighed.

“All over America?” he prompted.

“When you compete in ice skating, you go where the venues are. Other skating clubs host various competitions called sectionals. Then there’s a competition for the eastern and western divisions, then there’s Nationals. If you score high at Nationals, you get a shot at the Olympic team.”

He stared at her. “That what you and your partner are aiming at?” he asked, and he was seeing doors closing. If she planned to compete, it would mean a lot of travel.

Karina stared at him and felt a pang of misery. “Well, yes,” she confessed reluctantly.

“You can’t work here and travel all over the country competing,” he pointed out.

Janey wore a look of sudden anguish. The thought had just occurred to her, too.

Karina bit her lip. Suddenly her Olympic dreams were being overwhelmed by the family she’d never had. Janey and Micah had become that family, without her even realizing it until now, right now.

He drew in a breath. "How long?" he asked.

"Excuse me?"

"How long before the first competition?"

She wasn't sure. Since she and Paul had placed so high at the last world competition, the national figure skating authority might waive some of the competitions and let them compete at Nationals. The next Nationals would be just before the Olympics, and that competition would determine if she and Paul could get a slot in the pairs figure skating roster. But Paul had wanted them to compete at Grenoble and Lake Placid. That would be sooner than she liked.

"We have two international competitions that we want to enter," she said after a minute. "Nationals aren't until next January. It will mean a lot of practice. A lot. I've been off the ice for months, and I'm having to relearn all the moves I used to do without even thinking about them."

He relaxed a little. So there was time. Time for what, he wondered suddenly. He was engaged. Lindy was a royal pain. Karina was too young for him. She worked for him. Janey loved her. She was nurturing, gentle, sweet. There was that young partner who was buff and handsome. He blinked. His own thoughts were strangling him.

"Well, it's nothing we have to talk about tonight," he said finally. "I've got half a dozen calls to return. Need anything else?"

She picked up the little pharmacy bag. "No, but

thank you. And thanks for the meds. I'll pay you back."

"Patching up the hired help goes with the job description," he teased, making light of it. It also reminded him that she was an employee. Not fair game.

She felt those words painfully, but she smiled and pretended that she didn't. "Okay."

He shrugged. "Get well. She'll drive us both nuts if she's away from that skating rink for very long," he added, indicating Janey.

"I know," Karina laughed.

"You. Out. Go watch a movie," he told his daughter.

"Awww, Daddy," she protested, following him to the door.

"You can't get sick. School Monday."

She made a face.

"Study tonight and if she can't take you to the rink tomorrow, I'll take you," he volunteered.

"You mean it?" she asked, excited.

"You bet I do."

She hugged him hard. "Thanks, Daddy."

"Anything for my best girl," he teased, kissing her dark hair. "Now, scat."

"Okay. Call me if you need me, Karina, okay?" she said.

"I will. Thanks, sweetheart."

"Just yell. One of us will hear you," Micah added. "Need more juice?"

She shook her head and smiled. "This is still nice and cold. I love orange juice."

"Burt squeezes oranges to make that," he said.

"He doesn't like premade juices, is how he puts it," he chuckled. "Get some rest."

"I will."

He paused at the doorway and looked back at her. She was very pretty in that modest blue gown. She reminded him of a fairy princess he'd seen in a movie once. He ground his teeth together. She worked for him. He was engaged.

He had to keep reminding himself of those two things. He went out and closed the door.

KARINA FINALLY MANAGED to drift off to sleep. But she was feverish and she fell back into the same old nightmare, the one that had dragged her out of a sound sleep not long ago. She saw her parents there, in the wreckage of the plane, torn and twisted, pale, dead…she screamed.

CHAPTER ELEVEN

SHE WAS TRYING to get up, to get help, but her leg was broken. She sobbed as she felt again the pain that had been agonizing. Her parents were surely dead. But if they weren't, if there was still a chance…why couldn't she get up?

She moaned. Someone was calling her name. She felt hands pulling her up, hands on her shoulders, big warm hands. Comforting hands.

"Wake up!"

She gasped and opened her tear-filled eyes. Dark eyes looked back into her own, from a hard, dark face.

"What happened?" Micah asked.

She swallowed, took a breath and swallowed again. "I was there. In the snow. The plane crash."

"The one that killed your parents," he guessed.

"Yes." She drew up her knees under the covers and leaned her forehead against them. "My leg was broken. Help didn't come until late the next morning. I couldn't walk. I couldn't help them." Tears rolled down her cheeks.

"Good God," he whispered reverently. "I didn't realize you were there overnight with them."

"It was horrible," she sobbed. "They were so pale. So still. Dad was still strapped into his seat. Mama was thrown out of it. She was twisted up in the wreckage. She looked…like a broken doll."

"My poor girl," he said gently. He drew back the covers, picked her up and sat down with her on the edge of the bed. He held her tightly. "Let it out. You just need to let it out. I'm here. I won't let anything hurt you."

She sobbed. It was new, having someone want to take care of her, even for just this little time. Paul had comforted her. So had Gerda. But it wasn't like this. Micah was strong and tender, and the way he held her made her feel as if nothing in the world could ever threaten her again. She nestled close to him, her cheek against the soft material of his shirt, and let the tears fall.

"When I crashed my own plane, and my wife died, there was nothing I could do to save her. I tried. God, how I tried," he gritted. "The doctors said, after the autopsy, that there was fatal internal damage. Nothing I did would have helped. But I carried the guilt, that I survived and she didn't. I know how it feels."

"I'm sorry for your loss."

"I'm sorry for yours," he replied softly. "The only consolation I had was that we didn't take Janey with us. I love my daughter. I was fond of my wife, but the feelings I had for her didn't last much longer than the honeymoon," he added ruefully. "She wasn't happy living on a ranch, and I couldn't cost my workers their only means of support by selling up. She got even in the worst way. Boyfriend after boyfriend. I didn't even care enough to be jealous."

"My parents were married for a long time," she said. "They were happy together. Neither of them ever cheated on the other."

He shrugged. "Maybe it works out for some people. I had a raging desire for Lindy. I thought, hoped, it would make up for some of her more unpleasant traits. Not sure it has."

The mention of Lindy made her uncomfortable. "Don't you love her?" she asked.

"What is love?" he scoffed. "An illusion. I'll take cold hard facts any day over feelings." He shifted her in his arms. "Have you ever been in love?"

"Yes, with Roger Dantry when I was in fifth grade. He moved away and broke my heart. Since then, I've just loved skating," she added with a tiny laugh.

As the tears dried up, she started noticing things that had slipped past her senses. He smelled of expensive cologne and soap. He was wearing the same shirt and slacks he had on earlier. Hadn't he been to bed at all?

"What time is it?" she asked drowsily.

"Three in the morning," he said. He kissed the top of her head. "We have to stop meeting like this."

She laughed softly, involuntarily. He felt so good close to her. She loved the strength of his big body, the tenderness of his hands on her back, his lips in her hair.

"Why are you still up?" she asked.

"Lindy called," he muttered. "Made me mad. So I worked instead of slept."

She let her head fall back into the curve of his arm. "You work too much," she said, searching his dark eyes. There were equally dark circles under them. "You should turn your phone off at night and let people call you at a decent hour."

He smiled gently. "Should I, then?"

She smiled. "You should."

He drew in a long breath. His eyes were appreciative on the pert rise of her breasts under the thick silk gown. She was enticing like that, with her pale hair long and waving around her pretty face. The gown was cut straight across at her collarbone, but the lacy insert revealed delicate contours, the color of the inside of a conch shell. He wondered how it would feel to hold her with that bodice lowered.

She felt shivery at the way he was watching her. Involuntarily, her body reacted to his interest. She caught her breath and arched just slightly, on fire with needs that came on like a lightning strike, out of nowhere.

"Yes," he whispered, as if she'd actually spoken.

He drew her close, his lips in her hair. One big hand went to the buttons of his shirt and loosened them, pushing the edges apart, revealing hard muscle thick with curling black hair. His breath came quickly, roughly, as he eased the wide straps of the gown down her rounded arms, gently pushing it to her waist.

He dragged her against him, feeling her nipples go hard at the contact, feeling her breath jerk, her nails biting into his shoulders as she experienced the intimacy of the way he was holding her.

His mouth ran down her cheek to the soft curve of her throat. He put his lips against the throbbing artery there, where her life force lifted to meet them.

"Oh…gosh," she whispered shakily.

He brushed his mouth against her soft parted lips and lifted his head to look down at her. She lay in his arms like a doll, soft and responsive, and…shocked. He frowned as he searched her eyes.

"You haven't done this before," he said with sudden knowledge of her.

She swallowed, hard, and shook her head. Her body was trembling against him. He drew back just enough to let him see the hard-tipped little breasts buried in the thick hair of his chest. She had beautiful breasts. They were taut, topped by a dusky hardness that made him ache even more.

His hand smoothed over one of them, enjoying the silky feel of her skin, the warmth of her young body. It had been a very long time since he'd wanted a woman so much. He thought of babies. How odd. He never thought of them with Lindy. But, then, Lindy wanted bright lights and loud music. She didn't like children. She didn't even like Janey.

He bent his head to her yielded body, smoothing his lips over the taut rise of her breast, enjoying the faint scent of roses that clung to her, the way she lifted to him, shivering and hungry. He liked making her hungry. He liked being the first…

His mouth opened on the rise of her breast and took it inside, his tongue rough against the hard nipple as he suckled her.

She arched up to him, gasping for breath, drowning in pleasures she'd never known in her life, hungry for something, anything, that would ease the ache he was increasing with every movement of his mouth on her body.

"Micah," she moaned, digging her nails into his shoulders.

His mouth grew rougher. The sound of his name on her lips incited him. She made it sound sweet.

She wanted him. He felt the need in her, as he felt it in his own body. He dragged her to him, wrapped her up tight and felt for her mouth with hungry lips.

Her head went back against his shoulder, driven there by the devouring pressure of his mouth, biting into her own. He groaned. A little more, he thought, and he wouldn't be capable of stopping at all. He was wildly aroused already, throbbing with hunger.

In his arms, she trembled, her breath escaping into his mouth with little jerks as she yielded completely to his ardor.

It was hard to draw back. It was almost impossible. He throbbed all over. It was painful, the arousal he couldn't, didn't dare, satisfy with her. It was like that night he'd found her in the kitchen, making coffee, and his ardor had burst its bonds. She was sweeter than honey. She wanted him. He could have her. She was a virgin. A virgin!

He lifted his head and looked down at the soft treasure in his arms. There was a faint tremor in his own. He sucked in a rough breath and the eyes that met hers were glittery with hunger.

She didn't try to cover herself. She let him look at her, transfixed by the purely male appreciation she saw in his face. He loved looking at her. She felt it.

"Beautiful," he whispered as he drew his fingers over one pretty little breast, reddened by the hungry pressure of his mouth. "I left marks. I'm sorry. I haven't been so hungry in…well, in a long time," he confessed quietly.

"It's all right," she whispered back, surprised at the admission.

He traced around a hard nipple, making her shiver. "I haven't wanted Lindy since you walked in the door and upset my life," he murmured.

Her heart jumped.

He smiled slowly. "Are you surprised? So was I." He bent and kissed the pale flesh tenderly. "I want you."

"I know," she said huskily.

"And do you know what I'm going to do about it?" he asked.

Her lips parted. "What?"

He bent and kissed her soft mouth. "Absolutely nothing," he said against her lips.

He lifted his head and pulled up her bodice,

smoothing the straps into place with an odd tenderness.

Her pale gray eyes looked into his with wonder and something more, something deep and mysterious.

"I don't seduce employees," he said, hating the words even as he said them. He put her back under the covers and pulled them up to her chin.

"Oh," was all she could manage.

His lips made a thin line. "Don't let me do that," he said firmly. "I'm engaged. Even if I wasn't, you work for me."

She nodded mutely.

"Besides that, you're what, twenty-three? I'll be thirty-four my next birthday." His face was solemn. "There's no future in this. It's just a flash in the pan."

She tasted him on her mouth. He looked very sexy with his shirt open down the front, those hard muscles layered in thick curling black hair. She remembered how it felt against her bare breasts and she had to stifle a moan at the pleasure the memory prompted.

"It doesn't help when you won't stop leering at me," he said.

Her cheeks colored, but she managed a smile. "Sorry," she murmured.

He smiled tenderly. "You're not like Lindy," he said softly. "She really doesn't like being touched. She just wants it hard and quick." He shrugged. "I feel like a paid stud sometimes." He watched her face color even more. He grimaced. "Sorry. That isn't something I should be discussing with you."

He cocked his head. “You’ve never had a man, have you?”

She shook her head and her eyes fell.

“Why?”

She looked up, her eyes wide and surprised. “My…my parents were very religious,” she said. “We went to church, even though it’s not something a lot of people still do.”

He pursed his lips. “I see. Sex is a sin.”

“Outside of marriage, yes,” she said simply, and hated the amusement in his face. “Please don’t make fun of me,” she added with quiet dignity. “We’re all products of our upbringing. We inherit attitudes.”

He sighed. “I suppose we do. My father raised me like a soldier. It comes in handy sometimes, that discipline. But it makes it hard for me to deal with people. With some people,” he added, staring down at her. “I’m patriotic. That’s almost my religion. I’m conservative, in a liberal world.”

She smiled. “Me, too.”

“Puritan,” he accused, but he smiled. His eyes sketched her face. “Do you want children?” he asked abruptly.

Her lips parted on a jerky breath. “Yes,” she said. She hesitated. “Someday, I mean. Right now, skating is my life…”

“Skating,” he scoffed. “You’re living wrapped up in dreams. I know about ice skating. It was all Lindy talked about when we first started dating. She won a regional competition. It took years for her to work up to it, and she couldn't go any further. She gave it up for me."

Her heart skipped. She stared at him with dying dreams. "I can't. Give it up, I mean," she faltered. "My parents sacrificed so much for me. Skating is very expensive, if you go into competition. They mortgaged everything they owned, to keep me going."

He made a face. "Honey," he said, and she melted at the unfamiliar endearment, "there are hundreds of skaters who dream of winning medals. There are only a handful who ever do. You're living a lie. You'd be lucky to win even a local competition. You're worlds away from the high stakes stuff."

Her face fell. He didn't believe in her. He thought she was a rank amateur, just starting out. He didn't understand. How could he? He lived in a black-and-white world. Hers was gray, full of imagination. His was solid and he never wavered.

"I'm not giving it up," she said stubbornly.

His expression hardened. "I don't remember asking you to," he said with icy sarcasm.

She flushed.

He got to his feet, lazily fastening his shirt as he looked down at her. His eyes narrowed. She played the virgin well. But was she really one? Or was she playing a part? She'd said that skating was expensive. He was rich. Was she looking for someone to stake her, to pay her way into the big time?

"Are you really innocent," he asked, "or is it an act that you put on for men, to make them feel protective?"

She averted her eyes. “You can think whatever you like.”

“I like the taste of you,” he said blatantly, “but I’m still engaged. And I don’t spend money on skaters who can’t cope with reality. You’ll have to find someone else to keep you while you waste your life hoping for gold medals.”

She didn’t lift her eyes. She had a gold medal. She was a world champion skater. But she wasn’t telling him that. Let him think she was a dreamer. She didn’t care.

He saw her face close up. He was being deliberately insulting. He knew it, but he couldn’t help it. He was thinking of impossible things. She was too young. She was ambitious and silly, chasing rainbows. She worked for him. He was engaged.

He felt guilty at what he’d done. Whether or not she was innocent, she worked for him. He drew in a breath.

“You okay now?” he asked curtly.

“I’m fine.”

She wouldn’t look at him. She seemed genuinely embarrassed at what had happened.

“Don’t let it go to your head,” he said with faint sarcasm. “Any woman can arouse a man. It’s not love’s young dream. Just hormones. We have some sort of mindless obsession with each other. I won’t let it happen again. I already have a woman. I don’t need another.”

She forced a smile. She couldn’t lift her eyes past his collar. “Don’t sweat it, Mr. Torrance. I’ll file it away under impossible dreams. Like a skating medal."

"You do that," he snapped.

He turned and walked out, closing the door roughly behind him.

She let out the breath she'd been holding. She touched her bodice and grimaced. He'd been a little rough, and her nipple was sensitive. She couldn't believe what she'd let him do. She must be out of her mind!

She lay back down and turned out the light. She had to keep her distance from him. She felt ashamed of herself, letting him be so familiar with her body. He was engaged. He was her boss. It should never have happened.

But it had been sweet. So sweet. She ached to have it again. She turned over and pulled the cover over her head. Sleep was what she needed. Just sleep.

WHEN SHE WOKE, it was barely dawn. She'd had only a few hours' sleep. She wanted coffee, but she wasn't about to go in the kitchen, in case he was there.

She had a shower and fixed her face. She heard footsteps but they weren't his. She knew his quick, hard tread very well, even after just a few weeks.

She stuck her head out the door. Burt was in the kitchen, making breakfast. At least she'd have company if the boss showed up.

She went into the kitchen, pretty in a yellow sweater with black jeans, her hair down her back like a pale waving curtain.

“Good morning,” she said brightly.

Burt grinned. “Morning, sunshine,” he teased. “Hungry?”

“I could eat. But I’ll settle for coffee while you cook.”

“I just made a pot. Help yourself.”

She poured herself a cup. She sat down at the table, noting that there were only three places set. She let out a faint sigh of relief. It would be embarrassing, seeing the boss after last night.

“Boss gone again?” she asked, working to sound casual about it.

“Gone, and good riddance,” he muttered. “In a temper he was, slamming things around and cussing a blue streak.” He made a face. “I guess Lindy got to him again. She called first thing this morning. Needed a ride to a meeting in Minnesota. He went with her, just for fun, he said.”

Her heart jumped. Then it sank. Lindy again. Well, he was engaged, wasn’t he, after all?

Burt glanced at her and frowned. “You better this morning?”

“Much,” she said. “It was just a twenty-four-hour thing, apparently.”

“Boss said you woke up in the night. Had a nightmare.”

His face was bland, but he was making assumptions. She could see them in his expression.

“I dreamed about my parents,” she said, averting her eyes. “I was in the plane with them all night, after the crash." She swallowed. "They were both dead. My leg was broken. I couldn't move."

"Dear God," he said huskily. "I didn't know. I'm so sorry."

She fought tears. It had been three years, but the dream brought it back with a vengeance. "It's a bad memory. Paul and I disappointed them at the Olympics. They never said a word, but I could see it in their faces. They spent a fortune helping us get there."

"Parents love their kids. I'm sure they were proud enough that you just made it that far," he said, trying to comfort her. "I guarantee they weren't disappointed for themselves. Just for you."

"You really think so?" she asked.

He nodded. He smiled at the faint relief he saw on her strained face. "Yes, I really do."

She drew in a breath. "Thanks, Burt."

"You'll go all the way this time," he said firmly. "I know it."

She brightened. "Okay."

"You just give it your best. Practice and work hard. Muscle memory will pull you through every time."

She frowned. Muscle memory. She'd heard that from a skating coach, long ago.

"Like in the service," he said, going back to the stove, where the bacon was just about done. "We were taught self-defense. Muscle memory was part of it. They said when we got in desperate situations, we'd remember what to do. They were right," he added, and his face was bland for a minute. "Yes, they were."

"You were in combat," she guessed.

He nodded. "Years ago, in the Middle East." He smiled sadly. "I don't speak of it."

She smiled back. "I wouldn't ask you to. We all have our traumas, of one sort or another. We live with them."

"We do. Some are harder than others. Boss crashed the plane and Janey's mom died. He has to live with that. He has nightmares, too."

"I remember." She shivered inwardly, remembering how angry the boss had been when she woke up Burt to see about him. He'd been furious with her. Last night, he'd talked about it, even more. She wondered if he'd ever told Lindy how he felt.

He glanced at her, reading, accurately, the discomfort in her expression. "Boss can be a pain," he added. "But he's a good man. Too good for that Lindy creature," he added curtly. "Hates kids. The boss would like more kids than Janey, but he'll never get them. Lindy already told him she wasn't risking her figure or her business for the sake of a squalling baby."

She winced. "That's sad. He loves children." She recalled Micah asking if she wanted children. She did. But first, she had competitions to get through. She couldn't let Paul down. She couldn't let her parents down. She was torn.

"What sort of business does she have?" she asked to break the awkward silence.

"Real estate," he muttered. "Goes all over, selling big properties. Won't even handle anything under two million."

She sighed. "It must be nice. There would be quite a commission on a sale that big, right?"

He laughed coldly. "She's never sold a damned thing. Boss pays her way. She uses her license as an excuse to get him to take her places. Then it's casinos or shows or Broadway theater. Boss likes opera. She hates it."

"I like opera," she said softly. She smiled. "My parents took me to the Met one night, long ago, when I was skating in competition in New York State." She had a dreamy look. "There was a man playing bagpipes, behind a huge potted plant at a hotel. We were on our way there, walking. It was a haunting sound, in the darkness. We never got a good look at him."

"New York City is a magical place," he agreed. He ladled bacon and scrambled eggs onto a platter, and put fresh biscuits on another. He put them on the table. "Which opera did you see?"

"Semiramide," she said, making a face. "I don't like Rossini, but the sets were beautiful. We sat in the dress circle. It was really something to see!"

"I saw *Madame Butterfly* there," he replied. "I'm a Puccini fan."

She laughed. "Me, too. I liked *Turandot* even more. That song, 'Nessun Dorma,' was my favorite. I loved the way Placido Domingo sang it."

"So did I. Did you get to see it onstage?"

"Well, once, but it wasn't in New York. I can't

remember where I saw it. A local theater company from a college staged it. The sets were gorgeous, and the singers were very good, though."

"You must have traveled a lot."

"All over the country and around the world," she agreed. "I've seen places that still haunt me with their beauty. Kyoto comes instantly to mind. We visited a lot of temples."

"You skated in Japan?"

"Yes. And all over Europe. I've had enough bright lights and society to last me a lifetime," she added with a laugh. "It was wonderful. But I'm just as happy here, out in the middle of nowhere, surrounded by cattle."

"Cattle and bears," he added, laughing. "You and a stick and a bear." He shook his head. "They'll be telling that story two generations down."

She colored. "I had to save Dietrich. Janey would never have gotten over losing him."

"Neither would the rest of us," he confided.

"Want me to wake her up?"

He nodded. "Almost time to get her to school."

"At least the roads are clear. For now," she added, laughing.

"Cross your fingers that it lasts. Weather's tricky to forecast these days."

"Tell me about it!"

She knocked on Janey's door. A doggy whine came from the other side of it. She opened it and peered in. "Breakfast," she called softly.

Dietrich nosed her hand so that she'd pet him. Janey stirred in the big bed and yawned. "Bacon and eggs and biscuits?" she asked sleepily.

"The same. Come on before I eat it all," she teased.

"Dietrich loves bacon," she said.

"I'll make sure Burt gives him some. Come on, sweet boy," she added, letting Dietrich out into the hall.

"I'll be right there," Janey promised, throwing back the covers and reaching for her bathrobe.

IT WAS A QUIET, pleasant meal, with no complaining Lindy or snippy boss to mar the peace. But Karina missed him. The house lost all its color when he was gone. She wondered at her own reaction to him. The boss was almost eleven years her senior. He didn't really believe she was innocent; he'd said maybe she was pretending. It cheapened what had happened between them, marred a sweet memory and made it shameful.

"You're really quiet," Janey remarked.

Karina caught herself and laughed. "I'm thinking about all the hard work Paul and I are going to have to put in, to get ready for competitions."

"It sure is hard," Janey agreed. "You can watch it on TV and it looks so easy. But when you're trying to stand up on skates on ice, it gets a lot harder. I never knew how hard, until I put on skates and tried to get out into the rink," she added, laughing. "Two thin little blades, and blades have outside and inside edges. You have to jump just so, so that you take off on one edge on one foot and land on the opposite edge on the other foot…it's so complicated! I can't imagine how you and Paul do that so easily."

"Years and years of practice, since I was three years old," Karina told her, smiling. "I started out just like you, nervous and unsure of myself, and terrified that I was going to fall and break something."

"You broke your ankle," Janey recalled.

"Yes, I did, and at practice, not even in competition." She sighed. "I hope I never repeat that stupid mistake. It was a long recovery. The doctor said I should put up my skates and never try it again. I believed him. Until Hilde Meyer told me that he says that to all the skaters."

"Why?" Janey asked.

"Skating is a dangerous sport," was the soft reply. "They like beginners to wear helmets, to protect against concussion. If you fall backward, that's a real possibility."

"That's why you told me to always lean forward on my skates." She made a face. "Lindy taught me everything wrong. Coach said I had to start from scratch. Well, from where you came in," she added, laughing. "He said you'd done a great job of preparing me. All he had to do was build on what you'd already taught me."

"That's very flattering. I like Chad," she added. "He earned his place as a coach. He won silver at the Worlds. That's hard to do."

She sighed. "I bet gold is even harder," she said absently.

Karina averted her eyes. Burt cleared his throat. She stared at him intently until he got the message and said nothing about her gold medal.

"Gold is hard," Karina agreed after a minute. "But the thing about skating is that you can have a perfect program and never miss a jump. One time you'll win, another you may not even hit the top three spots. It's unpredictable."

"Luck plays a part, that's for sure," Burt interjected. "But practice has a lot to do with it. Muscle memory. Karina and I were talking about that earlier. You practice the moves enough and you do them without thinking about it, so that they become as easy as walking or running."

"Muscle memory." Janey grinned. "I'll train my muscles to remember everything!"

Karina and Burt both laughed. Dietrich laid his head on Karina's lap and whined.

"Okay, you heartbreaker," Karina cooed at him. She gave him a piece of bacon. He wolfed it down and put his head back in her lap. His big brown eyes looked up at her hopefully.

"You're spoiling him," Janey chided. "He's learned that if he begs like that, he gets whatever he wants."

Karina smoothed over his silky head. "I'm just a marshmallow, I guess."

Janey looked at her with warm affection. "I like marshmallows," she said with a grin.

Karina just laughed.

After breakfast, she took Janey to school and then drove on to the rink. Paul was waiting for her in the stands.

"I thought you'd be along," he said. "I heard that you were very sick."

"I was. I caught what you had," she laughed. "Boss took me to his doctor and got medicine for it. I'm fine now."

"I'm glad." He cocked his head. "Your boss carried you out like treasure, Hilde said," he teased. "Is something building there, you think?"

"He's eleven years older than me, I work for him and he's engaged to be married," she recited, more for her own sake than his.

"And none of that matters if he wants you," he returned, laughing at her embarrassment. "Hilde thinks he does."

"Hilde doesn't know anything," she said.

He pursed his lips. "Okay. Be secretive. But I would love for you to be as happy as I am," he said softly.

She sighed and put her head on his chest, letting him hold her. "Life is so hard."

He hugged her close. "Yes. It is. You deserve some happiness, *chérie*," he added gently. "It is what Gerda and I wish for you, so much."

"I love Gerda and the boys," she replied. "I miss seeing them."

"You should come down for the weekend and stay with us, like old times," he remarked.

"I would love to. But I have a job. And I love Janey."

"Who also loves you, I note," he laughed. He hugged her with a brotherly affection and let her go. "And now, to business," he teased. "Here comes our coach," he indicated Hilde coming their way and grinning from ear to ear.

Unseen, a woman in the back of the rink pulled out her cell phone and walked out the door.

THEY PRACTICED HARD. Hilde made suggestions and revised a section of choreography so that they skated more perfectly to the music. They were poetry in motion, she thought, watching them. They'd skated together for so many years that they anticipated each other's movements and synchronized them without conscious thought.

Hilde was certain that they were going to medal in the Olympics. There was no doubt in her mind that they'd climb back to their former perfection. That they would win. She'd never seen skaters with such passion, such grace. She was proud to be their coach.

KARINA LEFT PAUL at the rink and went to pick up Janey at school.

"Can we go to the rink as soon as we get home?" Janey asked. "I thought of something I want to ask Chad if I can try."

"What?" she asked.

Janey grinned. "It's a surprise."

"Oh, boy," Karina chuckled. "I love surprises!"

"So do I," Janey replied.

BUT WHEN THEY got home, a surprise of another sort was waiting for them. When they walked in, Micah was sitting on the sofa. With an ardent Lindy in his arms. He was kissing her as if he'd gone starved for a woman for months.

He looked up as Janey and Karina walked in the door. And the smile he gave her was full of sarcasm.

"We're moving up the wedding," he said without preamble. He looked down at Lindy with pure hunger. "It's going to be next month."

Lindy gave Karina a cold smile as she moved out of Micah's arms. "When are you and your boyfriend going to make your affair legal?" she taunted.

Karina was blank for a minute. "My boyfriend?" she asked absently.

"Yes. You were all hugged up with him at the rink this morning. I have a friend whose son skates there. She heard you tell your 'skating partner' that you loved him. Everybody's gossiping about you. And he's married. Isn't he?"

Karina felt her whole life sinking before her as she met Micah's glittery eyes and saw the contempt and distaste there. He thought she was involved with a married man, and he hated her for it. His expression told her so, as plainly as if he'd shouted it.

He glared at her. "Did you know that your erstwhile partner was married?" he asked Karina. He smiled coldly. "Or does that add spice to the affair?"

She felt the blood drain out of her face. He believed that of her. He really believed that she had no more morals than to seduce another woman's husband.

CHAPTER TWELVE

KARINA DIDN'T KNOW how to save the situation. Micah was furious. He looked at her as if she'd committed all seven deadly sins at once. The memory of how it had been between them, in the early moments of the night, hurt even more now.

"No comeback?" Micah asked sharply.

"Would it do any good, if I had one?" she asked with resignation.

"Not much," he replied. He laughed coldly and stood up. "On your way to the rink?" he asked Janey.

"Yes, sir," she replied, glancing with apprehension at Lindy, who was smirking.

"It's a waste of money, those lessons," she told Micah. "And the company your daughter is keeping is not going to do you any good, with all the gossip."

Janey moved closer to Karina. "Paul's nice," she murmured, lowering her eyes.

"Paul's married," Micah shot back. He glared at Karina. "I want those practice sessions to stop, right now. Or you're fired."

She swallowed, hard.

"No!" Janey protested. "No, you can't do that! Please, Daddy, they're working so hard, to compete!"

"They plan to compete?" Lindy said with contempt. She looked coldly at Karina. "She can barely stand up on the ice. How is she going to compete?" she scoffed. "She doesn't have what it takes to make a champion. I did. I won Regionals," she added smugly.

Karina wanted so badly to throw her gold medal in the arrogant woman's face, but this wasn't the time.

"Paul and I are not involved romantically," she said finally.

"Oh, sure you're not," Lindy laughed. "Hugged up like lovers and confessing love openly. And he's married."

"His wife is my friend," Karina replied with quiet dignity.

"That's a joke, isn't it?" Lindy retorted. "You're lovers, and his wife approves. Pull the other one."

"You heard what I said," Micah replied icily. "You give up your pipe dream or you give up your job. You can let me know later which you choose. Right now, Janey has a lesson to get to."

"Daddy, please," Janey repeated, her eyes wide with worry.

"We'll discuss this later," he said shortly. "Get going."

She started to argue, but she knew her parent. She just grimaced and went to get her skating bag.

Karina went to get hers as well, feeling sick all over at the thought of giving up her job. She'd have to. She and Paul had worked too long, too hard, to give up now because of a prejudiced boss who thought the worst of her. She could prove that she and Paul weren't lovers. If Micah had really cared for her, he'd have known she wasn't like that. He'd have believed in her innocence.

But he hadn't. He'd taken Lindy's friend's word, that of a woman who'd manufactured scandal from an innocent act and statement. She and Paul had been affectionate, like brother and sister, it hadn't been a romantic interlude. She could tell Micah that, but he wasn't going to believe it. She saw that in his face. He'd condemned her without a trial, on circumstantial evidence.

Well, if he wanted to think she was scandalous, let him. She didn't care. Of course she didn't. His opinion of her didn't matter.

She sighed. Sure it didn't. And snow wasn't white.

She and Janey went out the front door. Micah was back on the sofa, holding Lindy's hand and looking as if she was his world.

"I thought she was gone for good," Janey said quietly as they got into Karina's car. "You aren't going to quit, are you?" she asked with evident anguish.

"Not unless I have to," Karina said finally. She drew in a breath, flattered by the child's concern. "But if it does happen, we'll keep in touch, I promise we will. I have email. You have email. You can get Skype as well, it's free, and we can talk to each other and see each other at the same time..."

"I already have Skype," Janey said excitedly.

Karina smiled. "Okay, then. You write down your

Skype address for me, and your email address. I'll keep them. Just in case."

"You won't have to use them," Janey promised as she scrambled into her seat belt and searched her bag for a pad and pen that she used to write down skating moves she'd mastered. She scribbled them onto a page, tore it out and tucked it into Karina's purse. "There."

"Thanks, sweetheart. It's okay," she added softly. "It will work out."

"Of course it will. I'll worry Daddy to death."

"Don't," she advised. "It will only make things worse. Especially now." She grimaced at the thought of Lindy marrying the boss so soon.

"He just can't marry her," Janey said, as if she was thinking the same thing. "It will be the end of the world."

"No, it won't," Karina replied. She forced a smile. "You'll get through it. You're tough, Janey. It will be all right."

Janey drew in a breath. She looked out the window silently, wishing her father wasn't such an idiot. If only he'd noticed Karina, who was twice the woman Lindy was, and Karina liked kids. She hoped against hope that her father would come to his senses in time.

She glanced at Karina worriedly. She knew her companion couldn't give up practice. Not now, when they were so good, when they had a shot at national competition. Paul wasn't romantic with Karina, he was affectionate. But like a brother. Not like a boyfriend. She wished her father could see the pair as she saw them. He was blind to Lindy's faults, and even blinder to Karina's virtues. It was going to be a rough time for her, if that marriage happened. She prayed silently that it wouldn't. Losing Karina would be like…well, like losing the mother she'd barely known. She glanced at the blonde woman beside her and ached at the thought that she might be soon gone. If she left, Janey would have nobody to talk to, nobody to share her hopes and dreams with. She could talk to Karina about things she wasn't comfortable talking about to her father, although she loved him very much. Karina was her best friend. If she left, it would be, she thought sadly, the end of the world.

PAUL WAS WAITING for Karina, all smiles. "So there you are! I'd almost given you up," he teased.

Karina smiled, but her heart wasn't in it. "We had a late start. Sorry."

"No problem," he replied easily. "I've been doing figures," he teased.

"Nice for discipline," Karina replied, glancing at Janey. "And there's Chad, waiting for you," she laughed. "Let's get our skates on!"

They did. Janey walked to the barrier and took off the skate guards. "The test is next week," she said with obvious reluctance. "Tests at school make me nervous," Janey added worriedly. "What if I don't pass?"

"You'll pass," Karina said with a smile, joining her at the barrier as she took off her own skate guards. “I’m sure of it. You’re really good. And I wouldn’t lie about it,” she added firmly. “Skating is my life. I take it very seriously. I wouldn’t tell you that you’re good if I wasn’t certain of it.”

Janey beamed. “Okay.” She flushed a little with embarrassment. “Thanks,” she added, and impulsively hugged Karina.

Karina hugged her back. “Have fun,” she said with a smile.

“I will!”

PAUL SKATED OVER to Karina. “Okay, spill it. You’re worried. Why? Boss take a bite out of you, did he?”

She flushed.

“Oho, my girl,” he taunted. “More than a bite, ha?”

She glared at him. “You stop that. He’s just my boss.”

“I might believe you, except for that scarlet blush,” he chuckled as they skated to the middle of the rink and took up their positions for practice.

“I always blush.”

“You do not.”

“Pay attention to the music,” she laughed as it began to flood the speakers. “And skate!”

He made a face at her, and then moved to his pose as they began to skate their program. Hilde came to the barrier to watch. Karina gave herself to the music and moved into position, smiling dreamily as the music washed over her and pushed her worries aside.

It had been like that all her life. No matter how

bad things got, and she'd had some upsets in her young life, she could always put on her skates and leave the world behind. It had worked when the assistant coach assaulted her. It had worked when she had to fly back and testify against him, with all his students and fellow coaches glaring at her. Although three other female skaters, encouraged by Karina's bravery, came forward at the last minute to testify against him and he drew two years in jail for his criminal act. It had worked after the loss at the Olympics and the death of her parents. Skating was her balm for any wound. It was helping now, when she faced losing the man she…loved.

Her heart jumped as she heard her own voice, in her mind, making a confession that she hadn't expected. She faltered a little but caught her balance as she went into a layback side by side with Paul.

"Clumsy," he teased.

She grinned. "Sorry. My left foot rebelled."

He looked worried. "Not hurting?"

"Oh, no. It's fine. I was just awkward. Honest."

He nodded. They continued.

Lost in the joy of the program, she forced herself to stop thinking about Micah. He'd issued an ultimatum. She couldn't give in. The memory of her parents compelled her to keep going, to win that Olympic gold they'd been so certain she could get. She couldn't let Paul down by forcing him to find a new partner—not after his one disastrous try to replace her.

If Micah was that petty, she decided, it was just

as well to get away from him. Besides that, he was marrying Lindy the following month. She felt an upwelling of rage and grief. Poor Janey. She would go crazy with Lindy in the house. She'd never be able to continue with skating, because Lindy would insist that boarding school was a good idea. She'd coax Micah into it, and Janey would be one less problem for Lindy to contend with. Next, Burt would go. She'd complain so much that Micah would hire someone to replace him. If he could toss Karina out so easily, nobody else's job was safe. Dietrich would be sold.

She swallowed, hard. She was making mountains out of molehills, as her father used to say. Tormenting herself wasn't helping the situation. There was nothing she could do, to save Janey or herself. Micah was like a steam engine going down a high grade when he made a decision, and he never backtracked. She knew him that well, after only a few weeks.

She knew the taste and smell and character of him. She loved him. It would wrench her heart from her body to leave him. But he was giving her no choice. He thought skating was a pipe dream. He didn't think she could skate. But, then, he'd never really seen her skate. Neither had Lindy. They'd been at the rink when she was still learning to get back on the ice. Neither of them knew how well Janey could skate, either. Lindy made fun of the little girl, told her she had no talent. Lindy, who'd won a regional competition, making fun of Karina, who had a gold from the World Figure Skating Championships.

Well, she'd show them both! She and Paul were not only going to compete at the Olympics, they were going to win that gold medal. She'd work herself to death, risk any injury, to throw that medal in high-and-mighty Micah's face! Not to mention Lindy's. It would vindicate her. And Janey would love it.

"You're smiling," Paul noted as they finished their routine, to applause from the other skaters, whom they acknowledged with waves. "Why are you smiling?"

"Micah and Lindy think I'm having pipe dreams about winning a medal," Karina told him. "In fact, Lindy rubbed it in my face that she'd won a medal at regional competition!"

"Wow."

"Not that it's an easy thing, to win a medal of any sort," she conceded. "But I do think a gold at the Worlds is a little more proof of ability than a bronze at Regionals. Just my little opinion."

He hugged her. "It's a great opinion, and, yes, we are going to win the Olympics," he chuckled, looking down at her affectionately. "And then I'm going to feature in ice shows for a couple of years while I finish my degree so that I can teach. How about you?"

"I'll do the same, so that I can get my own degree in history. Maybe I'll go on to master's work, so that I can teach elementary school."

He laughed. "I'll settle for teaching adult education with a bachelor's. The boys will be in kindergarten next year. I'll need to be home, or Gerda will never manage enough discipline to keep them straight."

"Gerda's no marshmallow," she teased.

"No, but boys are difficult. You'll find that out, one day."

Her face fell. "I don't want to get married," she said.

"Not even to your abrasive boss?" he chided softly.

She blushed and he laughed.

"Stop that," she muttered, moving away from him. "He's going to get married next month. He and Lindy moved up the wedding date."

He winced. "I'm so sorry."

"Life is hard."

"Then you die," he chuckled.

They were recalling famous lines from a retro television show, *Dempsey and Makepeace*, about an American peace officer who worked in London with a tough female one. They'd watched it on a popular internet site, along with Gerda.

"Such is life," Paul said philosophically. He glanced at his watch. "I suppose you have to get your charge home on time tonight," he guessed.

"I suppose so," she said reluctantly. "The boss was furious." She grimaced. "Somebody who's friends with Lindy was at the rink last night. She told Lindy that you and I were all hugged up in public, and that you're married. So the boss thinks I'm helping you commit adultery."

"We should tell Gerda at once," he said with mock fear. "She'll be furious!"

She hit him. "Quit that."

He laughed. "Suppose I go home with you and

talk to your boss?" he asked gently. "You should have just told him the truth."

"He wouldn't believe me," she said simply. "He wouldn't believe you, either." She sighed. "He's looking for a way to get rid of me, Paul. It comes down to that."

"But, why?"

"I don't really know. I suspect it's because Lindy doesn't like me and Janey does."

He sighed. "Perhaps he feels something he doesn't want to feel, yes?"

"I don't know," she repeated. She searched his eyes. "Without a job, I don't know how I'll manage!"

"You can coach on the side down in Jackson," he said. "I know two families who are desperate for coaches for their sons and the coaches at the rink are already overwhelmed. They're wealthy and they'd pay well." He pursed his lips. "Actually I already told them about you." He sighed. "I could see how things were going to go. His fiancée hates you."

"I noticed." She brightened. "Thanks, Paul. At least I have a safety net, if I need one."

He brushed back her disheveled hair. "Perhaps it will work out." He smiled. "He might realize his mistake and send his girlfriend out the door."

She cocked her head and smiled up at him with soft gray eyes. "Perhaps pigs might fly."

He chuckled. "Perhaps they might." He looked up. "Janey is just through with her lesson. She goes to competition next week, her very first. Are you going with her?"

"I hope I am," she said quietly. She had a cold feeling in her stomach about that. Micah had looked at Karina as if she were trashy. If he convinced himself that she was immoral, running around after a married man, he wouldn't want her around Janey. She was certain that Lindy would help him along with that conviction.

"Well, we wait and see, yes?" he asked. "Meanwhile, I will practice some more by pretending that you are skating with me."

"Get Hilde to skate my part," she teased. "She's still very good on skates."

"Indeed she is." He smiled at her. "I'm sorry things aren't going well for you. I want you to be happy."

Her eyes were sad. "The only times I've ever really been happy were when I skated. It's helped me keep going through much worse things than this."

He understood. "Then, I will see you tomorrow, yes?"

"I hope you will. I'll text you if things go wrong."

"You must try to be optimistic."

She didn't answer him. She smiled again, turned, and went to the barrier, where Janey was just taking off her skates.

"I guess we'd better go home, huh?" Janey asked sadly. "Daddy was in a foul mood. I'm sorry you and Paul won't get to skate again tonight. You're so good on the ice!"

"Thanks," Karina said, forcing a smile. "It takes a lot of practice."

"Don't let Daddy fire you," Janey pleaded. "I don't know how I'll manage if I have to actually live with Lindy. She'll never let me compete. She'll convince Daddy that I don't have the talent."

"You do have the talent," she replied. "Burt will be on your side. Get him to be your advocate."

"You can't leave," Janey repeated. Tears were welling up in her eyes. "You're my best friend!"

Karina pulled her close and rested her cheek on the child's dark hair. "You're mine, too, darling," she said softly. She drew in a painful sigh. "I don't want to leave. But you have to understand, I can't give up now. Paul and I have worked too hard, for too many years, to let this chance pass us by. It might never come again. And Paul's already tried to replace me. You know how that worked out."

"I do." Janey pulled back and wiped at her red eyes. "I do understand, too. It's not right that Daddy wants you to give up your dreams."

"I'm sure he thinks you deserve someone better," she replied gently. "And you do. I'm going to have to travel to compete." Her lips made a thin line. "I can't take care of you and do that as well."

"You could take me with you," Janey said wistfully.

Karina laughed. "Oh, I'd love to," she said, and meant it. "But it's not practical. You're in school. You can't miss weeks of it without repeating a grade. I want more for you than that."

"Thanks. I guess that was a pipe dream. But you and Paul are magic on the ice," she added. "I want you to win the Nationals and then come back here and throw your medals at Daddy."

Karina smiled sadly. She didn't mention that she had a gold medal she could throw at him. She wasn't going to do that. He'd jumped to conclusions and made assumptions without giving a care about Karina's feelings. She wasn't going to tell him anything. If she and Paul made it to the Olympics, he could watch them on television, with Lindy and Janey. Then they'd all know.

As satisfying as that scenario was, it was, as Micah had said, a dream. But it was one within reach and she wasn't giving up.

WHEN THEY GOT HOME, Micah and Lindy were still snuggled up together on the sofa watching the news.

They looked up when the skaters walked in the door.

Janey looked around. "Where's Dietrich?" she asked.

"You know that Lindy's allergic to him," Micah said curtly. "He's down at Billy Joe's cabin."

"Oh." Janey's face fell.

"Dogs don't belong in the house," Lindy said haughtily. "They're nasty."

"Dietrich is not nasty!" Janey shot back.

"Go to your room," Micah said icily.

Janey looked up at Karina with wet eyes, and Karina grimaced.

"Don't look to her for help," Micah said sarcastically. "You heard me."

"Yes, sir," Janey said miserably. She walked off with her skating bag and went into her room.

"No need to ask who's been teaching her how to backtalk adults," Lindy scoffed, glaring at her.

"No need at all," Micah agreed. He kissed Lindy and got to his feet. "In my office," he told Karina shortly and walked off, leaving her to follow.

She didn't look at Lindy on the way. She knew without even doing so that Lindy had a smug, satisfied expression on her face.

MICAH CLOSED THE door behind them. He went to his desk and sat down behind it, slinging his legs up onto it before he crossed them.

"I gave you a choice," he said. "Either give up the skating or give up this job. You can't compete in skating without a lot of travel. Lindy told me that. How are you going to babysit my daughter? You can't take her with you."

"I know that, Mr. Torrance," she said without meeting his eyes. She looked, and felt, totally defeated. Here it was. The choice. She'd dreaded it since she and Paul began practice.

It would have been a hard choice after the passionate interlude she'd had with her boss the night before. But now, it was made easier by the fact that he was actually marrying Lindy. Karina couldn't live in the same house with her.

She lifted her chin. "Would you rather fire me or just ask for my resignation?" she asked with quiet dignity.

He glared at her. He hadn't wanted an easy acceptance. He'd wanted her to deny that she had anything going with her married skating partner. He'd wanted her to fight, to defy him, to refuse to quit. He was disappointed, and he didn't understand why. He ached for her. He didn't understand that, either.

He got to his feet. "It might be better if you quit," he said flatly. He forced a sarcastic smile. "That way you can't draw unemployment."

"I wouldn't draw it if I could," she said simply. "I can work. I've worked since I was seventeen."

That needled him. She was young and healthy. Of course she could get another job. "Doing what?" he asked. "Waiting tables?"

"It's honest work."

"What would you know about honesty?" he demanded. He moved toward her and took her by both arms. "You're helping your partner commit adultery. How 'honest' is that?" he asked hotly.

The feel of his hands made her knees go weak. He could see it. She couldn't even help herself.

His hands became caressing, moving up and down her arms as he moved a step closer, so that she could feel his strength, the heat of his body.

"I'd never have believed you could be so shallow," he bit off. His eyes dropped to her mouth. "And I thought you were innocent!"

His mouth came down on hers, hard. It was instant passion, but without tenderness or respect. He dragged her hips against the raging arousal he couldn't even help, and he hated her for the way his body reacted to her. He wanted her beyond bearing. He was obsessed with her. And she was sleeping with that blond-haired, handsome, married man! It made him furious.

He was bruising her, humiliating her, with blind need that had no care for her feelings. And she was as helpless as he was. She reached up to his neck, pressing herself against the warm strength of him, moaning softly under his devouring mouth.

He groaned and lifted her against him. It was like the other time, like flash fire. He couldn't think past relief. He didn't want Lindy, who was beautiful and hot as a flame. He wanted this woman, ached for her, and could never have her. She didn't want a home and children, she wanted to pursue some stupid dream of skating fame while she romanced a married man.

He knew all that, but he couldn't resist her. He cradled her against him, his lips softened, became tender. He drew her closer and groaned against her mouth as the need almost brought him to his knees. His eyebrows drew together in an anguish of passion. He forgot her dreams, his responsibilities, everything, as he fought to satisfy a hunger that seemed to have no possible fulfillment.

He picked her up in his arms and walked to the sofa. He started to put her down, to smooth his body over hers, to have her. If she'd been sleeping with her partner, there was no need to worry about abusing her innocence. She was willing. He was hungry. He could have her, right here…

She felt the need in him. She knew what he was

thinking. She wanted to protest, but it was so sweet, feeling his hunger, his aching passion. She wanted nothing more than to give him what he needed. She loved him more than anything. Right now, if he'd asked her to give up skating and marry him, she'd have said yes without hesitation.

But before he could say anything, before she could get her fevered brain to work, there was a loud, impatient knock on the door.

"Micah? Are you ever coming out of there?" Lindy demanded, trying the doorknob.

Micah and Karina froze for a few seconds, staring at each other in faint shock. But it became apparent that the door was locked.

Micah was surprised. He didn't remember turning the key in the door. He looked down at Karina's swollen mouth and felt the hunger almost buckle his knees. How in the hell had this happened?

"I'm coming right out," he told Lindy, raising his voice.

"Well, hurry up," she snapped. "I want to get some sleep before you fly me out in the morning! I bought a pretty negligee, just for you!"

Karina felt shamed, soiled, as the seductive voice on the other side of the door made her intentions clear. She glared up at Micah, who was trying to fight his hunger and failing miserably.

She pushed at his shoulders, feeling weak. "Put me down, please," she asked huskily.

He set her on her feet a little roughly. He drew in a harsh breath, hating his own weakness, and hers.

"Well?" he asked. "Do you stay or go?"

She closed her eyes. "I go," she replied. She looked up at him with anger glittering in her eyes. "I'm not your toy!"

"No?" he asked with a faint, arrogant smile. "You could be."

She backed up a step, flushed and miserable at her own helpless attraction to him.

He was thinking, too. She had no resistance to him whatsoever. He touched her and she was his. Beyond that, her responses just weren't those of an experienced woman. Unless her paramour was a lousy lover. She might think she loved him, but she really didn't.

While he was trying to sort his muddled feelings, she was walking toward the door, hoping her swollen mouth wouldn't give anything away to Lindy.

"I'll leave first thing tomorrow," she said, with her back to him.

"You'll never win a competition," he said harshly, angry that she was really going. "Lindy's forgotten more about skating than you know, and she says you haven't got what it takes."

She turned, her face full of quiet pride. "One day, you may find out what I've got, Mr. Torrance. You, and Lindy as well."

"Fat chance, Miss Carter," he chided.

She only looked at him, filling her eyes with his face, memorizing it, because she was certain that she'd never see it again. "Goodbye," she said.

She walked out and closed the door behind her, shutting him out.

Lindy gave her a brief glance, stopping at the younger woman's red eyes. "So he fired you."

"No. I quit," she said shortly.

Lindy laughed. "Good. Now you can't file for unemployment, can you? My, my, how will you afford those expensive skating lessons with your coach now, Miss Carter?" she added, alluding to Hilde. "You'll never go anywhere in skating. I should know. I've been in competition."

Karina just looked at her, without saying a word.

Lindy made a face and went back to watching television.

KARINA PACKED, FIGHTING TEARS. She hoped that Lindy and the boss would be gone when she got up, so that she'd havc a minute with poor Janey. Dietrich was going to live with Billy Joe. Lucky Dietrich. Janey would adjust, but it would be a hard life with Lindy. Karina felt bad for her. She loved the little girl. It was going to be a wrench to leave her. She didn't try to think how it was going to feel, being without Micah. She didn't dare.

OF ALL THE mornings to oversleep, Karina thought as she looked at the clock and grimaced. She'd be late getting Janey to school. She assumed that she'd do that, one last time, and they could talk.

But when she left her bedroom, Janey was nowhere in sight. Fortunately, neither were Micah or Lindy.

"At least have breakfast before you go," Burt said sadly. "I made you those bacon and egg sandwiches you like so much," he added with a forced smile.

"You're so sweet, Burt," she replied, and fought tears. "I guess he told you, huh?"

"He did." He glowered at her as she sat down. "I was ready to tell him some things, too, but Lindy said they were dropping Janey off at school and going on to Vegas. They walked out without breakfast." He sighed. "Boss was so subdued I wondered if he was the same man I've been working for."

Subdued wasn't a word she associated with her boss. Not ever. She frowned. "Why?"

"Lindy must have upset him again," he said. "Stupid man. She'll ruin his life. Not to add what she'll do to poor Janey. He must be out of his mind!"

She sat down and started eating. "He's a grown man."

"He's an idiot. Lindy said you'd quit," he added, sitting down with black coffee in a humorous mug. "Did you? Or did the boss force you to?"

"He said I could quit or get fired," she replied. "He says I'm living in a dream world, that I'll never win a skating competition. It's hard to even win a local one, he added. Besides, Lindy says I don't have what it takes."

"And she knows that because she won a medal at regional competition," he scoffed. "Should have thrown your Worlds gold in her face."

"It wouldn't accomplish anything," she replied sadly. "It wouldn't change anything." She looked up at him. "Don't tell them anything about me," she pleaded. "Just take care of Janey. She's the one I'm worried about. Lindy wants to put her in a boarding school."

He didn't comment. He wasn't sure anybody could stop the boss from doing that. "He grew up without love," he said. "His mom died when he was a baby, his dad was career military. The general used a belt on the boy if he cried at all, even when he was little." He smiled sadly. "Boss hasn't ever been in love. Not really. He thinks love is something that happens in bedrooms."

"That's sad."

"Sadder than you know." He shook his head. "He was going to break it off with Lindy. Told me so last week. Then he brings her home with him last night and they're all cuddled up together. I don't know what's gotten into him."

"Well, it's not my problem anymore. I'm going back to my apartment in Jackson. Paul will go, too. I hope Hilde can come down to coach us."

"She will," Burt said. "You're a winning team. You'll see. And when you win the Olympic gold, I'll sit the boss in front of the TV, tie him to a chair and hit Replay on the recorder. I'll make him watch it until he turns blue!"

She laughed. "Oh, Burt. I'll miss you."

"I'll miss you, too, Karina." He sighed. "I wish you could stay."

"I do, too, for Janey's sake. Take care of her."

"You know I will. You take care of yourself."

KARINA CLIMBED INTO her car, waved goodbye to Burt, standing in the doorway, and drove to the rink. Paul would be waiting. She had sad news for him and for Hilde. She didn't cry. But it was hard. She'd never see Janey or Micah again. It broke her heart.

CHAPTER THIRTEEN

HILDE WAS BELLIGERENT. "He would fire you for such a petty reason?" she huffed. "When you and Paul are world champions in pairs, and he wants you to give it up because it is a pipe dream?"

"He doesn't know who I am," she told Hilde sadly. "I'm not sure he'd even care. He and his fiancée are getting married next month. I'm just sad for Janey. I didn't even get to say goodbye," she added, fighting tears. "At least I have a way to contact her, unless they stop her from associating with me."

"There, there," Hilde said, hugging her. "It will be all right. You and Paul go on to Jackson. I will find someone to manage the rink here and I'll get an apartment there, so that I can go on coaching you."

"I hate for you to have to do that," Karina said worriedly. "It's your livelihood. We're paying you to coach us, and we get a stipend from the national organization to help with it, but..."

"I still have some money left over from my career. I invested wisely. Besides," Hilde added with a grin, "if I coach a team that wins pairs at the Olympics, think what I can charge my future students."

Karina chuckled. "I want to win for that reason alone."

"You also want to win to show your unpleasant boss that he's no judge of character," Paul added with a grin. "Not to mention, his fiancée as well."

"Yes, I do," Karina said. Her mouth made a straight line. "I'll work harder than I've ever worked in my life. That gold medal, I *will* throw in his face! And hers!"

Paul chuckled. It amused him to see his partner's fury. She was eloquent when she lost her temper. But it gave away the hurt underneath the words. She was in love with the man. He was sorry for her.

"I've already interviewed ten potential managers for the rink," Hilde added, laughing at their shocked faces. "Well, you know, I always planned to go with you to the competitions. I had to find someone to stay here and take care of my business. He'll just be doing it for a little longer than I thought. It's not a worry. We'll all go to Jackson and skate at the big rink there."

"That will be one worry less, for me, having you coach us there so we don't have to commute to Catelow for lessons," Paul said, and Karina nodded. "We can't lose you now. Too much is at stake."

"Yes, it is," Karina said. "I'm so happy that you'll do that for us. It will make more problems for you."

"No, it won't," Hilde said brusquely. "We all have things to prove to other people." She laughed. "I'm going to prove to all my former skaters that I'm not over-the-hill. And you two are going to prove to one stubborn rancher that you don't have impossible aspirations!"

They all smiled. It was a goal to win. Now they had purpose and ambition and determination. All it needed was much work and practice. Jackson would give them that.

BURT WENT TO pick up Janey at school. She knew without Burt telling her that Karina was gone.

Her father and Lindy were nowhere in sight when they got home. She was glad. She was very angry and she wouldn't be able to hide it. Lindy would be impossible.

"I'm so sorry, honey," Burt told her gently.

"I'm supposed to go down to Jackson next week for my first test," she wailed. "They'll never let me go, now!"

"If they won't, I'll drive you myself," Burt said haughtily.

"Oh, Burt, you sweetheart!" She hugged him and then turned away toward her room. "I was so happy," she said miserably, glancing back at him. "Why is life so hard?"

"I wish I knew," Burt said softly. "Want some milk and cookies?"

"Thanks. But no. I don't want anything." She went into her room and closed the door. She cried until her heart felt broken. She was furious at her father. Why had he insisted that Karina give up skating, when he knew how much she loved it? Why? He'd never seen her skate with Paul. If he had, he'd know that they had the talent to go all the way. She could tell him that, but he was unapproachable in these moods. And Lindy would find ways to keep Micah and his daughter apart, as she always did when she spent weekends with them. She was so jealous of Micah that she even saw his own daughter as an obstacle. Janey had learned to hate her visits. They always ended in misery.

A beep alerted her to an incoming email. She had very few friends that contacted her that way. She pulled out her cell phone and looked. It was from Karina!

"I'm back in my apartment in Jackson. Paul and I got here safely. Don't worry about us, okay? If you have to, get Chad to talk to your father about that competition. He knows you're good enough. He'll fight for you. Don't forget me, okay? I love you."

The tears came back, full force. Janey pulled up the reply screen and sent back a message of her own, ending it with, "Wish you were here. I love you, too."

At least they could still speak to each other. She'd have to make sure that her father didn't know. He was perfectly capable of hiding or destroying her computer and cell phone to keep her away from Karina.

AT THE RINK, Paul and Karina practiced every single day, for hours at a time. They were getting to the point now that they remembered each detail of the program without having to have Hilde remind them.

Karina was improving by the day. She was almost back to her old level of perfection. Her ankle bothered her a little, the injury resulting in arthritis in the joint. But she had anti-inflammatories for that, and they worked. She had to regulate the dosage carefully, though, and only take them when she wasn't skating. The loss of even a tenth of a second in the rink could mean disaster. Her mind had to be clear.

The Nationals were in January. They had less than two months to train, which would mean pushing practice to the limit. Fortunately, all the skating Karina had done with Janey had helped her regain her strength and speed in the rink. Now it was just a matter of perfecting the moves in unison, which settled into place with ease since she and Paul had skated together for so many years.

It was exciting. Karina was certain that she and Paul would manage to get into at least the top five at the Nationals. If they did, that score, added to their scores at the World Championships and the Four Continents Championships earlier in the year, would almost certainly give them a shot at Pyeongchang in February. They were consistent in their programs and they always received high marks in any competition they entered.

Maybe it was a long shot, but Karina didn't think so. She was far more confident than she'd ever been before. And the biggest incentive was that she wanted to show that doubting rancher that she could skate far better than his snippy fiancée. It would be worth all the aches and pain and stress to get that Olympic gold medal. If she and Paul managed it, she was going to have a poster made of them on the podium with their medals sent to Mr. Arrogant Rancher, express. Then let him belittle her talent!

The worst of it was that she missed him. Days had passed without a word from Janey. And then, on the very next day, she had an excited text from Janey.

"Chad came to the house and talked to Daddy, so he's taking me to Jackson for my competition! Chad's coming, too. I'm so excited! I'm wearing that special skating costume that Daddy bought for me, the one I showed you. Lindy's coming, too," she added with an emoji of a frowning face. "But I'm just going to ignore her and skate my best. You were right about having Chad talk to Daddy. Lindy got mad, but Daddy said he was taking me anyway and she could just shut up. Daddy's not eating. Burt thinks Lindy is spoiling his appetite. Maybe I'll see you while I'm at the rink!" She added the time she and her father were going to come to the rink.

"We can't practice from two to four tomorrow," Karina told Paul quietly.

"Why not?" he asked, puzzled.

"Janey has her first test," she said. "And her father's coming with her. I don't want to see him."

"Pauvre petite," he said softly. "I'm so sorry."

"I thought maybe he'd regret what he said," she replied, downcast. "That really was a pipe dream," she added on a hollow laugh. "I don't think he regrets anything."

"Sometimes men don't know what they want until they lose it," he replied.

"And sometimes they just wave it off and never

look back," she laughed. "It doesn't matter. We're doing really well. Hilde thinks we're ready for Nationals right now. That's high praise, coming from her."

"We've put in a lot of practice, and you've bounced back far quicker than I thought you would."

"I've surprised myself," she agreed. "I can't forget how afraid I was to go out on the ice again."

"All skaters who suffer injuries have those doubts and fears. But most of us conquer them. You recall my broken arm seven years ago?" he asked.

She smiled. "You came back even quicker than I did."

"Well, I didn't have to land on my arm," he said, tongue-in-cheek.

"But you did have to lift me, which you couldn't do until it was totally healed."

"Also true. Nobody escapes bruises and sprains in this sport."

"But it's worth every bump," she replied.

He smiled. "So it is."

THE RINK WAS crowded the next day. Karina didn't go down to the rink until she was certain that Janey's test was over. She hated missing the child's big moment, but she was too raw to encounter Micah.

Paul was waiting for her. She skated onto the ice with him for practice.

"Did you see her?" she asked.

He shook his head. "Are you certain it was to be today?"

"Yes. At least, I thought it was. Maybe I got the day wrong."

"Maybe so. Come. We have an area roped off for us."

He led her over to it. Hilde had already started the music for them, the beautiful Rachmaninoff piece that set the stage for their routine.

She skated with her whole heart. This was her life. How had she thought she could ever give it up? It was in her blood, her mind, her very soul. She gave in to the music and let it take her, following Paul's movements so perfectly that they might have been attached to each other with silken cords.

When they finished, Karina was flushed and winded, but happier than she'd been in days.

"And so, you become better and better," Hilde remarked with a grin as they skated over to her at the barrier. "I am so proud. You will certainly go to the Olympics. And you will win," she added with firm conviction.

"I must confess that I think the same," Paul replied. "In fact..." He broke off as he stared over Karina's head. "Oh, dear."

She turned around and there was Janey, skating toward her like a comet.

"Janey!" she exclaimed.

She caught the child in her arms and held her close, hugged her tight. "Janey!" she exclaimed, her face alight with happiness. "I'm so happy to see you!"

"I'm so happy to see you! I passed!"

"You passed? I'm so proud of you!" she exclaimed. "But when did you skate?"

"Oh, two hours ago," Janey replied. "I didn't see you. I'd hoped you'd be here, but I guess you didn't want to be. Because of Daddy."

"I'm sorry," Karina said and meant it.

"It's okay," the child replied. She sighed. "Daddy's been horrible. Just horrible. He yells, he curses. And she's always around. Burt's quitting. He says he can't live with her. Daddy's away more than he's home. I can't even have Dietrich in the house. I'm just miserable."

"I'm so sad for you," Karina replied quietly. "But life has storms. We just have to get through them. You're tough. You can do this. It isn't forever. In a few years, you'll go away to college."

"Or I'll go away to the Olympics," Janey teased.

Karina laughed. "College is necessary. I only lack a semester to finish my bachelor's degree. Paul already has his bachelor's. We plan ahead. You can't compete forever."

"Are you going to the Olympics?"

"We hope so," Karina said. "Our scores from the other competitions this year place us very high. We'll have to wait and see."

"We're a shoo-in," Paul chided. "She's a pessimist."

"True," she had to confess.

Janey was looking behind her. She grimaced. "They're back. I told them I wanted to watch the other kids skate. I thought you and Paul would probably be here. I wanted to see you."

"I'm glad you came back," Karina said softly, smiling at the child.

"You should let Daddy watch you skate," she said. "He'd change his mind."

She looked past the child at a glowering Micah on the other side of the rink, holding hands with a smug Lindy. "I don't care what he thinks," Karina said quietly. "But I do care about you. I'm very proud of you. Keep up with practice. In no time, you'll be back down here taking the next test up."

"I hope I will. Lindy says I need to quit wasting time at the ice rink and spend time on my homework."

Karina smoothed back the child's hair. "Let each day take care of itself, sweetheart," she said softly. "Don't gulp your life down. Savor it. One day at a time. Okay?"

Janey managed a smile. "Okay." She hugged Karina again. "I'll write. You write me, too, okay?"

"Okay. I promise."

"See you!"

She turned and skated back across the rink to where her father and Lindy were waiting. Karina turned away. She couldn't bear to look at Micah.

HE SAW HER and hated her. She was still bound and determined to pursue a career in ice skating. She didn't have the talent, Lindy said. She'd never make a contender. He had to confess, he couldn't see her in the difficult climb to stardom, not as gentle and soft-spoken as she was. Lindy likened it to prizefighting.

There were always people trying to trip you up, keep you down, disillusion you. Karina didn't fight back.

It hurt him to let her go. But he knew he couldn't make her stay. She'd chosen a career, a dubious one, over him. He'd been willing to toss Lindy over, to marry Karina, to have children with her. And then he found out she was sleeping with her married partner. It had destroyed his dreams. He'd never have thought her capable of being so two-faced. But he had proof.

She wouldn't look at him. He didn't want to admit how much it hurt. He missed her. He was miserable without her. He'd deliberately brought Lindy back into his life and nobody was happy, including himself. Janey was sad all the time, Burt was outraged and determined to quit. Micah couldn't bring himself to touch Lindy, not after his headlong reaction to Karina. It was a huge mess, and he'd made it all by himself.

Hurt pride counted for a lot, he thought. Karina had turned away from him. She wanted her partner. He was second best to a low-rent skater who apparently didn't even have a job. What did she see in the man?

"I said, are you ready to go?" Lindy asked impatiently. "They didn't even test the child properly. No wonder she passed!"

Janey bit her lower lip.

"Leave her alone," Micah said, and his voice and his expression made threats.

Lindy cleared her throat. "Oh, all right. Can we

just go? I've wasted a whole day. I could be out selling properties."

"That would be a first," Micah said bluntly and glared at her.

She caught her breath, shocked.

"Let's go," Micah said gruffly. He walked out ahead of Lindy and Janey. He was more than ready to go home.

"BURT, I PASSED, I passed!" Janey said excitedly when she saw Burt in the kitchen.

He grinned at her. "You go, girl," he teased. "I'm proud of you."

"Have you got supper ready?" Lindy asked irritably. "And I hope it's not swimming in grease again!"

"Actually, I made pork barbeque," he said with a raised eyebrow, "and French fries."

"My favorite," Micah chuckled. "Thanks."

"Well, make me a salad, then," Lindy huffed. "Because I'm not eating barbeque!"

"I made a salad already, to go with the barbeque," he told her.

"Stop being a harpy, sit down and eat," Micah told Lindy shortly. "And stop complaining every damned minute of the day about everything around you!"

She caught her breath. "How dare you!"

"How dare I what?" he shot back, and he looked absolutely dangerous.

She just stared at him.

"If you don't like it here, go get your stuff together and I'll have the company jet fly you back to Vegas tonight. In fact," he added, "that sounds like a good idea to me. You can keep the engagement ring. Just don't come back."

"But we're getting married…" she stammered.

"No, we're not," he said flatly. "I'll be damned if I'll spend the rest of my life with a shrew like you!"

"Well! Well!" she burst out. "Well!"

"That's a deep subject for a shallow mind. Get packed!"

He pulled out his cell phone and called his pilot. There was a brief conversation. "He'll be here in thirty minutes. I'll drive you to the airport myself," Micah added.

"But we're engaged," Lindy said. "You bought me a ring."

"Temporary insanity. I'm cured, now. You go back to Vegas and find yourself a more biddable millionaire to order around. And make sure he doesn't have kids, first. Because you're the worst example of a potential stepmother I've ever seen in my life!"

Lindy had visions of all that sweet money burning around her feet. She forced a smile. "Now, Micah, you're just under a lot of stress. I can help you with that."

"Not unless you're a licensed psychiatrist," he shot back. "I told you. We are no longer engaged. Now get packed."

She stomped her foot. "Well, thank you for nothing!" she yelled. "Just because I didn't sweet-talk your brain-dead daughter, you're dumping me! That suits me very well, because having to live with her wouldn't be worth it. No matter what that dumb skating coach and that idiot babysitter have been telling her, she has no talent. And that goes double for the babysitter. She'll never get close to a medal!"

Janey bit her tongue. She didn't want to get into more trouble, and her father already looked as if he was ready to go up in flames.

"I'm going!" Lindy yelled. "And I'm not coming back this time, even if you beg me!"

"Don't worry," Micah said. "I'm not that desperate for a woman."

Lindy flounced off without even answering him.

MICAH DROVE HER to the company jet and put her on it. They hadn't exchanged five words all the way.

He watched it take off with a feeling of unequaled relief. How could he have been so blind to her faults? He'd let her savage Janey and Burt. He'd let her poison his mind against Karina. He felt liberated.

But there was still the nagging emptiness he'd felt since he pushed Karina out of his life. He hated what he'd done to her. He hadn't asked why she was so certain she could have a career as a figure skater. In fact, he'd never seen her skate. He recalled her saying that her parents had mortgaged their home to pay her expenses as she entered into higher competitions. Would even deluded parents have risked so much for a woman who had no talent?

He needed to talk to her. He phoned Burt and told him he had some business to conduct and that he'd be late, to make sure Janey did her homework and got to bed on time. Then he started for Jackson.

THE RINK HAD only a few skaters on the ice. It was near closing time. He settled down on the back row, hoping that Karina might be down there. He didn't want her to see him and run, so he sat in the shadows. There was a couple nearby, elderly and friendly.

He smiled and turned his attention back to the rink. The music had just started. What was it, Rachmaninoff? It was a beautiful piece, but he couldn't recall the name.

A couple he hadn't noticed was just starting a practice routine, by the look of it. He frowned. They were professionals, by the look of them. They skated as if they were joined by a string, going fluidly from balletic grace to incredibly athletic jumps, all performed without a hitch. He leaned forward, fascinated. He'd only seen skaters of that quality looking over Janey's shoulder as she watched Olympic pairs competition in reruns on television.

"Aren't they great?" the elderly woman whispered.

"Who are they?" he asked.

"That's Paul Maurice. His partner is Miranda Tanner," she added. She chuckled softly. "We call her the 'Wyoming Legend.' She's from near Jackson. Her mother was a two-time gold medal winner at the Olympics in figure skating."

He frowned. Paul was the name of Karina's partner. Had he just been leading her on, and was he in competition with yet another woman?

"Of course, that's not her real name," the woman continued. "It's the name she uses in competition, so she's not hounded by sports reporters. Her real name is Karina Carter."

He felt the blood draining out of his face. He was remembering what he'd said to her. That she was a rank amateur who'd never go anywhere in figure skating, that she was pursuing a pipe dream.

"They won the gold medal at the World Championships this year, before she was injured," the woman continued, oblivious to the shock in her companion's face. "We're very proud of them. They're almost certain to go to the Olympics next year."

Olympics. They were gold medalists in international competition. He'd said she'd never get anywhere in skating. He couldn't remember feeling so ashamed of himself. He'd sent her running, demeaned her, separated her from Janey. She loved Janey. Janey loved her, too. All that, because of Lindy's lies.

"He's married, someone said," he murmured absently.

"Oh, yes. He and Gerda have twin sons. Karina's their godmother." She laughed, while he was cursing himself for his folly. "She and Paul and Gerda were best friends from grammar school. Karina said that she and Paul had to make sure not to make eye contact when they were doing that romantic stare they end their performance with, because the one time they did, they burst out laughing and lost points. They're like brother and sister."

"They'll win the gold this time," the man accompanying the old woman said firmly. "Didn't place in the top five at the last one, but they'll make up for it this time."

Last time. Karina and her parents had gone to the last Olympics. Because Karina had competed in them. He'd gotten the wrong end of the stick, all the way around.

"Been watching skaters come and go here for thirty years," the elderly woman said gently. "Never saw anybody skate like those two."

"I see what you mean," he replied.

Karina and Paul finished their routine and skated off the ice. Two small boys and a blonde woman went to meet them. Karina bent and lifted one of the boys, kissing his rosy little cheek and laughing.

Micah wanted to go down and see her, talk to her. But he knew that if he tried, she'd walk away. He'd hurt her badly. He'd have to bide his time and try to work his way back into her life, somehow. It wasn't going to be easy.

BURT HAD JUST finished cleaning the kitchen when Micah walked in, his steps dragging.

"Janey did her homework," he told the boss.

Micah sat down at the table. He was giving the older man a curious look. "Did you know?"

"Excuse me?"

"Did you know that Karina skated under a different name?" he persisted.

Burt flushed.

"Thank you the hell very much for telling me so that I wouldn't make a fool of myself!" Micah growled. "I told her she was chasing pipe dreams!"

"She made me promise not to," Burt said, grimacing. "She was hounded by sports reporters just after the accident. She wanted to get away from sports. Never planned to skate again, she told me. But Janey wanted to learn how to skate and you made her drive Janey back and forth to the rink. She got pushed back into it."

"I watched her skate with Paul." He sighed. "He's got two little boys. Karina is their godmother. Paul's wife is her best friend."

"Did you talk to her?"

He hesitated. Then he shook his head. "She turned her back on me when I picked up Janey this afternoon at the rink in Jackson. I don't blame her," he added. "When she's had time to get over it a bit, I'll try again."

"Are they good?" Burt asked.

"Good." He sighed. "I've seen Olympic contenders who weren't half as talented. It was like watching ballet."

"Karina's mother used her maiden name when she skated. Irene Tanner." Burt smiled. "I watched her skate, the second year she took the gold medal. She was like a fairy on the ice, graceful, poised, elegant. I had something of a crush on her."

"Does Janey know?" he asked after a minute.

"No. Karina was afraid she might mention it to someone."

Micah leaned back in his chair. "Lindy fed me a lot of bull. I was already jealous of Paul. She threw gasoline on the fire."

"If I can say so, I'm glad Lindy's gone. Got tired of hearing her run down Janey."

Micah sighed. "I spent so damned much time making money that I didn't notice my daughter was being pummeled by a woman who didn't even want her around. Lindy mentioned boarding school and I told her my daughter wasn't being raised by strangers. It bothered me even months ago that she'd mention such a thing." He laughed shortly. "She was hot. But there are more important things."

"Plenty of them."

Micah got up. "Well, I guess I'll turn off the phone and go to bed."

Burt's eyebrows rose. "Turn off the phone at night? There's a famous first."

"Karina's idea. She said people had no right to bother me when I was trying to sleep. I didn't think about it until then."

"Back before portable phones, people didn't call you at two in the morning to conduct business," Burt said. "No wonder so many businessmen have heart attacks. They get no rest."

"I don't sleep much anyway. But a few peaceful hours aren't bad." He pursed his lips and his dark eyes twinkled. "She chased a grizzly bear away with a stick," he chuckled. "They'll be talking about that when my grandchildren are in school."

"No doubt."

"That reminds me, call Billy Joe and have him bring Dietrich up here. Put him in Janey's room."

"She'll be happy about that. Broke her heart that he wasn't allowed in the house anymore."

"I've been blind as a bat," Micah said. "But my eyes were truly opened tonight. I was going to try and talk to Karina. I sat in the back beside an elderly couple who were watching Paul and Karina practice. I got an earful. Do you know what they call her, down in Jackson?"

"No. What?"

"The 'Wyoming Legend,'" he said with affection. "I guess I'm going to have to eat some cold stringy crow before this is all over."

"She isn't the sort to hold grudges," Burt replied. "She's just hurt. You did lay it on pretty thick. And having Lindy here to rub it all in didn't help a lot."

He grimaced. "No, it didn't."

"For my part, I'm glad I don't have to give up my job," Burt chuckled. "I was ready to. No way I could live under the same roof with that woman, carping about everything. Especially about my cooking."

"I'm amazed that it took me so long to see through her," Micah said.

"You were being led around by your libido," Burt mused.

"That's one way to put it." He shook his head.

"Well, I'm not anymore. But I still have no idea how I'm going to get Karina to listen to me while I eat crow."

"Give it a little time," Burt said.

"I will. And hope it does the trick." He didn't add that it was going to be a lonely time in between. The house already seemed devoid of color.

PAUL AND KARINA practiced and practiced. Thanksgiving came and went, a boisterous and fun time with Karina at the Maurice home for turkey and dressing. Janey sent love and greetings and a photograph of her practicing for her next test. Karina returned one of herself with Paul and Gerda and the boys laughing as they trimmed the Christmas tree. Gerda always put it up at Thanksgiving.

It was a quiet Thanksgiving at the ranch in Catelow. Micah was home, for a change, and Billy Joe came up to eat with Micah and Janey and Burt. Dietrich had a plate of deboned turkey of his own. But it was a somber celebration without Karina.

The one bright spot in Micah's life was that Janey showed him the photo of Karina with the Maurices, decorating a Christmas tree. He didn't notice Janey's delighted look as he stared at the photo on her computer with rapt attention.

Janey mentioned that look to Karina when she sent a digital photo of herself and Micah and Burt, taken by an obliging Billy Joe. But Karina didn't say anything about it.

Privately, Karina downloaded the photo and printed it out. She found a frame for it and put it on her bedside table. Life without Micah was colorless.

CHAPTER FOURTEEN

CHRISTMAS WAS A quiet affair at the ranch. Janey had a present from Karina, which she placed under the tree. She'd sent one of her own to Karina's apartment. There was a small present that accompanied Janey's, with no tag. Karina assumed that it was from Burt. Until she opened it on Christmas morning.

It was a charm bracelet. She frowned as she looked at the little figures on its links. There was an ice skate with what looked like crystal chips. There was a dog, very obviously a German shepherd,and what looked like a bear. The last charm was a crow. She wondered what the charms meant. Probably Janey liked crows. She smiled. It was a pretty bracelet. It appeared to be sterling silver. But she examined the clasp, which said 18k gold. That was when she realized that the chips weren't crystal. They were diamonds.

She couldn't believe that Janey had talked her father into buying Karina something so expensive. Janey's present had been a skating sweater, in Karina's size, black with a pair of skates outlined in crystals, and a friendship bracelet that had obviously been handmade by the giver.

There was a note from Janey, tucked in the Christmas card that accompanied the gifts. "The sweater is from me. I crocheted you the friendship bracelet. I hope you like them. Dad sent the charm bracelet. He says crow probably tastes terrible." There was an emoji of a smile.

Karina studied the charm bracelet again. Crow. Eating crow. Why would he want to eat crow?

It occurred to her that it was a roundabout apology. But for what? He'd said she'd never make it in skating. Had he changed his mind?

Fat chance, she thought. Lindy would be buying a wedding gown by now and thinking of all the ways she could get rid of Janey. Karina had wanted to ask about that, but she didn't want to pry, or bring up a subject that would be painful to her young friend. So instead she just wished Janey a happy Christmas, thanked her for the presents and said she hoped that Janey liked hers.

Karina had sent Janey a skating costume, an expensive one from the boutique where Karina had her costumes made. It was white with crystal accents, which would look beautiful on the little girl, with her dark hair and pale olive complexion. Janey had raved about it.

Janey wrote her back, a long email about Dietrich being back in the house and Lindy being gone for good. She asked if Karina had liked the charm bracelet, adding that her dad had spent a lot of time having it made to his own specifications by an artist who worked for an exclusive jeweler in Denver.

Karina's heart jumped when she read that. Micah had designed it himself. It wasn't something he'd just bought, ready-made. She turned it over in her hands, fascinated. She didn't understand.

There was a postscript to Janey's email. It read, "Dad saw you and Paul skating in Jackson. He said it was like watching ballet. He knows you're going to win a gold medal. We're all going to be at the Olympics to cheer you on. And don't bother saying you don't know if you'll get to go. All of us are sure that you will. Love to Paul. Lots of love to you. Janey."

Karina put the charm bracelet to her lips and tears rolled down her cheeks in her lonely apartment. She knew that she'd cherish the piece of jewelry as long as she lived. Micah was sorry he'd misjudged her. That was nice, but an apology was all it was. He hadn't suddenly discovered passionate love for her. He and Lindy had broken up before, she recalled, and he'd always taken Lindy back. Karina was under no illusions that she was going to fill Lindy's place in his life. That really was a pipe dream.

She thanked Janey for both gifts, said that she and Paul were practicing hard for Nationals and wished Janey a happy New Year.

KARINA WAS ALL NERVES. Paul just smiled.

"We know our routine backward and forward," he chided as they waited their turn to skate. "We know we're good. But this isn't a competition. We're just going out there to skate for Janey and show her how good we are."

She looked up at him. “What? Janey’s here?” she exclaimed.

“Somewhere,” he said, nodding. “Burt, too.”

Her heart jumped. Dear Burt! He’d made sure that Janey could see them compete. She didn’t think about whether Janey had asked her father to fly them here. Likely he was off somewhere with Lindy…

“Heads up,” Paul said, as they were announced, after the bouquets of flowers and stuffed animals meant for the previous skaters had been cleared off the ice.

They skated out onto the ice, momentarily half-blinded by the lights all around. Karina wanted to look into the stands, to see if she could see Janey. She didn’t dare. Now she had to concentrate on what she was doing. Every second counted.

The pair had finished second in the short program on Wednesday night. Scores on that one would be added to those of the free skate, which was tonight, Friday night. Then, tomorrow, the Olympic contenders would be named. A lot was riding on their scores here. They had to hope that all the training, all the hard work, would pay off.

“We’re good. We’re great. We will win,” Paul whispered to her as they assumed their starting pose. “So smile and let’s show them who we are!”

She laughed softly. “Okay.”

AND THEY DID. They skated a perfect program. Up in the stands, Janey was almost jumping up and down as she watched them speed across the ice, into flawless jumps.

"They're so good!" Janey whispered. "They're perfect!"

"Yes, they are," Burt agreed.

Micah didn't say a word. He was watching, wishing them all the luck he could muster even while he thought of a future that couldn't contain Karina. She was beautiful on the ice, a fantasy of balletic movement. How could he ask someone with that sort of talent to give it all up and live on a ranch in Wyoming and have children? He'd said her skating aspirations were pipe dreams, when what he wanted of her was the true dream. No wonder she couldn't give it up. She'd worked her whole life to get here, to this point in time, to be the best in the world.

He was morose, even as he cheered when they finished the free skate and moved off the ice to wait for their scores.

"Look! They're in first place!" Janey enthused.

"Now all they have to do is hold on to it," Burt said. "But as long as they can stay in the top three, they'll still have a shot at the Olympics."

"When will we know?" Janey asked.

"Tomorrow morning, they'll announce it," Burt said. "But you have to consider that they won the Grand Prix again in November, and they won the Worlds back in March. Those combined scores will decide it in their favor, I'm pretty sure."

"Oh, I hope you're right!" Janey said.

In fact, he was. Paul and Karina held on to first place, winning the gold in the U.S. Figure Skating Championships. The next morning, the US Olympic teams were announced. Paul and Karina would go to Pyeongchang.

Karina and Paul were delighted to be chosen. This would be their second Olympics, but they were hoping to do better than last time. Hilde could hardly contain her enthusiasm. Her skaters had overcome so many obstacles to win the event. And it was her coaching, her choreography, that had won the day.

Other skaters came by to speak to her. So did other coaches. Hilde felt vindicated. Perhaps she wasn't as out of touch as people had thought!

Karina and Paul were to fly out Sunday from San Jose, back to Jackson. Saturday night, they ate at a five-star restaurant with Gerda and the twins and Hilde. Sitting nearby at another table were Janey and Burt and Micah.

Although Paul had told her that Janey was in the audience, Karina was surprised to see Micah there. She tried to avoid looking at him, but he was staring in her direction. After the waiter took their orders, Janey went over to congratulate them.

"You're going to the Olympics! I'm so proud of you!" Janey exclaimed, hugging Karina, who laughed and hugged her back.

"So this is your young friend," Gerda said, opening her arms to hug Janey, too. "I'm Gerda. I'm very happy to meet you. I've heard much about you."

"I've heard about you, too. Your little boys are so cute!" Janey exclaimed.

"A handful," Paul chuckled, "but our greatest joy."

"Dad said to say congratulations, too," Janey told Karina. "We're all proud of you both."

"Thanks," Karina said huskily. She started to pick up her water glass and Janey saw what was on her arm.

"You're wearing the bracelet," Janey noted. She grinned.

Karina flushed. "It's very pretty," she faltered.

Janey didn't say anything else. She laughed as she went back to the table with Burt and her father.

"She's wearing it," she told Micah.

His thick eyebrows arched.

"The charm bracelet," she added.

He cleared his throat. "Oh." He felt as tongue-tied as a teenager. It pleased him that she'd even put on the bracelet. Of course, it was pretty.

Sure. That was it. She liked it because it was pretty. He'd done so much damage to their relationship that he couldn't expect more than that.

As THEY FILED out of the restaurant, Karina hugged the boys and Gerda and Paul and waved them off to their hotel room. She was going to her own, upstairs, because they were staying at different venues.

"Need a ride?" Micah asked gruffly as he and Janey and Burt came outside.

"I'm upstairs," she said, flushed, as she averted her eyes.

"So are we," Burt said. "Janey, didn't you want to look at a doll in the shop over here?" he added, indicating a shop window, whose business was still open.

"Yes, I did!"

He and Janey walked away, stranding Karina with Micah.

He stuck his hands deep in the pockets of his dress slacks and looked down at her from his formidable height. "You like it, then."

She glanced up, hesitantly.

"The bracelet."

"Oh. Well, yes," she faltered, lifting her wrist. "I didn't realize it was so expensive."

His big hand caught her wrist and held it gently as he studied the bracelet on her arm. "I noticed that you like white gold," he said.

"Yes, I do."

He drew in a long breath. "I'm sorry," he bit off.

Her pale gray eyes searched his dark ones.

"I watched you and Paul skate in Jackson, the night I put Lindy on a plane and broke the engagement," he continued. "There was an elderly couple sitting near me. They told me about the gold medal. About Paul's wife and the twins." He averted his gaze. "I felt like a fool."

"Lindy didn't help," she said. "I hug Paul all the time. He's the brother I never had. But I don't feel romantic about him. I never did. Gerda's my best friend in the world. I'm godmother to their twin boys."

"I was jealous."

Her eyes widened.

He glared down at her. "He's younger than I am, handsomer than I am, and he skates as beautifully as you do. He's part of a world I know nothing about. I deal in oil wells and cattle, business matters." He averted his eyes. "I felt bad when I realized the truth. I'd told you that you'd never make it into competition without once watching you skate." His eyes lowered to hers again. "You're like poetry when you're on the ice," he said, faint wonder in his tone; that, and something deeper. "Mobile art."

She flushed. "Thanks."

"You and Paul skated in the last Olympics, didn't you?"

She nodded. "We had a new coach. We'd just finally left one who was loud and abusive. We weren't really ready. After that, my parents died and I broke my leg, so I was off the ice for a couple of months. It was a bad time."

He moved a step closer, so that she could feel the heat of his body, the strength of it. "You weren't going to skate again, after you broke your ankle. That's why you came to work for me."

She grimaced. "I was afraid," she confessed, looking up at him. "If it hadn't been for Janey wanting to learn to skate, I don't know if I'd ever have had the courage to try again. Even my doctor said I should give it up."

He drew in a long breath and laughed hollowly. "That's what I was really asking you to do, when I fired you." A faint flush covered his high cheekbones. "I'd had my fill of Lindy's sharp tongue and demanding attitude, not to mention the way she was with my daughter. I thought…" He stopped, unwilling to voice what he'd thought.

She reached out a hand and touched his hard cheek. "You thought…?" She looked up, with her heart in her eyes.

His teeth ground together. She was beautiful, in a way that had nothing to do with surface attraction. She was beautiful inside. "I thought you wouldn't have a chance at real competition. I wanted more kids than just Janey. I…"

Her heart ran wild. "You…?"

His big hand moved to her cheek and rested there, his thumb moving sensually over her soft mouth. "You love Janey. She loves you. The ranch is isolated. If you were just an amateur skater, a hopeful, I thought you might not mind giving it up. Getting married. Having kids." He removed his hand. "That was before I knew how good you were." He smiled sadly. "No wonder your parents sacrificed so much for you, Karina. I've never seen anything like you and Paul on the ice."

She was melting at his feet. He'd wanted to marry her. To have children with her. He'd been planning to ask her to stay, to give up skating for him, for Janey. He didn't realize that she'd have done it, even then. She loved him.

"But it was impossible," he continued, retreating with a bland, public smile. "You have a great career here," he indicated the ice arena in the distance. "I don't doubt that you and Paul will get that gold at the Olympics."

"Thanks," she said, her tone subdued, her eyes losing their excited, happy sparkle.

"I'll make sure that Janey and Burt get to Pyeongchang to cheer you on," he added gently.

Her eyes searched his, and the disappointment in them was blatant.

He frowned. "What is it?" he asked gently.

"You aren't coming, too?" she blurted out.

His sensual lips parted as he stared down at her. His breath caught in his throat. "Do you want me to?" he asked huskily.

"Oh, yes," she whispered.

Ignoring the crowd around them, the snowflakes that began, very lightly, to settle on them, he framed her face in his big warm hands, and bent to her mouth. He kissed her with breathless tenderness, so tenderly that tears rained from her eyes and ran down her cheeks in pale rivulets.

He lifted his head when he tasted them. "What?" he whispered.

"Joy," she whispered back, her eyes glistening, but not with sadness. "It's overflowing."

He smiled slowly. "Oh."

She laughed inanely. Life was sweet again. Life was glorious!

He loved the change in her. He loved knowing that he'd caused it. He smiled slowly. "Okay. I'll go with them. To Pyeongchang."

"Okay."

They laughed, a little self-consciously when they noticed the smiles they were getting from people around them. They moved apart.

"I guess it will be practice from now until next month," he guessed.

She nodded. "Hours every day. It takes a lot."

"You take care of yourself," he said.

She smiled. "You do the same."

He sighed. "I'd take you home with us, if I could," he added.

She smiled. "I'd go, if I could."

His heart lifted. He caught her wrist, the one that held his charm bracelet. "Do you like it?"

"I love it," she said. "But you could have left off the crow."

He chuckled. "I'll think of something to replace it."

"I like crows. Not for lunch."

He grinned. "Me, too."

He brought her wrist to his lips and kissed it softly. "Stay away from bears."

She had to think a minute to remember. She'd chased a bear away from Dietrich. She laughed. "How's Dietrich?"

"Happy to be back in Janey's room at night." He shook his head. "Men can be blind," he confessed. "I certainly was."

"Wear a raincoat when it rains," she returned softly.

He got lost in her pretty gray eyes. "I will."

They just stared at each other while snow swirled

around them. Karina never wanted to leave. She wanted to stand there and look into Micah's dark eyes forever. But of course, she couldn't.

Janey came running back, grinning when she saw her two favorite adults gazing at each other.

"It's a pretty doll," she announced.

They both looked down at her, smiling.

"But I like skates better," she added. "I want to skate like you when I get big," she told Karina, and hugged her.

Karina hugged the little girl back. "You can do whatever you like in life," she said gently. "You just have to believe in yourself."

"You and Paul are going to win. I just know it!"

Karina smiled, but her eyes were sad when they met Micah's. He looked depressed. She wondered why. But before she could ask, the snow came harder.

"We'd better get some sleep," Micah said. "We leave early in the morning. I have to stop off at Phoenix for a conference. Don't worry," he told a crestfallen Janey with a laugh, "you and Burt can take the jet home, I'll have it come back for me."

"Okay, Dad. Thanks!" Janey exclaimed.

"I'll second that," Burt drawled. "I've got some things to do at the ranch."

"How's Billy Joe?" Karina asked.

"Off limits, that's how he is," Micah growled.

Karina looked up at him and suddenly she broke into a beaming smile. He understood that expression without words. He smiled, too.

"Maybe we can take in a movie after the Olympics," he suggested.

She grinned. "Maybe we can."

Janey didn't say a word. But she was smiling from ear to ear. So was Burt.

TRAINING INTENSIFIED IN the weeks that followed. There were meetings and public appearances in between.

Paul was amused at his partner, who spent a lot of time texting Micah during their rest periods.

"I'm amazed that your fingers haven't given out," he teased. "What in the world do the two of you find to talk about?"

"Janey," she said, laughing. "Well, mostly."

"And when it's not just Janey?"

She shook her head. "Just ordinary things. Dietrich. The ranch. Business. How many cities he's seen." She hesitated. "How lonely he is."

"Good."

Her eyebrows arched. "Good?"

"Yes. If he's lonely, that means he's not seeing someone else, yes?"

She pursed her lips. "Actually, yes," she agreed, nodding. "Very astute!"

He made her a mock bow. "Gerda and I did the same," he recalled.

"You and Gerda talked all the time," she chided. "You talked too much to reduce it into a few lines of text on a cell phone. Besides, cell phones weren't as efficient then as they are today."

"All too true. Not so many apps."

She laughed. “Truly.” She drew in a breath. “I’ve never talked about after Pyeongchang,” she began.

“But of course you have,” he corrected. “We are going to do a couple of ice shows to keep us going financially, then I’m going to teach adult education and you’re going to finish your degree.”

“Well, I’ve talked to you and Gerda about it,” she agreed. “But I haven’t said anything to Micah. He seems to think that you and I will go on in competition for years yet, especially if, God forbid, we don’t win at the Olympics.”

“Either way, I have no such plans. Neither do you. Why don’t you tell him?”

“I’m not so confident. I mean, he wants to go out with me when we’re back from Pyeongchang, but he hasn’t really mentioned anything more than that. Well, except for wanting more children than Janey…”

His eyebrows met his hairline. *“C’est vrai?”* he asked, laughing.

She flushed. “Actually, I’d like children, too. A lot of them.”

“But he thinks you want to continue skating.”

She nodded. “I can’t think of a way to tell him how I feel without coming off, well, brassy.”

“Chérie,” he said softly, “it won’t sound ‘brassy’ coming from you.”

“After we get back from Pyeongchang,” she said. “I’ll think of something.”

His eyes twinkled. He imagined that Micah would think of something a lot sooner than that. But he didn’t say so.

JANEY CONTINUED HER LESSONS, and Chad thought she was ready for the next test. He and Micah spoke while Janey practiced on the ice at Catelow.

"She's very good," Chad told her father. "I've very rarely seen such dedication in a child so young."

Micah smiled. "She's inspired. Having a world-famous skater for a friend has kept her focused," he chuckled.

"Yes, Karina is unique. So was her mother," he added. He shook his head. "I never had the honor of watching her skate, but there are videos of her on YouTube. She was amazing. Two-time gold Olympic champion in singles. You know, Karina started out to follow in her footsteps." He made a face. "Then there was the assault in New York at sectionals competition." He shook his head. "That was why she and Paul teamed up. Paul protected her."

"I mistook that relationship for something worse," Micah confided. "I gave her a hard time over it. I should have known better. She isn't the type to help a man commit adultery."

"Not her. Karina's parents were both deeply religious. She doesn't speak of it much, but she's like that, too."

He smiled slowly. "I noticed."

"So. Do you want to take Janey down to Jackson for the test Saturday?"

"Do I ever!" Micah exclaimed. "Karina and Paul will be at their last practice before they fly to Pyeongchang. I wouldn't miss that for the world. Even if I need an excuse to barge in on them."

Chad's eyes twinkled. "Trust me, you wouldn't need an excuse."

Micah's eyebrows arched in a question.

"I text Karina about Janey's progress. Every other text, she asks if I've seen you and how you are."

Micah grinned. "Well!" he said.

PAUL AND KARINA were just finishing their last practice when Micah and Janey walked down to the barrier. Chad was waiting beyond it, on the ice, having preceded them to Jackson.

Karina spotted Janey and her father, and she raced to the barrier to hug Janey. "I'm so happy to see you!" she exclaimed, her eyes going helplessly to Micah's face.

"We're happy to see you, too!" Janey exclaimed. She waved at Paul and blew him a kiss, which he returned. He was headed to another part of the rink, where Gerda and the boys were waiting for him.

"Janey's here for her test. Which she's going to pass," Micah said with easy confidence.

Janey reached up to hug him. "Of course I am! I'll never get to the Olympics if I don't pass all my tests, so I work hard. I want to follow in my inspiration's footsteps," she added with a grin at Karina, who laughed.

"Okay, it's time," Chad called.

"Wish me luck!" Janey said, pulling off her skate guards and handing them to her dad, along with her coat.

"You won't need luck," he replied.

She grinned and skated off toward the small group of skaters also waiting to be tested.

"She watches videos of you and Paul on YouTube all the time," Micah told her. He shrugged. "Me, too."

She flushed. "Gerda filmed us and uploaded it."

"Good for Gerda. It makes up for not being able to see you," he said huskily.

"You could come down here..." she began.

He shook his head. "Not while you're training," he said. "No distractions. I want you to win. Even if winning takes you far away," he added with a resigned sigh.

She looked up, searching his eyes. "It will only take me to Pyeongchang."

"I mean after that," he corrected. He stared at her almost hungrily. The feel of her body so close was making him uncomfortable. He wanted more. Much more. "You'll go on in competition, won't you?"

The way he said it, he sounded as if he expected her to do that. Her self-confidence took a nose dive. "Well, if we lose, I suppose we'll keep trying," she confided. "If we win..." She hesitated. "Well, there would be public appearances and exhibitions, and there's an ice show that a lot of amateur skaters take part in, after they finish competing."

"That would mean a lot of travel," he said.

She sighed. "I'm afraid so. I've lived out of a suitcase most of my life," she added. "Going from one competition to another."

He stuck his hands in his slacks pockets and

looked past her at Janey. "I'm sure that the medals are worth it," he said and smiled.

She'd hoped for something more than that from him. But she forced a smile. Had she been reading too much into those casual text messages? She'd thought they were on the brink of a new relationship, but he was backing away.

She drew in a breath. "Well, we sacrifice quite a lot for the medals," she said finally. "We're obsessed with them, I suppose."

"It's understandable, when you've trained for so many years toward a goal like that."

"Do you still have goals?" she asked hesitantly.

He shrugged. "Not so many as I did," he confessed. "I want to have enough time to spend with Janey, while she's growing up. I've been remiss, there. Business has consumed me. I'm just beginning to realize how much time I've spent on the road, on business."

"Janey knows that you love her."

"She does. But it takes more than an occasional visit to make the point," he replied. He looked down at her with a guarded expression. "You're doing it as much for your parents as for yourself, aren't you?"

She nodded slowly. "They were so proud of me, so happy when Paul and I were chosen to go to Sochi, in the last Olympics. Everything went wrong. I know they were disappointed. They hid it very well..." Her voice trailed away as she recalled bitterly the day the plane had crashed. "Even then, they were looking forward to the next Olympics. They had such faith in Paul and me." She shifted restlessly. "I wanted to justify their faith in me, all the sacrifices they made so I could compete."

"You'll make them proud, at this Olympic Games," he said with certainty. "You'll win. I know you will."

She looked up at him with sad gray eyes. "We'll do our best," she said. "That's all any of us can do."

He started to say something else, but Janey came skating toward them like a streak of light.

"I did it, I passed!" she exclaimed. "I flubbed up on one jump, but I still passed!"

Karina laughed. "The judges are tolerant of little mistakes," she said, hugging the child. "I should know. I made my share when I was your age!"

Micah looked at his watch. "I hate it, but we have to go. I'm on a plane to New York tonight. I know," he said when Janey made a face. "I promised there would be less travel. I'm working on that. I have to make sure I delegate efficiently, so that I can step back and let the company earn its keep. Okay?"

She smiled. "Okay, Daddy."

"That's my girl." He looked back at Karina. "I'd wish you luck. But you won't need it," he said quietly. "This is your year."

"Thanks," she said huskily.

"And we'll be there to cheer for you!" Janey added. "I can't wait!"

"Neither can I," Karina lied. She could wait. It had just dawned on her that, more than winning an Olympic gold, she wanted Micah. It was almost physically painful to smile at him as he followed Janey up into the stands to take off her skates.

She didn't watch them leave. Her heart would have broken right in two, in her chest, to see Micah's broad back walking out of her life. She'd had such hopes. Then, in the space of a few minutes, everything had changed.

Paul skated over to her. He frowned. "Is everything all right?"

She forced a smile. "Certainly! Now where were we…?"

CHAPTER FIFTEEN

So soon, practice was over and Paul and his family and Karina flew to Pyeongchang.

The city was fascinating to all of them. This was one of the few places on earth Karina and Paul had never been. They discovered some of the most delicious food they'd ever eaten, after the excitement of the opening ceremony with its parade of athletes and music.

They mingled with the other skaters and wished each other luck. Many of them had been in competition for years, just like Karina and Paul, and they'd become casual friends. One of the things Karina loved about the international competition was the sense of family, even when competing. They all had the same goal, the same hope, the same sense of history in the making. But only one gold medal got awarded. So there was also the obsession to win, to be the best.

"What if we lose?" Karina asked Paul nervously.

They were waiting their turn to skate. It was the short program. The arena was full. It was noisy. The skaters before Paul and Karina had just received their marks, to wild applause. Their bouquets and stuffed animals were scooped off the ice. Everything was ready for them.

"WE DO THE best we can, and that will be all we need to do," he whispered. "Now smile! And don't worry! Janey's up there somewhere watching. We skate just for her, and for Gerda and the boys and Hilde. Right?"

She took a deep breath and forced a big smile. "Right!"

They skated onto the ice, took their positions, and went into their routine. It was a fast-paced, saucy skit, much different from the one they used in the free skate. But during one of the throws, Karina landed a little awkwardly. She recovered quickly and grimaced as she and Paul came back together.

"Don't sweat it," he whispered. "Smile! Everybody fumbles!"

"Not everybody," she chided.

"Skate!"

She laughed and continued to the end. Then she and Paul waited nervously for their marks, sucking at bottles of water while Hilde sat on tenterhooks with them.

The marks came through. Even considering the fumble, they were very good. Just not good enough for first place.

"Wait," Hilde told them patiently. "Just wait. After the free skate, you will pick up. You'll see."

Karina sighed. "Oh, I hope so!" She looked around the stands. "Are Micah and Janey here?" she asked.

"I haven't seen them," Hilde said.

Karina's spirits fell. Micah had promised. Had something happened at the ranch? Was one of them sick, injured? There was another possibility as well. What if Micah had only been appeasing Janey? What if he'd never meant to come to the Olympics in the first place?

She grew morose. He'd intimated that they were going out together after the Olympics. That had been before they'd discussed what lay ahead for her and Paul. Afterward, he'd been more hesitant. What if he was having second thoughts? What if he was missing Lindy?

"Stop brooding," Paul said softly. "If he isn't here, there's a reason. Don't let it matter. We've come so far. Let's go all the way, yes?"

She looked up at her partner, her friend, and she smiled. "Yes."

THEY ATE OUT, very late, and went to bed. Nobody had called. Karina didn't sleep well, worrying whether Micah and Janey and Burt were even going to come. Twice she picked up her phone to try and text Micah, but twice she put it back down. He had her number. He could call her, after all, if he wanted to. It seemed brassy to chase after him.

She and Paul and Gerda and the boys did some sightseeing and shopping, and Karina tried to put the last competition out of her mind until it was upon them. She was all thumbs as they waited once again for their turn on the ice.

It seemed ages until they were ready to start the free skate. During that time, Karina's eyes had glanced through the audience, hoping, praying, for a glimpse of familiar faces. But she hadn't seen them.

Worse, she'd had no texts from Micah since she and Paul had left the States. That was worrying. But she couldn't afford to dwell on it. She had to concentrate on her skating. She and Paul, her parents, Gerda and the boys, they'd all sacrificed so much to get to the Olympics, to compete here. They had supporters from all over the States, from the skating authority, the fans. They couldn't let themselves, or all those people who believed in them, down. If Micah didn't show up, he didn't show up. There was nothing she could do about that.

In fact, she had a worse worry. Lindy could have been forgiven. She could be back in Micah's life, wearing his ring again. After all, he'd taken her back before. All the things he'd said to Karina could have been forgotten if Lindy had come back and aimed her cap at him again. Men were susceptible to beauty, and Lindy was beautiful.

"You must stop brooding," Paul said just before they went out onto the ice. "You must concentrate. This is it, kid."

She laughed. "Yes. This is it, and I'm not brooding. I'm just nervous. I slipped last time..."

"You won't slip this time," he said with supreme confidence. He grinned. "The world is ours. I've never believed it more than now. We are going to win."

She caught his enthusiasm. She smiled. "Yes. We are!"

THEIR NAMES WERE CALLED. They skated onto the ice, moved into position, waited for the music. The first strains of Rachmaninoff began to play, so beautiful that they were almost painful to hear. They lifted the heart, and the soul.

Karina looked at Paul. He was her anchor, her focus. She looked at nothing else. There was only the music and the program. There was nothing else.

They had little to lose. They were in third place. At least, they were likely to get the bronze. So even a slip wouldn't matter anymore. They threw themselves into the program and skated as they'd never skated before, expecting nothing, hoping for nothing, just living in the moment and wringing the last ounce of joy out of their spectacular performance.

When they finished, the audience was on its feet. People were screaming. Digital cameras were flashing. There was thunderous applause. Karina looked at Paul and tears streamed down her cheeks.

"Perfect," he whispered.

She smiled. "Perfect," she replied.

She scanned the audience, not really looking for anyone as she and Paul took many bows. Her eyes lit on a Stetson. Next to it was a small girl. Micah and Janey! They were here! They'd seen!

"Micah's here!" she whispered excitedly. "So is Janey!"

He chuckled. "I told you."

She just laughed.

They skated off the ice. Hilde hugged them both. "We're going all the way. I know we are!"

"Fingers crossed," Karina whispered.

"No need," Paul said as their scores were flashed on the big screen. "What did I tell you? First place!"

They hugged each other.

"Now if we can just hold the lead…" Karina whispered.

"Have faith," Hilde said, hugging her. "It's our night. I know it is."

AND, SURE ENOUGH, at the end of the programs, after the scores were tallied, Paul and Karina were still in first place. They'd done it. Gold!

The ceremony was exhilarating. The three pairs skated onto the ice, one at a time, receiving their accolades from the audience as they took their places on the podium. Each pair hugged the other pairs, a show of grand sportsmanship that acknowledged the pain and glory of competition.

As the gold medals were looped over Paul and Karina's necks, they looked at each other and then away, as tears rolled down their cheeks to the throbbing applause of the audience. First in the world. Amazing!

THERE WERE INTERVIEWS that seemed to go on forever, when all Karina wanted to do was get to Micah and Janey. But business came first, this time.

She and Paul smiled for the cameras, displayed their medals, congratulated the other skaters on their fine performances, and thanked all the people who'd helped them get to the Olympics. It was a long list.

Finally, there was a little free time. Karina went looking for Micah and Janey, but she didn't see them anywhere.

In desperation, she sent a text to Micah. "Are you and Janey in one of the restaurants here?"

It was almost five minutes before she got a reply. "Sorry, only had time to watch you win. On our way back to the States. Congratulations."

And that was all. She'd hoped that they might have time to sit and talk together, to discuss whatever had started him backing away from her. But he was already gone. She fought tears.

"I am so sorry," Paul said when he saw her face and guessed what was wrong. "They didn't stay?"

"He said they had to get home." She wiped away tears. "Well. Gold! Best in the world!"

He smiled. "Yes!"

"The ice show made me an offer," she began.

He laughed. "They made me one, as well."

"And?"

"I'll do it if you want to," he said.

"I'd like to get an endorsement or two, just to make enough for several semesters of college," Karina replied. "I can teach at the rink while I attend classes."

He sighed. "I was thinking the same thing. I'm tired of living out of a suitcase. I want to teach as an adjunct, teach adults. I can also coach at the rink."

"So, let's do what we want to instead of what people expect us to," he suggested.

She smiled. "Let's."

IN THE END, they did sign on for brief appearances at select events, including a stint at the ice show. They were up front about their participation as well, noting that they didn't plan to skate professionally or even compete at an amateur level again. They had careers in mind now.

That attitude was applauded. After all, they could still skate when they wanted to. And the ice show made them a promise; they could make guest appearances if they liked. Karina did like, to help with her college fees. And Paul liked the idea of some cash to put back for the boys' education.

They laughed and promised to think about it.

Then they went home.

KARINA KEPT IN touch with Janey. She'd dreaded hearing that Micah and Lindy were engaged again, but no such announcement was forthcoming. That was a relief. At least, until Janey mentioned that her dad had brought one of his female personal assistants home with him to see the cattle. Janey liked the woman, and at least she didn't yell. But it was early days yet.

The certainty that Micah was seeing someone else made her miserable. She threw herself into her class work. One of the adjunct professors who taught geology asked her out. Miserable and lonely she agreed.

They had little in common, but they ate hamburgers and fries and discussed rocks until Karina was ready to throw one at the man. He took her home early and didn't even attempt a goodnight kiss. Just as well, because she was measuring her shoe against his head. It had been the most boring date of her entire life.

She mentioned the date to Janey, but not the misery it had been. If Micah could see other people, there was no reason that she couldn't, too!

She hadn't told Janey that she was enrolled in a degree program at the local college. It wouldn't matter to Micah anyway. He and his PA apparently were happy together. At least, maybe the woman would be kind to Janey. That was all that mattered.

SHE'D JUST FINISHED her last class and was headed toward her apartment, walking, when she noticed a very expensive sports car sitting in front of the building. Apparently someone had a rich visitor.

That reminded her of Micah and she sighed, still miserable. She hadn't seen him in months. It had depressed her so much that she only went to skate occasionally now, having even lost her passion for the ice.

She unlocked her door just as she heard a car door open behind her. She turned, and there was Micah, dressed in a very becoming dark blue business suit with a white shirt and silk tie. He was without the familiar Stetson for a change. Her heart started racing, double time, as he approached her.

He frowned, noting the textbooks in her hands. Most of her classes had digital textbooks, but two of them required paper ones because they hadn't been converted digitally.

"What are those?" he asked. "Been to the library?"

"To class," she replied.

"Class?"

"I'm finishing my history degree," she said.

He looked down at her with faint surprise. "I thought you and Paul were working the ice show circuit."

"Only long enough to pay my way through college," she said. "It's expensive."

His face changed. "I thought you were going to keep on the circuit."

"We're tired of living out of suitcases," she said simply. "Paul wants to watch his sons grow up, and not from a distance. He misses Gerda, too, and she can't travel now that the twins are in pre-K."

"I see." He didn't, but it was something to say.

"Do you want coffee?" she offered.

"I'd love a cup. I've been sitting out here for an hour, hoping you'd show up. I went to the rink, but you weren't there."

"Janey told you I was back in Jackson," she guessed as she let him in and went to the kitchen.

"Yes."

She started a pot of coffee. "Is she doing well in school?"

"So far," he said. He perched himself on a stool at the counter and watched her move around the kitchen. In fact, he couldn't seem to take his eyes off her.

"That's good."

He drew in a rough breath. "Okay, what's this

about a geology professor you're seeing?" he shot at her.

Her lips fell open. "Oh, yeah? What's this about your PA coming to spend the night at the ranch?" she shot back.

The light in his eyes that had gone out, came back abruptly. He laughed, deep in his throat.

She flushed.

He slid off the stool and took her by the waist, drawing her lightly to him. "I hoped it might provoke a reaction."

She bit her lower lip. "You didn't stay, in Pyeongchang," she said.

"I wanted to!" he replied. "But you were surrounded by reporters and I didn't want to rob you of your fame. It was hard earned, I know."

"I would have chucked it all, to see you," she said huskily.

"Oh, honey," he ground out. "I've missed you!"

He bent and kissed her hungrily. She reached up, linking her arms around his neck, and she kissed him back as if she was doomed and this was the last time she'd ever see him. Apparently he felt the same way, because he didn't come up for air for a long time.

His mouth slid down her throat as he rocked her in his arms. "You had the whole world. Why are you in college?"

Her arms tightened around his neck. "I want to teach grammar school," she said. "I have one semester to go, to get my Bachelor of Arts degree, then another two or three years to get my teaching certification."

He lifted his head and searched her pale gray eyes. "You don't want to skate anymore? But you've got the whole world!"

"No. I haven't." She reached up and traced his chiseled mouth with her fingers. "It's very lonely, fame."

"It is?"

She nodded. "I missed Janey. I…missed you, too. Janey said you brought the PA home with you…"

He chuckled. "So she'd tell you."

She caught her breath. "What?"

"I thought if you lost her temper, it might mean that you cared, just a little," he confessed. He sighed. "But Janey wrote you and you didn't say a word."

"Until today."

He nodded. He cocked his head and studied her pretty, flushed face. "So you don't want to make a career of ice skating, not even when you have an Olympic gold medal?"

She smiled and shook her head.

He pursed his lips. "You want to teach."

She nodded. "Very much. I love kids."

"Interestingly enough, so do I."

She drew in a long, happy breath, because his dark eyes were saying a lot more than his lips were.

His arms loosened. "I have an idea," he murmured.

There was a whimsical note in his deep voice. She pulled back, uncertain when she saw the wicked look in his eyes.

"Listen," she said, clearing her throat as she anticipated an imminent seduction attempt, "I know I must sound terribly old-fashioned and stuffy, but..."

"Turn off the coffee pot and come with me."

He let her go.

"But it's just finished making," she protested.

"It will keep. Come on."

He took her by the hand and drew her along with him, waiting patiently while she fumbled the key in the lock and turned it before they left.

"Where are we going?" she asked.

He chuckled. "It's a surprise."

He put her into the sports car and climbed in behind the wheel.

"You're being very secretive," she said.

"It's a happy secret."

"Okay, then."

He smiled at the easy way she accepted things. Totally unlike Lindy, who never lost an opportunity to argue. He felt for her hand and held it tightly. She clung to it, sighing.

"What about Paul?" he asked.

"He's not as ambitious as I am," she laughed. "He just wants to teach college as an adjunct. Adult education. It doesn't require a master's degree."

"I see."

"He's going to teach skating on the side, as well."

"You could do that yourself," he said.

"Well, not if I'm teaching school full-time," she began.

"Here we are."

He pulled up in front of the courthouse. She frowned. "Why are we here?"

"You mentioned wanting a job working with children," he said, opening her door for her. "I have just the thing."

She laughed. "Working for the city?" she asked, all at sea.

"Wait."

He led her into the probate judge's office. The clerk greeted them with a smile.

"Can I help you?" he asked.

"Yes," Micah said. "We'd like to apply for a marriage license."

"Very well!"

Karina's eyes began to tear up. She'd never expected that he was anywhere near ready for that sort of commitment. She looked up at him, all eyes.

"It's okay," he said softly, and he smiled.

She drew in a breath. She smiled back.

They got the license. He paid the fee. They went back to the car, and he drove them to a local jewelry store.

"Rings," he said. "They go with the marriage license."

"Oh."

He tugged her into the shop with him and led her to the most expensive wedding sets in the case.

"It's forever," he said quietly. "So get something we can hand down to Janey."

Tears boiled over in her eyes. He drew her close. "Overflowing joy?" he teased.

"Overflowing joy," she agreed.

SHE PICKED OUT a white gold set with sapphires instead of diamonds. She'd never seen anything more beautiful.

"One more stop," he added when they were back in the car. "But first…" He took the engagement ring out of the box and slid it onto her ring finger. He kissed it tenderly. "I haven't asked. But will you?"

"Oh, yes," she whispered with all her heart. "Yes!"

He bent and brushed his mouth gently over hers. "I'm really glad that you said yes."

"Why?" she asked absently.

"Well, I hired a band and a caterer, and I've got a minister scheduled to do the service at the ranch this Sunday…"

She gasped. "But, but…"

"But if you love me, and I'm pretty sure that you do, you'll be as impatient as I am to get married."

She was still staring at him. "How did you…?"

"Janey tells me everything, you know," he said smugly.

Everything. She recalled a few embarrassing texts that she'd sent to Janey, worrying over Micah and if he was well, and if he was pushing himself too hard. "She showed you the texts," she groaned.

"Every single one. I was sure you'd never want to settle down on a deserted Wyoming ranch with a ready-made family. Not when you'd just won an

Olympic gold. I guess I looked as depressed as I felt. Because Janey brought me her phone and left it with me, turned to all your messages."

"The little minx," she laughed.

"She loves you." He brushed back her hair. "In fact," he said solemnly, "so do I. With all my heart. I've made a hell of a lot of mistakes with you. But if you're willing, I'll spend the next fifty years or so trying to make up for them. And we could have a few more kids. You know, to inherit the ranch and the oil business."

"Oh, I'd love that," she said huskily.

He pursed his lips. "Me, too. So now that we're engaged…?"

"No."

He lifted both eyebrows.

She flushed. "No," she repeated. "I want the whole nine yards. The wedding ceremony, the anticipation, the nerves, the wedding night—all of it."

"Why, Miss Carter," he exclaimed. "Did you think I was working up to seduction?"

She cleared her throat. "Well," she began.

He chuckled. "I want you to come up for the weekend. You can have your old room and Burt and Janey will guard your virtue. We can even put Dietrich on guard duty and he can sleep with you, if it makes you feel safer."

She burst out laughing and hugged him, hard. "Oh, I do love you."

"I noticed. Now. Last stop."

He drove them to a couture shop, the only one in

town. "She has a wedding gown in the window," he said. "I've been staring at it every time I came down here with Janey. I've pictured you wearing it."

"But it might not be my size, and if we're getting married on Sunday...?"

"I checked," he whispered. "It is your size. Let's go inside. I'll prove it to you."

He walked her into the shop. The designer's eyebrows arched and she chuckled as she saw Karina. "So, Mr. Torrance, she said yes?"

"She said yes," he replied. "And I didn't even have to make her feel guilty by telling her I commissioned the wedding gown in her size."

"You did?" Karina exclaimed. "Oh, my goodness!"

"I feel that I know you already," the shop owner laughed. "He talks about you all the time."

Karina looked at him with her heart in her eyes. "I do the same thing," she confessed.

"Here, come and try it on, let's just be certain that it fits. But if it needs adjustments, I can have it ready by tomorrow," she promised.

KARINA TRIED IT ON. It fit perfectly, but she was superstitious enough not to let Micah see her in it.

The proprietor wrapped it up neatly in a hanging bag and gave it to her, after returning Micah's credit card to him. "I wish you the happiness I've had for the past thirty years with my own husband," she told Karina and hugged her.

"Thank you. The dress is beautiful."

"I'll want a photo for my window," she teased.

"I'll make sure you have one," Micah assured her.

HOURS AND A few passionate kisses later, Karina snuggled close to Micah in the armchair they were sharing and sighed. "I wish I could go home with you," she said. "But I have a nine o'clock class in the morning and a lab I have to study for."

"The weekend will come soon enough," he mused. His tie was off, his shirt half unbuttoned. Her blouse was undone, her bra unfastened. He bent and put his lips tenderly to her soft breast. "We seem to be very compatible."

She laughed. "We do." She touched his mouth. "I must seem ridiculously old-fashioned."

He kissed the words away. "I want to do it right, as well. For Janey's sake. I haven't set her a good example with Lindy." He shook his head. "That was a near fatal mistake. I still can't believe I was so blind."

"Sometimes we don't see what's right in front of us," she said soothingly. "You love Janey. She knows it."

"She'll like having brothers and sisters," he said softly, smiling at her. "But we can wait until you're through school, if you want to."

"Pregnant women can still study," she pointed out. "In fact, I could do distance education for a good part of my master's work. I, uh, asked about it already."

He chuckled. "Thinking ahead, were you?"

"Hoping," she confided. She sighed as she studied

him. "I wanted you more than I ever wanted skating. That's a lot."

"Same here." He kissed her hungrily, one last time and then stood up, taking her with him. "It's been a long dry spell and I don't trust myself too far right now. So I'm going home. I'll come down to get you Friday. What's your class schedule next week?"

One of my professors is having surgery, so I only have one class, next Thursday morning."

"Nice," he remarked with twinkling eyes. "We can fly down to Nassau for three days and have a brief honeymoon."

"But, Janey..."

"She's going to stay with Gerda and Paul," he remarked. "And, yes, I asked."

"Well! And Gerda never said a word!"

"I swore them both to secrecy," he chuckled. "She'll be in great hands."

"Yes, she will. Nassau?"

"Yes. Have you been there?"

"Actually, it's one of only a handful of places I haven't been," she confessed. "There were pirates in the Bahamas. History," she emphasized.

"I can wear an eye patch and get a parrot for my shoulder, if you like," he teased.

She pressed close. "That's very sweet."

"Yes, it is," he chuckled, hugging her close. "I'll see myself out. Study hard."

"I will. Drive carefully."

"I always do." He lifted her engagement ring to

his lips and kissed it softly. “A few more days. And then, fireworks!”

Her gray eyes twinkled. “Promise?”

“Cross my heart.”

She grinned.

CHAPTER SIXTEEN

IT WAS THE sort of wedding Karina had dreamed of having. The altar in the living room was decorated with white roses and lilies, and all the cowboys and most of Micah's business associates came down for the wedding.

Burt led Karina down the aisle to the strains of the "Wedding March," played by a small band hired for the occasion. Karina said her vows with tears in her eyes behind the lacy veil that obscured her from Micah's eyes. If only her parents could have been there, to see this. But she felt that they knew, somehow, that she'd landed well in life.

Gerda was the matron of honor and Janey was the maid of honor, beaming as she watched from the sidelines. She was wiping away tears as well, when Micah spoke his vows and bent to lift the veil and kiss his new wife.

Karina thought that she'd never known such happiness in her life. Not even winning the gold medal at the Olympics was so poignant.

Paul and Gerda hugged them both. The twins were headed to the kitchen with Janey, where Burt was just putting finger foods on trays to be carried out to the tables where the wedding cake waited to be cut.

A photographer hired for the occasion took snapshots of them feeding each other cake. He did candid shots of the guests as well.

"The jet's flying in this afternoon at three," Micah told her. "We're headed for the Bahamas. Janey's going back with Paul and Gerda and the boys."

"What about Burt?" she asked.

"He gets several days of full control of the television set and no people to complicate his life," he told her. "He's ecstatic."

She grinned. "I don't know what we'd do without him."

"Neither do I."

"Do you dance, Mrs. Torrance?" he asked, using her married name for the first time as the band tuned up in the rec room, which had been cleared as a dance floor.

"Not very well," she confessed. "I mean, I can do ballet, but it's not the same thing."

"I'll teach you," he whispered softly, and his eyes were saying that he had in mind teaching her more than just dancing.

She flushed prettily. "Okay," she said.

He chuckled as he led her onto the dance floor.

TIME FLEW. THEY were on the jet and headed for Nassau so quickly that the whole wedding seemed like a dream.

"Happy?" Micah asked.

"So happy," she replied.

They were both wearing casual clothes, comfortable for the trip. They hadn't packed much because, as he remarked, they could buy anything they needed once they were at the hotel.

"Where are we staying?" she asked.

"The British Colonial Hilton," he replied. "It's right on the beach. You can watch little tugboats turn the big cruise ships as they head out of the harbor to the open sea," he chuckled.

"It's right downtown?"

"Yes, on the site of old Fort Nassau."

"History!" she exclaimed.

"Yes, and there might even be ghosts!"

"You'll have to protect me from them," she said with twinkling eyes.

"Honey, I'll protect you from the whole world," he said softly. "I'm the luckiest man alive right now."

"I'm definitely the luckiest woman."

They held hands almost the whole way.

IT WAS MADDENING to get checked in. Apparently half the world had decided to check in at the same time. But eventually they were taken up to their room, overlooking the bay.

"What a view!" she exclaimed at the window.

He tipped the bellboy and closed and locked the door behind him. "The view inside is even better," he mused.

She turned as he pulled her into his arms.

"I don't know very much," she blurted out. "Is it all right?"

He framed her face in his big warm hands. "Yes, it's all right. And I'll treat you like fragile porcelain. I promise. Don't be afraid."

"Will it hurt?" she asked, a little apprehensively.

"Even if it does, you won't mind."

She cocked her head, not understanding.

He just smiled as he bent to her mouth. "You'll see..."

SHE HADN'T DREAMED that her body was so capable of pleasure. His hands were slow and tender as they worked on her nudity, learning her, exploring her, in a heated passion without words.

She arched up to his mouth, shivering as he took her from one plateau to the next, learning all the ways that love was expressed with kisses and caresses and building hunger.

She felt his lips on the soft inside of her thighs and was astounded by the sensations they provoked. She moaned and began to shiver with increasing hunger. He laughed softly, deep in his throat, at her exquisite responses. It had never been like this with a woman. To her, it was all new and exciting and mysterious. Even his first wife had been experienced; Lindy had lived with several men before Micah became engaged to her. But Karina was innocent. It excited him beyond bearing to know that.

His mouth slid up her soft thigh to her belly and pressed there, hard. He thought of babies. He'd loved

Janey so much when she was born. He couldn't help wanting another child, several more children.

He nuzzled her firm, hard-tipped breast and his hands slid under her hips as he moved slowly down against her.

He touched her in a way he never had before. She jerked a little, but she didn't resist. Yes, she was ready. More than ready. It shouldn't be too difficult.

Her nails bit into his upper arms. He felt her stiffen.

"It's all right," he whispered in her ear. "Don't be afraid. I won't hurt you."

As he spoke, his hips moved, very gently. He felt the ease of his passage, despite the tightness that he'd anticipated. His breath sighed out at her lips as he felt her body resist for just a few seconds before it relaxed and allowed him to penetrate it.

"God!" he exclaimed, shuddering at the poignancy of the moment. He lifted his head and looked into her wide, shocked eyes. He was fighting to breathe. His heartbeat was shaking him. But he held back the avalanche of need, giving her time to adjust to him, to her first intimacy. "Okay?" he whispered huskily.

Her nails stopped biting into him. She swallowed. "O...okay," she whispered, dry mouthed.

His nose nuzzled hers. "First times are hard. It gets easier."

"It does? Oh!" She gasped and shivered when he moved suddenly, spreading her thighs even more as he shifted up against her and went deeper into the sweet, dark heart of her.

"Better?" he whispered, smiling tenderly.

"Yes...yes...better!" she panted. Her eyes widened as the sensations began to build on each other, until she was climbing and climbing and climbing, so high that the fall would surely kill her!

He framed her face in his hands as he moved, his body fencing with hers in a rhythm that very quickly sent her right off the edge of the world.

She cried out helplessly, a sweet, keening cry of ecstasy that made him wild with pride. Her first time, and he could feel her climaxing under him. "Micah!" she sobbed as he moved deeper, faster. She couldn't bear it. What she'd thought was fulfillment was only a step up a long path to unbelievable delight. Her eyes rolled back in her head and she arched and shuddered rhythmically, sobbing as she felt a kind of pleasure she'd never dreamed could exist.

He gave in to his own need as he satisfied hers. His hands dug into the mattress at either side of her head as he went into her roughly, quickly, bringing the pleasure crashing down on him like a wall. He groaned out loud and whispered her name, over and over again, as he endured the most delicious ecstasy he'd ever known in his life.

They lay together in the aftermath, drenched with sweat, shivering together.

"Oh, gosh," she whispered, shaken.

His mouth moved lazily up her chin to cover her soft, swollen lips. "Well?" he murmured dryly.

"Well, what?"

"Did it hurt?" he asked amusedly.

He lifted his head and looked down into her wide, fascinated eyes.

She drew in a long shivery breath. Her whole body felt as if it had exploded and then suddenly relaxed into lethargy. "No," she whispered. "Oh, no, it didn't hurt!"

He grinned. He kissed her tenderly. "I forgot to ask."

She linked her arms around his neck. "What did you forget?" she murmured, smiling against his warm mouth.

"To ask if you wanted me to use something."

She cocked her head and searched his dark eyes. "We talked about that before. I'd love to have children with you."

He sighed. "Me, too." He smoothed his hands under her relaxed body, feeling the delicious softness of her skin. "I wasn't sure you'd want them this soon."

"We've already agreed that pregnant women can go to college," she teased.

"Well, yes."

"And that I can do distance education for my master's work," she added.

He ran his fingers through her damp hair. "I wouldn't have asked you to give up skating," he said solemnly.

"I know that. But I don't want to be away from you and Janey most of the year," she replied. "And when the first baby comes, I want to be home all the time."

He smiled. "We both will," he promised. "I'll make sure I put good people in key positions, so that I can delegate authority when I need to. No more letting the business run my life. I'll run the business instead."

She smiled back. "Why did you draw back after we came home from San Jose?" she asked curiously.

He traced her eyebrows. He looked very somber. "You have a rare talent," he began. "I didn't want you to be distracted while you were spreading your wings on the ice, seeing what you and Paul could do." He grimaced. "Too, I wasn't sure you could give it all up to live on a ranch and have babies. It isn't a glamorous life I'm offering you."

"I've had glamour," she replied. "And fame. And fortune. Know what?" she added. "They're very lonely. Paul had Gerda, always cheering him on, looking after him, comforting him. I had nobody."

"And now you have a ready-made family," he said.

She laughed. "I love my ready-made family," she assured him. "All of it. Even Dietrich. I can't think of anything that will make me happier than just being with you for the rest of my life."

"I can second that." He brushed his mouth over hers and his hips shifted.

She caught her breath. He was capable again. Something stirred in her, a new hunger, a new need.

He raised both eyebrows.

She laughed softly and arched her hips.

He laughed, too, as his mouth covered hers once more.

THEY ARRIVED BACK at the ranch, tired and content, the day before Karina's next class in Jackson.

Janey hugged her and hugged her, aglow with all the presents Karina had brought for her. There were colorful skirts and blouses and sashes, with lace and embroidery. There were coin purses and a big woven bag with a hat that matched in shades of purple. There were sea shells and T-shirts and even a pearl necklace.

"I'm rich!" Janey exclaimed, going from present to present like a bee searching for pollen. "Thank you, Karina!"

Karina hugged her warmly. "You're very welcome. I'd have brought you skating stuff, but it's rather the wrong climate for it in Nassau," she teased.

"Oh, I'm happy with what I've got! This hat is so cool!" She tried it on and grinned up at Karina and her dad.

"It suits you," Micah told her warmly.

"Welcome home!" Burt called as he came in the back door. "Everybody hungry?"

"We had peanuts on the plane," Micah sighed.

"He had four bags of them," Karina added, indicating Micah.

"They wouldn't have filled up a hollow tooth," Micah sighed. "We need to do something about food service on the company jet."

"Take it up with the board of directors next meeting," Burt suggested. "I've got a whip and a chair around here somewhere…"

Micah chuckled. "Next time, we'll pack in some sandwiches," he said, compromising.

"I'll rustle up some grub," Burt said. "How was Nassau?"

"Fascinating," Karina replied. "I loved every minute we spent there. We saw forts and one night, he took me to the casino on Paradise Island. I lost five dollars," she added on a sigh. "I guess I'm not cut out to be a gambler."

"Good thing," Burt replied. He hesitated. "I, uh, have a confession to make," he said worriedly.

Micah's eyebrows rose. "What sort?"

Janey grinned. "Tell them!"

"Well, you know that really great photo we got of Paul and Karina on the podium, accepting their gold medals at the Olympics?"

"Yes," Micah replied. "We used the telephoto lens on that new camera Janey talked me into."

"Well, I sort of sent a copy of it to someone."

Karina and Micah both looked at him while Janey laughed.

"I thought Lindy should know that somebody besides her could win a medal." His wicked smile was contagious.

They burst out laughing.

"What did she say?" Karina asked.

"I don't know. She blocked my number," Burt chuckled.

"Well, that made my day," Karina confessed.

"Mine, too," Janey said.

Micah shook his head. "All those pointed comments about how neither of you would ever be able to skate in a competition." He smiled at Karina and

Janey. "I learned something from the experience as well."

"What?" Karina asked softly.

He leaned toward her. "That crow tastes terrible," he said in a stage whisper.

She laughed along with the others and hugged him warmly.

"I have to study when we get through with supper," Karina said as she pulled back. She grimaced. "I've got a class first thing in the morning."

"I'll have the jet take you to Jackson and bring you home," Micah said with a smile.

"Don't you have to be at some meeting in Denver?" she asked suddenly.

He waved a hand. "They can have a meeting without me for once. I'm going to Jackson with you."

"You are?" she asked, and her face brightened.

He chuckled. "I don't want to let you out of my sight. Not just yet."

"In that case, I won't mind going."

"Can't I come, too?" Janey asked plaintively.

He pursed his lips and looked at Karina. "What do you think?"

"I think she can come, too," Karina laughed. "You can take her to the rink while I have my class, and then we can have lunch somewhere."

"Do you like sushi?" Micah asked.

"I love it!" she exclaimed. "We had it in Kyoto, when we went there a few years ago."

"It's one of my favorites, too," Micah said. "I had grilled eel in Osaka."

"So did I," she laughed. "It was delicious, wasn't it?"

"We are not eating raw fish in this house," Burt announced with mock hauteur.

"Well, you won't," Micah agreed.

"Good enough," Burt added as he finished making sandwiches. "I catch fish with my bait. I don't eat it."

"Spoilsport," Micah chuckled. "And what's the difference between raw fish and raw steak?"

"I like raw steak. That's the difference," Burt chuckled.

Karina sat down with the others at the table and smiled while Micah said grace before they dug into their sandwiches. She was part of a family. She only wished her parents could see her now.

Fame and fortune were lovely goals, but they were lonely goals. No amount of them was enough to compare with a loving family and the comfort of a home, a real home.

She smiled and picked up her sandwich. The future looked very bright indeed.

SHE FINISHED COLLEGE, got her Bachelor of Arts degree and enrolled in distance education to begin her master's work.

That was just before she started losing her breakfast. Micah found her in the bathroom, assuming the position in front of the toilet, and he let out a whoop that brought the other occupants of the house running.

"What is it?" Janey asked worriedly. "Karina, are you okay?"

"I'll say, she's okay," Micah chuckled, wetting a washcloth for her. "She's pregnant!"

"We don't know that…yet…" She had to pause for another round of nausea.

"You're never sick," he pointed out, handing her the cloth.

"A baby," Janey exclaimed. "Wow! I'll have a brother or a sister! I won't be an only child anymore!"

Micah hugged her warmly. "Whichever it is, you'll be Big Sister," he told her. He smiled affectionately. "Love is better when you spread it around."

"Yes, it is," Karina laughed weakly. She struggled to her feet, with Micah's help.

"Can I get you something to settle your stomach?" Burt asked worriedly.

"Some ginger ale, if we have any."

She stopped and only then noticed that there were three other people in the bathroom besides herself. "This looks very strange," she pointed out as she went to wash her face.

"No, it doesn't," Micah said with a grin. "It's a big bathroom."

She laughed. "Okay. I'll give you that."

She rinsed out her mouth. Micah swung her up in his arms. "Bed for you," he said softly.

"I'm not an invalid," she protested.

He kissed her nose. "Shut up. You're an invalid until your stomach settles down. Deal?"

She managed a wan smile. "Deal." She snuggled close as he walked down the hall and placed her gently on their big king-sized bed.

"How about some soda crackers?" Janey asked, hovering. "They always help me when I'm sick."

"That would be lovely, sweetheart," she said, smiling at the little girl.

"Back in a jiffy!" Janey laughed, and went to fetch them.

"She's over the moon," Micah remarked. "So am I." He shook his head. "You know, it's almost a year since you walked in the door and I jumped at you with both feet."

"You were very disagreeable," she pointed out.

"I was stunned. You were like a ray of sunshine, the first time I saw you. I was engaged and unhappy, and all at once I felt as if I'd walked into fire." He shook his head. "I knew you were going to be trouble."

"I knew you were, too," she returned. She smiled. "But nice trouble."

"Thanks." He bent and brushed his mouth over her eyes. "Rest now. I'll go yell at a few people on the phone and be back before you know it. You have to see the doctor tomorrow. I'll have Grace make you an appointment."

Grace was his PA, who turned out to be not only very nice, but also very married, with three little girls. He'd confessed that, sheepishly, after they were married.

"I can make my own appointment, thank you," she teased.

"You're not still jealous?" he chided.

She laughed. "Of course I'm jealous. You're the

most gorgeous man in Wyoming and I'm married to you. No other woman gets close. Ever."

He brushed back her hair. "I promise."

She reached up and touched his mouth. "It's going to be a boy or a girl," she said.

"No!" he exclaimed.

She flushed. "Well, I mean we don't get a choice. But I'd like a boy, to go with our girl."

"We'll take what we get and be happy," he returned.

She beamed. "Okay."

He chuckled. "Tummy settling down?"

She nodded.

Burt came in with ginger ale and ice in a glass, followed by Janey with a small bowl of saltines.

"Thanks," she told them.

"No sweat," Burt replied. "It's the least we can do, seeing as how you're providing us with a whole new dependent at tax time," he added, tongue-in-cheek.

She burst out laughing. "Oh, that's cold, Burt. Really cold!"

"I'll do penance," he promised. "How about a nice hot bowl of soup to go with those crackers? Chicken soup fixes most everything."

"Not sure if it works on morning sickness," Karina replied.

"Let's find out," Micah suggested.

They all beamed at her. She laughed and sipped her ginger ale. "Okay," she replied.

Micah sat down beside her and held her hand.

Janey perched on the edge of the bed and smoothed her hair.

"You two are spoiling me rotten," Karina remarked. "And Burt's helping."

"We're not spoiling you," Micah said easily. "We're pampering our Wyoming Legend."

"Oh, is that it?" she chuckled.

"That's exactly it. And we all live happily ever after," he added with a grin.

Which they did. All of them.

* * * * *

After a disastrous breakup, Keena Whitman leaves town to pursue her dreams. She returns seven years later, successful and as irresistible to her ex, Nicholas Coleman, as ever. As sparks fly, true love is in the air...

Read on for a sneak preview of A Waiting Game, *a classic romantic novella in* Any Man of Mine, *coming in February 2019 from* New York Times *bestselling author Diana Palmer*

CHAPTER ONE

KEENA WHITMAN'S DAY had gone backward from the moment she got out of bed. Two of her best sketches had been destroyed when Faye turned a cup of hot coffee over on them. Naturally, the sample-room staff had been livid when they had to wait for Keena to redo the sketches so that they could make up the rush samples for the salesman. Like all salesmen, he was impatient and made no attempt to disguise his annoyance. She'd missed her lunch, the seamstresses had missed theirs and to top it all off, she'd gotten the specifications wrong on a whole cut of blouses, and they had had to be redone with the buyers incensed at the holdup. By the time Keena was through for the day and back home in her Manhattan apartment, she was smoldering.

She kicked off her high-heeled shoes and threw herself down on the long, plush, blue-velvet couch with a heavy sigh. How long ago it seemed that she'd worked at textile design and dreamed of someday working for a big fashion design house. And now she had her own house and was one of the most famous designers of casual wear in the country. But the pleasure she should have been feeling simply wasn't there. Something was missing from her life. Something vital. But she didn't even know what. Perhaps it was just the winter weather making her morose. She longed for the freedom and warmth of spring to get her blood flowing again.

She lay on her back and stared at the ceiling. She was slender with short black hair and eyes as green as spring leaves. Her complexion was peachy, her mouth as perfect as a bow. At twenty-seven, she retained the fresh look of innocence, despite her sophistication. At least Nicholas said she did.

Nicholas. She closed her eyes and smiled. How long ago had it been when Nicholas Coleman had offered her the chance to work as an assistant designer in his textile empire? It was well over six years ago.

She'd been utterly green at twenty-one. Fresh out of fashion design school in Atlanta and afraid of the big, dark man behind the desk of Coleman Textiles in his Atlanta skyscraper.

It had taken her a week to get up enough nerve to approach him, but she'd been told that he was receptive to new talent, and that he was a sucker for stray animals and stray people.

Even now she could remember how frightened she'd been, looking across the massive desk at that broad leonine face that looked as if it had never smiled.

"Well, show me what you can do, honey," he'd dared with a cynical smile. "I don't bite."

She'd spread her drawings out on the glass surface of the cluttered desk, her hands trembling, and watched for his reaction. But nothing had shown in his dark face, nor in his dark brown, deep-set eyes. He'd nodded, but that was all. Then he'd leaned back in his swivel chair and stared at her.

"Training?" he'd shot at her.

"The—the fashion design school, here in town," she'd managed to get out. "I…that is, I worked on the third shift at the cotton mill to pay my way through. My father works for a textile mill back home—"

"Where is back home?" he interrupted.

"Ashton," she replied.

He nodded, and waited for her to continue, giving every impression of being interested in her muddled speech.

"So I know a little about it," she murmured. "And I've always wanted to design things. Oh, Mr. Coleman, I know I can do it if someone will just give me the chance. I know I can." Her eyes lit up and she put her whole heart and all her youthful enthusiasm into her words. "I realize there's a lot of competition for design jobs, but if you'll give me a chance, I promise I won't let you down. I'll design the sharpest clothes for the lowest cost you've ever seen. I'll work weekends and holidays, I'll—"

"One month," he said, cutting into her sentence.

He leaned forward and pinned her with his level gaze. "That's how much time you've got to prove to me that you can stand the pace." He threw out a salary that staggered her, and then dismissed her with a curt gesture and went back to his paperwork.

He'd been married then, but his wife of ten years had died shortly thereafter of a massive heart attack. Rumors had flown all over the main plant, where Keena worked, but she ignored them. She didn't believe that an argument had provoked the heart attack, and she told one of the women so. Mr. Coleman, she assured her tersely, wasn't that kind of man. He had too much compassion and, besides, why would he keep a picture of his wife on his desk if he didn't love her?

Somehow the innocent little speech had gotten back to him and the next week, he'd sought her out in the canteen on the pretense of asking how everything was going.

"I'm well on my way to making you fabulously wealthy," she assured him with an impish grin as she held her plastic coffee cup between her hands.

"I'm *already* fabulously wealthy," he replied.

She sighed. "In that case, you're in a lot of trouble."

He'd smiled at that—the first time she'd seen him smile since his wife's death. The late Mrs. Coleman had been a beauty—blonde and delicate, a perfect foil for his size and darkness. Since her death he'd been strangely lost, and his temper had become legendary. He spent more time at the plant than at his office, and threw himself into the accumulation of other plants to complement it. His holdings and his wealth had mushroomed in the months between, and the pressure was telling on him. His hair was growing silver at the temples; his eyes were boasting dark shadows. His tireless business dealings were becoming the talk of the plant. Mr. Coleman was out to become a billionaire, some said. Mr. Coleman was after a business rival, others said. Mr. Coleman was going to make his empire the biggest in America, if he lived, others commented. But only Keena seemed to see through the relentless businessman to the lonely, grief-stricken man underneath. The other employees might think Mr. Coleman was indestructible, but Keena was certain that he wasn't. She would run into him occasionally in the elevator or in the cafeteria. She recalled one time in particular when his eyes had seemed to seek her out. With his coffee in hand, he strolled over to her table and sat down beside Keena and her friend Margaret as naturally and easily as if the three met for a coffee break every day.

"How's it going, Miss Future Famous Designer?" he asked Keena with an amused glance.

Keena had laughed and given him a flip reply, something about an interview in *Women's Wear Daily*. Hadn't he seen it? Margaret finished her coffee and excused herself quickly.

"Did I say something I shouldn't have?" Nicholas asked, staring after the young woman.

"The company brass makes most employees want to run for cover," Keena explained in a dry tone.

"You aren't running," he observed.

"Ah, yes," she agreed. "But then, I've never had much sense."

He chuckled into his coffee, taking a long sip of it. "The patternmakers sing your praises, by the way.

They told me your specs were the first they'd had in five years that were written in English."

"High praise, indeed, and I hope I'm going to get a ten thousand dollar a year raise as an inducement to keep them in a good mood?" She grinned.

"Cheeky, aren't you?" he asked with narrowed eyes.

"It's my dimple," she replied in all seriousness.

He shook his head in mock despair. "Incorrigible."

She looked at him—so businesslike and somber in the vested gray business suit that strained against his massive, muscular frame—and dropped her eyes almost at once.

After that day he'd made a point of having coffee with her once in a while. Infrequently, he'd invited her out for a meal, and they'd talk a great deal. She'd asked him once if he had any family, and he'd replied stiffly that what there was of it wasn't to his liking.

"It still hurts, doesn't it?" she had asked quietly then.

He stared at her, his face closed up. "I beg your pardon?"

She met his eyes with compassion and utter fearlessness. "You miss her."

He seemed to see right into her mind in the long minute that followed, and the hauteur slowly drained out of him.

"I miss her like hell," he admitted finally and with a faint, fleeting smile. "She was the loveliest creature I ever knew, inside and out. Generous to a fault, shy." He sighed heavily, his face darkening. "Some women can tear a man down with every word. But Misty made me feel every inch a man every time she looked at me. We married because it was necessary to keep the businesses in the family. But we grew to love each other desperately." He glanced at her. "Yes, I miss her."

She smiled at him. "You were lucky."

He scowled. "Lucky?"

"Some people go through life without ever touching or being touched emotionally by another human being. To love and be loved in return must be magic," she finished gently. "And you had that for ten years."

His eyes had searched hers before they fell. "I never thought of it that way," he said simply.

"Shouldn't you?" Her voice had been gentle and low. And while he was still thinking about it, she changed the subject completely, telling him about some ridiculous mix-up that had occurred in the cutting room that afternoon.

It was sad that he and Misty hadn't been able to have children, she had always thought. They would have made him less lonely. But she could see that he seemed to find solace in her company, and they had worlds of things in common, from a mutual love of ballet and the theater to classical music and art. She found in him a mentor as much as a friend, a tutor and a protector. Nicholas never made a pass at her himself and was fiercely protective. He scrutinized the few suitors she had over the years and gave her his advice, welcome or not, on the men she went out with. If she had to work late, he escorted her home himself. And when he felt that she was ready, he'd found her a job as an apprentice designer in one of New York's grandest fashion houses. He'd encouraged her, pushed her, bullied and chided her, until she climbed straight to the top, which was quite a climb for the only child of a poor, widowed textile worker in the small Georgia town of Ashton. She didn't like to remember her childhood at all. In fact, Nicholas was the only person she'd ever told about it. But then, Nicholas was like no one else. In a real sense he was the only true friend she'd ever had since she left Ashton. And shortly after she'd come to New York, she was relieved to know that Nicholas maintained an apartment in the city.

The phone rang, and she barely heard it, so deeply was she immersed in memory. She was used to Mandy getting the phone, making coffee, serving meals, but this was Mandy's day off, and it took her five rings to realize it. She dragged herself to the end table and picked up the receiver.

"Hello?" she murmured, stifling a yawn.

"That kind of day, was it?" came a deeply amused voice from the other end of the line. "Get on something pretty and I'll treat you to dinner at The Palace."

She felt her spirits revive. "Oh, Nicholas, we haven't gone there in months! And they make the most marvelous chocolate mousse."

"Can you make it in half an hour?" he asked impatiently. "I've got to catch the eleven o'clock plane to Paris, and we won't have much time."

"Has anyone ever told you that people who don't slow down get ulcers?" she asked, exasperated.

"They would have to catch up with me first," he told her. "Half an hour."

She stared at the dead receiver. "Nicholas is an enigma," she muttered as she slipped into a long green velvet gown with a deep V neckline and a side slit. He was every inch the high-powered executive, and he had millions, but he wouldn't delegate any responsibilities. If a deal had to be closed, he'd close it. If there was a labor relations problem at one of his plants, he'd negotiate it. If there was an innovative process being presented, he'd go to see it. He pushed himself relentlessly even now, a habit left over from those first horrible weeks after Misty's death. He wouldn't slow down; he wouldn't take time off. It was as if he was afraid to stop, because if he did, he'd have to think and that wouldn't please him. He had too much that he wanted to forget.

Keena was dressed and waiting when the doorbell rang. She opened the door and mentally caught her breath at the sight of Nicholas in evening clothes, as she always did. With his dark hair and eyes, his bronzed complexion in that leonine face, his towering, wrestler's physique, he was the stuff of which feminine dreams were made. And perhaps if Keena hadn't been so wary of men, so unforgetting of that humiliating adolescent romance and the humiliating incident that had followed it, she might have fallen head over heels in love with him. But she'd seen Nicholas in action, and she knew the effect his dark charm had on women. She'd seen his occasional conquest swoon, fall, succumb and be heartlessly discarded too many times to risk joining that queue herself. Nicholas had found safety in numbers since Misty's death, and he was apparently risking no emotional involvement by confining himself to one woman. Keena preferred the position of being just Nicholas's friend and confidante. It was much safer than being added to the notches on his bedpost.

His own eyes were busy, sliding up and down her body with his usual careless appraisal.

"Delightful," he said with a cool smile. "Shall we go?"

"I'm starved," she told him as they got into the empty elevator and Nicholas pressed the main floor button. "I feel as if I haven't eaten for days."

"You look it, too," he growled, eyeing her from his lounging position against the rail. "Why the hell don't you give up that diet and put some meat on your bones?"

"Look who's talking!" She glared. "It would take a forklift to get you up a hill!"

He moved toward her with a dark look in his eyes under that jutting brow. "Think it's fat, do you?" he taunted. He caught her hands and dragged them to his shoulders. "Feel. Show me any flab."

It was like discovering fine wine where she had expected to taste water. She'd never noticed just how broad Nicholas's chest and shoulders really were, or how the scent of tobacco and expensive cologne clung to him. She'd never noticed how chiseled his mouth was, or how exciting it could be to look into his dark eyes at close range. It had been safer not to notice. But her hands touched him through the smooth fabric of his evening jacket and lingered there when she felt the hard muscles under it.

"Well?" he asked, a strange huskiness in his deep voice as he looked down at her.

"You… I never realized how strong you were," she stammered. She looked up into his eyes and time seemed to stand still for a space of seconds while they looked at each other, discovering facial features, textures, expressions, in an unfamiliar intimacy, in the quiet confines of the elevator.

It took several seconds for them to realize that the elevator had stopped and the door had opened. Self-conscious and a little clumsy, Keena managed to get out a little ahead of him and lead the way to the front of the building where his white Rolls-Royce waited with Jimson at the wheel, staring straight ahead stoically.

"Doesn't Jimson ever get a day off?" she asked Nicholas when they were inside the car with the glass partition up, giving them total privacy.

"Not lately. I've been working twenty-five-hour days," he replied.

"I'll never get used to this car," she sighed, leaning her dark head contentedly back against the leather as he was doing.

"What's wrong with it?" he asked curtly.

"Nothing! It's just that few people ever get to ride around in a Rolls—white, no less." She laughed.

He half turned in the seat, one big arm over the back of it, his eyes gleaming, though his smile had not completely disappeared. "And what's wrong with that?" he asked with deliberate slowness.

She braved his glittering eyes. Why did he look so suddenly predatory to her? So dark and menacing? "Nothing—except that I feel as if I were on display every time I ride in it. That's all."

"You should be on display, Keena." Something in the way he fairly growled her name sent a warm, unfamiliar tingle up her spine.

"Because I'm rich and famous now, you mean, and everyone back in Ashton would hardly recognize *this* Keena Whitman?" She laughed shortly, her words underscored with a note of self-derision.

Her answer hadn't pleased him. It was in the hard lines of his face, the narrowing of his eyes. "No, not at all, though you needn't take that Little-Miss-Nobody-from-Ashton tone with me. You know what you are and what you've accomplished. And that you're a very beautiful woman," he said in that hard, matter-of-fact way of his.

If he had been looking at her, then he would have seen the shock register on every feature. Keena was suddenly thankful for the darkness between them and the sudden blare of a horn that had broken Nicholas's steady gaze for just that instant.

"Damn city traffic," he muttered half to himself. When he turned back to her, it was with a faintly puzzled expression. "Surely, you've had men tell you that before, that you're beautiful? Scores of them, I'm afraid." His words broke off abruptly, his gaze dropping to her slender body, outlining it with a masculine approval that was new and frightening.

"Why are you looking at me like that?" she asked in a faint whisper.

His dark, quiet eyes eased back up to meet hers. "I was wondering what it would feel like to make love to you."

Don't miss Any Man of Mine *by Diana Palmer, available February 2019 wherever Harlequin® books and ebooks are sold.*
www.Harlequin.com